y

Praise for the Novels of Rachel Caine

Undone

"Fast-paced . . . plenty of excitement. . . . A cliff-hanger ending will keep fans eager for the next installment."
—*Publishers Weekly*

"This is a good read, full of nail-biting action, some really creepy kids, and a final chilling revelation."—*Locus*

"A lot of action and a fast-paced plot. The cliff-hanger ending will make you want to find out what happens next." —SFRevu

"Ms. Caine takes readers on a fabulous new journey and introduces us to a powerful new heroine who's been forced into a reality she's not equipped to handle. . . . *Undone* well exceeded my expectations, and I'm really looking forward to seeing where the series will go from here." —Darque Reviews

"A fantastic start to another auto-buy series. Whether a newbie to the world of the Wardens and Djinn, or a veteran of the series, *Undone* will capture and thrill you."
—The Book Smugglers

"Superb ound Reviews

continued . . .

2010

The Weather Warden Series

"You'll never watch the Weather Channel the same way again.... The forecast calls for ... a fun read."
—#1 *New York Times* bestselling author Jim Butcher

"[As] swift, sassy, and sexy as Laurell K. Hamilton ... Rachel Caine takes the Weather Wardens to places the Weather Channel never imagined!"   —Mary Jo Putney

"A fast-paced thrill ride [that] brings new meaning to stormy weather."   —*Locus*

"An appealing heroine, with a wry sense of humor that enlivens even the darkest encounters."   —SF Site

"Fans of Laurell K. Hamilton and the Dresden Files by Jim Butcher are going to love this fast-paced, action-packed romantic urban fantasy."
—*Midwest Book Review*

"A kick-butt heroine who will appeal strongly to fans of Tanya Huff, Kelley Armstrong, and Charlaine Harris."
—*Romantic Times*

"A neat, stylish, and very witty addition to the genre, all wrapped up in a narrative voice to die for. Hugely entertaining."   —SF Crowsnest

"Chaos has never been so intriguing as when Rachel Caine shapes it into the setting of a story. Each book in this series has built-in intensity and fascination. Secondary characters blossom as Joanne meets them anew, and twists are revealed that will leave you gasping."

—Huntress Book Reviews

"The Weather Warden series is fun reading . . . more engaging than most TV." —*Booklist*

"If for some absurd reason you haven't tucked into this series, now's a good time. Get cracking." —Purple Pens

"I dare you to put this book down."

—*University City Review* (Philadelphia)

"Overall, the fast pace, intense emotion, cool magics, and a sense of hurtling momentum toward some planet-sized conclusion to the overarching story are keeping me a fan of the Weather Warden series. I continue to enjoy Joanne's girly-girl yet kick-ass nature."

—Romantic SF & Fantasy Novels

Books by Rachel Caine

Rachel Caine

UNKNOWN

OUTCAST SEASON, BOOK TWO

A ROC BOOK

ROC
Published by New American Library, a division of
Penguin Group (USA) Inc., 375 Hudson Street,
New York, New York 10014, USA
Penguin Group (Canada), 90 Eglinton Avenue East, Suite 700, Toronto,
Ontario M4P 2Y3, Canada (a division of Pearson Penguin Canada Inc.)
Penguin Books Ltd., 80 Strand, London WC2R 0RL, England
Penguin Ireland, 25 St. Stephen's Green, Dublin 2,
Ireland (a division of Penguin Books Ltd.)
Penguin Group (Australia), 250 Camberwell Road, Camberwell, Victoria 3124,
Australia (a division of Pearson Australia Group Pty. Ltd.)
Penguin Books India Pvt. Ltd., 11 Community Centre, Panchsheel Park,
New Delhi – 110 017, India
Penguin Group (NZ), 67 Apollo Drive, Rosedale, North Shore 0632,
New Zealand (a division of Pearson New Zealand Ltd.)
Penguin Books (South Africa) (Pty.) Ltd., 24 Sturdee Avenue,
Rosebank, Johannesburg 2196, South Africa

Penguin Books Ltd., Registered Offices:
80 Strand, London WC2R 0RL, England

First published by Roc, an imprint of New American Library,
a division of Penguin Group (USA) Inc.

First Printing, February 2010
10 9 8 7 6 5 4 3 2 1

PUBLISHER'S NOTE
This is a work of fiction. Names, characters, places, and incidents either are the
product of the author's imagination or are used fictitiously, and any resemblance
to actual persons, living or dead, business establishments, events, or locales is
entirely coincidental.

The publisher does not have any control over and does not assume any responsibility for author or third-party Web sites or their content.

If you purchased this book without a cover you should be aware that this book is
stolen property. It was reported as "unsold and destroyed" to the publisher and
neither the author nor the publisher has received any payment for this "stripped
book."

The scanning, uploading, and distribution of this book via the Internet or via any
other means without the permission of the publisher is illegal and punishable by
law. Please purchase only authorized electronic editions, and do not participate
in or encourage electronic piracy of copyrighted materials. Your support of the
author's rights is appreciated.

To Alan & Sivi Balthrop, and their lovely family, with much love and respect. Thank you for giving me such constant, loving support!

To A. J. Merrifield, for being just so damn cool.

ACKNOWLEDGMENTS

There are too many debts to acknowledge in the course of writing this book, but I would like to gratefully recognize the following virtues:

Prudence (from my mother, Hazel, who keeps me grounded)

Justice (from my beta readers, blessed be they)

Courage (from my agent, Lucienne Diver, who surely needs it to deal with me)

Faith (from my husband, Cat, who replies to all my complaints about the progress of my book with a simple "I know you can do it.")

Hope (from the Sales & Marketing Department)

Charity (from my lovely editor, Anne, who gave me the time I needed)

I am nothing without these virtues.

WHAT HAS GONE BEFORE

MY NAME IS CASSIEL, and I was once a Djinn—a being as old as the Earth herself, rooted in her power. I cared little for the small, scurrying human creatures who busied themselves with their small lives.

Things have changed. Now I *am* a small, scurrying human creature. In form, at any rate. Thanks to a disagreement with Ashan, the leader of the True Djinn, I can only sustain my life through the charity of the Wardens—humans who control aspects of the powers that surround us, such as wind and fire. The Warden I'm partnered with, Luis Rocha, commands the powers of the living Earth.

I have made mistakes, in my short existence as a human. I have made promises I could not keep. I have lost those I learned to love.

I will not let it happen again.

Even if every instinct tells me I must.

Chapter 1

SO MANY MISSING CHILDREN.

Their faces looked at me from the flat surfaces of posters and flyers, tacked to a long board opposite the row of chairs—a sad parade of even sadder stories.

Although several young girls with brown hair and vulnerable smiles looked back at me, Isabel Rocha's picture was not on the wall. I found some comfort in that. *I will find you,* I promised her, as I did each day. *On your mother and father's souls, I will find you.*

I had allowed her mother and father to be murdered. I would not allow Isabel to share the same fate.

I sat with Luis Rocha in the hallway outside of the offices of the FBI, which he had carefully explained was a place where I could not, for any reason, cause trouble. I failed to understand why this hallway should be different from any other in the city of Albuquerque, but I had agreed, with a good bit of annoyance.

Luis was in no mood to debate with me. "Just do it," he snapped, and then fell into a dark, restless silence.

I watched him pace in front of me as his dark gaze took in the wall of photos, a tense, revolted expression on his face. He stopped, and the expression altered into a frown. He pointed one flyer out to me. "That's Ben Hession's kid. Ben's a Fire Warden."

I nodded, but I doubt he noticed. He lowered his finger, but his hands formed into fists at his sides, emphasizing the sinuous flame tattoos licking up and down his arms. Once again, I wondered at the choice; Luis Rocha controlled Earth, not Fire. In that, he and his brother Manny had been alike, though Luis's power outstripped Manny's by leagues.

Manny had been my Warden partner, assigned to me by the highest levels of his organization to teach me to live as a human and use my powers—for I still had some, although nowhere near as many as I had as a Djinn—usefully. How to become a Warden in my own right. Manny had been a sweet, patient soul who had given of himself to sustain me in this new life.

And I had let him die. Now it was Luis's responsibility to look after me, and mine to never allow such a thing to happen again.

A tired-looking man in a rumpled suit stepped outside of his office and gestured to us. As he did, his coat swung open to reveal the holstered butt of a gun attached to his belt. For an ice-cold instant I had an unguarded memory, a sense-memory of the shock and rage washing over me as I watched the bullets strike Manny, strike Angela . . .

It's a memory I don't care to relive.

Something must have changed in my face or my manner, because his altered in response. His eyes sharpened their focus, narrowing on me, and his hand moved closer to his body. Closer to the weapon.

I looked away, at Luis. "He has a gun," I said.

"He's FBI," Luis told me, and folded his arms across his chest. "He has to carry one. It's a tool for him."

"I don't like it," I said. He shrugged.

"Deal."

The FBI man stared at me as if I had said or done something that alarmed him, then transferred his attention back to Luis. "Luis Rocha?"

Luis nodded and walked toward him. I rose to follow. "That's Cassiel," he said. "You might have heard."

"I heard," the FBI man said. "I just didn't believe it. Guess they weren't kidding." He offered me a half-nod—not a welcome, just an acknowledgment. I returned it exactly. "Inside. I don't want to talk in the hall." He looked right and left, as if someone might be listening although no one was in view except the silent, sad wall of photographs. Luis moved ahead of him into the office.

I stopped for a moment to lock gazes with the man again. He was tall, though only an inch or so taller than I, and whipcord thin. He had a bland, quiet face and dark, oddly empty eyes, as if he hid everything except what he wished me to see. His clothing was just as bland—a plain shirt beneath a plain dark suit and tie.

"Inside," he repeated. "Please."

There was something about him I could not explain, something beneath the surface. It occurred to me, finally, as he swung the door shut behind me, closing the three of us within a plain box of a room with tinted windows along one wall. I turned and said, "You're a Warden."

"Undercover," he said. "It pays to have a few of us seeded inside the various intelligence-gathering agencies, so we can keep on top of things. First time I've been contacted directly, though." His gaze found me again, very briefly. "Also the first time I've met a Djinn face-to-face."

"You still haven't," I said. "I am no longer a Djinn." It still hurt to say it.

"You're not exactly human either, the way I understand it. Close enough for government work," he said, and indicated the chairs on our side of the plain, institutional desk as he took the battered one behind it. "So, why come to me?"

"Because the FBI investigates cases of missing children," I said. "And we have a missing child."

"We," he repeated a little slowly. "The two of you."

Luis cleared his throat and leaned forward, elbows on his knees. "Yeah, well, the missing girl is my niece," he said. "Cassiel's an interested party. And my partner." He let two seconds go by, then added, "Not that way, okay?"

"Okay," the FBI man said, without a flicker of expression. The nameplate on his desk read SA BEN TURNER. "So tell me what you've got."

I let Luis tell it, in his own way—the abduction of his recently orphaned niece, our pursuit, our discovery that the children of Wardens were being selectively abducted and taken to a hidden location, where they were being trained. Molded.

Turner did not interrupt. Not once. He listened almost without blinking, and when Luis finally paused, he said, "So who is this you're talking about? What's their goal?"

Luis looked at me.

"The one who leads them was once a Djinn," I said.

"You would call her Pearl. She . . . is extraordinarily dangerous, and she is insane. As to goals, I think the children—and all humanity—are insignificant to her. Her goal is much larger."

"Larger," Turner repeated, and shook his head. "And that's officially out of my depth. So let the Djinn stop her."

"They can't," I said. "Or won't. She's already gained enough of a foothold in this world that she can destroy any Djinn who approaches too closely. I believe that is her goal, to destroy the Djinn and replace them in the Mother's affections. She would welcome an open war, which is why Ashan ordered me to destroy her power source."

Turner's eyebrows rose. "Sounds like a plan. What's her power source?"

"You," I said. "Humanity. How do you feel about the plan now?" I let that sit in silence for a moment, then said, "I declined."

Turner sat slowly back in his chair, staring at me, and then looked over at Luis again. "She's serious?"

"As fucking cancer," Luis said. "It's still her nuclear option, if we can't get this under control and find a way to stop Pearl."

"*So* out of my depth," Turner muttered, and shook his head. "And you've been in touch with Headquarters? Lewis?"

Everybody knew Lewis Orwell, the head of the Wardens organization. Everyone also assumed that Lewis was a sort of magic button to press whenever one wanted a particular outcome. Nonsense. Lewis might be a supremely powerful man, but he was only a man. This was far beyond him, and the Wardens as a whole. They were being used, yes, but Pearl was not interested in them, except as levers to move the world in her direction.

"Most of the high-level Wardens are out of contact, including Orwell," Luis said. "We're not going to find the answers there. We're on our own to deal with this, and that means we have to get creative. That's why I'm here."

Turner was looking steadily less comfortable with the turns the conversation was taking. "If your niece is in the system as a missing or abducted child, she's already getting the full-court press from the FBI as well as local law enforcement," he said. "What else do you want me to do?"

"Make it your case," Luis said. "You're a Warden. These are Warden children. I'll give you a list of those we've identified so far as missing, but there may be more. Maybe a lot more, if some of them were foster children, orphans, nobody to miss them. Here's the catch: In at least one case we know of, one of the parents was complicit in the kidnapping. They're recruiting fanatics, and they've been successful. Think terrorists, only with potential Warden powers."

"Christ," Turner whispered, and briefly shut his eyes. "You've got no idea what kind of night sweats I've had thinking about that for the last ten years, anyway. We've got some contingency plans, but I still don't think they're up to the job, not for a serious threat." He focused attention back on me, speaking directly. "What can you tell me about their organization?"

"Well armed," I said. "Paramilitary, at the very least. And they've recruited some disaffected former Wardens, or possibly artificially enhanced the powers of some who were not gifted enough to be recruited as Wardens in the beginning."

"Like the Ma'at."

I nodded. The Ma'at were a separate organization, a kind of shadow of the Wardens, built out of those with *some* hints of latent power who were not deemed to be either strong enough to train as Wardens, nor dangerous enough to receive the Wardens' typical treatment for those they rejected—a kind of psychic surgery to rip away their powers. The Ma'at had discovered it was possible to combine powers in groups, especially with the voluntary assistance of Djinn, to right the balance of the forces of the Earth—forces the Wardens seemed often to neglect to keep in the proper proportions.

In a certain way, the Ma'at were the maintenance workers of the supernatural world around us. I had always had a small amount of respect for their efforts—as much as I had ever harbored for any human endeavor, in any case.

"They're our next stop," Luis said. "We're paying a visit to their top guys, seeing if we can get an organized effort around this thing."

Turner shrugged. "Good luck with that. Okay, here's what I'll do: I'll take your list, start digging, and see if I can make any more connections with missing kids. If you're right, though, there may be a whole lot of this that's off the FBI radar right now. How much do you want me to wave the flag?"

"Hard and fast," Luis said, and stood up to offer his hand for a farewell shake. "We're going to need every damn advantage we can get if we're going to make this end well."

Turner's eyes flicked to me again, and I knew what he was thinking—not because I could read his thoughts, but because I understood his fears. "No," I said, in answer to his unvoiced question. "Luis cannot stop me, if I choose to accept Ashan's assignment and destroy your people. No one can stop me. Agreement is all I need to regain my powers as a Djinn."

No one could stop me except, possibly, the enemy we all feared.

Pearl.

Turner didn't offer any kind of commentary about that. He just said, "I'll make your niece my top priority," and ushered us out of his office. I followed Luis down the hallway, past all those silent, haunting pictures, to the elevators. He pushed the button, but I kept going, to the sign that marked access to stairs. With a sigh, he fell in behind me.

"You know, we need to talk about your claustrophobia," he said.

"I am not claustrophobic," I said. "I do not care for small spaces that operate at the mercy of thin cables and human engineering, and are easily manipulated by my enemies." The door slammed and locked behind him, sealing us in the silent cool stairwell, and I turned to him on the broad concrete landing.

He looked little different than he had the first moment I had met him—strong and lean, with skin the color of caramel and dark, secretive eyes. Hair worn a bit long around his sharply angled face. On his muscled arms, the flame tattoos caught the light in shadowy flickers.

"You think he'll help?" I asked. Luis shrugged.

"No idea. But we've got to pull every string we can reach."

"And if he is working for Pearl and her people?"

"Then they know we're serious. Can't think that's a bad thing. They already know we're not going to quit. I want her to know we're prepared to take drastic measures if we have to, to stop her."

Except Luis didn't believe it. He still, deep down, did not believe that I would shed my human form, rise up as a Djinn, and destroy humanity.

Luis did not know me at all.

"So we go to the Ma'at," I said, and took the first flight of steps, heading down six floors. "By plane, yes?"

"It's faster," he said. "Hopefully, nobody will try to kill us today."

"That would be a different kind of day."

In fact, I suspected that someone *would* try to kill us, possibly even in the narrow confines of the concrete and metal stairs, but we reached the bottom-floor exit without incident, and walked out into the open lobby. We turned in our visitor badges at the security desk and exited through a heavily armored door, out into the Albuquerque afternoon sun. The dry air held the scent of fragrant mesquite wood burning in fireplaces, the sharp bite of pine, the greasy and ever-present stench of car exhaust. Overhead, a jet painted orange and blue climbed the clear sky and left a contrail behind.

Luis and I walked to the distant parking lot where we had left his large pickup truck—black, with dramatic bursts of colorful flames on both sides. He'd recently had it washed and polished, and it shone like ebony in the sun. I thought longingly of my motorcycle, which

I'd reluctantly left behind; I preferred the simplicity and freedom of that transportation, not the enclosed space of the narrow metal box. But the windows did roll down, and although the day had grown cool, it was not yet cold.

It would be soon, though.

Before we reached the car, two people stepped into our path—a tall, wide man and a shorter, darker one. They held out black leather cases with gold-washed badges of identification.

Police.

I glanced at Luis as we both came to a stop, and he knew what I was asking: *comply, or fight and run?* I was unimpressed by human authority figures, except that I understood they could complicate my ability to operate in the already complex maze of human existence. Prison would be inconvenient.

Luis held out one hand to me, a clear *wait* gesture. I held myself ready to follow his cues.

"Detectives," he said, and nodded to the two men. "How can we help you?"

"You can get your ass up against the truck," the shorter one said. "Hands on the hood. Feet apart. You two, Pink."

He was referring, I assumed, to the fading shade of pink that still clung to my pale hair. I had not yet decided whether or not to scrub the last of it away, or renew it into a hot blaze of magenta. The contempt in the way he addressed me made me want to turn *his* hair into a burning pink bonfire.

Perhaps literally.

I smiled, instead, and as Luis moved to obey the orders,

I did as well, placing my hands on the cool, slick finish and spreading my feet to a distance of about a shoulder's width. When the shorter detective stepped up behind me, I said, very quietly, "I don't enjoy being touched."

"She's not kidding," Luis said. "You really don't want to test her on that."

"Got to pat you down for weapons," the detective said. "And if you resist, I'll Taser your fine albino ass and haul you to the county jail. Is that clear?"

"Oh man," Luis sighed. "Just roll with it, okay?"

I supposed he meant that for me. I wasn't quite certain what he wanted me to do, but I gathered, from the way he caught and held my eyes, that he wanted me to do nothing.

So, with a great deal of distaste, I allowed the stranger to put his hands on me, moving up my sides, across my back, down my legs and back up between them. *Calm*, I told myself. *Remain calm*. That was a great deal harder than I'd expected, but by continuing to stare hard into Luis's wide, dark eyes, I found a certain measure of balance.

The detective stepped back. "She's clean. Okay, your turn, Rocha."

Luis smiled, very much as if he was used to this sort of treatment. "No problem. I know you enjoy this kind of thing."

That drove whatever good humor there had been in the stranger completely away, and he slammed Luis forward with the bar of his forearm against Luis's back, crushing him against the hood of the pickup truck.

I leaned back, taking my weight off the balls of my feet, and said, "I wouldn't do that."

"Shut up, punk," the older, broader man said. "Hands on the hood. *Hands on the hood!*"

"Why?" I didn't comply. As much as I hated being touched and treated with contempt, my fury was well and truly ignited now not for myself, but for Luis. The shorter man was slapping his hand down Luis's sides and legs with more violence than he'd shown me. "What have we done?"

"You think I need a reason to roust a Norteño asshole?" he shot back. "Think again."

"I'm not Norteño," Luis gritted out, face still smashed against the truck. "Haven't been for years. Better get a new playbook, detective."

"If you're not Norteño, then why did the gang shoot up your brother and sister-in-law? Just for the fun of it?"

"I left. They didn't like it. I just got back in town. You can check it out."

The older man nodded to the younger, who let Luis go and stepped back. Luis got himself upright again and stepped back from the truck turning to face the two men. "What's this about?" he asked.

"You." The older man pointed at me. "Name."

"Leslie Raine," I said. It was as good as any, and I had Warden-produced identification to prove it was mine.

"Where you from?"

"Here."

"Yeah, you look like a fucking native." He dismissed me and turned back to Luis. "What are you doing hanging around the Federal Building?"

"I'm not hanging around," Luis said. "We just came from seeing the FBI. Special Agent Turner. He'll verify that."

The two men exchanged a fast, unreadable look. "How's an asshole like you rate time with a fed?"

"It's not your business," I said, with all the cold hauteur an eternity of being immortal had taught me.

That got me a longer appraisal from both men. "So what are you, some kind of a fed? Rocha's some kind of informant?"

I smiled, slowly. "Do you really want to talk about this here? In the open?"

On the street, people were slowing down in cars to stare at us; in a storefront opposite, someone stood still, taking a photograph with his cell phone. I sent a pulse of power over the distance between us, squeezing metal and glass, and the phone gave a sad little electronic *pop* and died. The man frowned at his dead device and shook it impotently, as if he could shake life back into it. Then, seeing my expression, he quickly moved on.

I don't like it when people stare.

Whether the two policemen believed me or not, they opted for caution. The older one nodded, and the younger one walked to an anonymous gray sedan nearby and opened the back door. "Inside," he said.

"Are we under arrest?"

"Why? You got something we ought to arrest you for?"

I shrugged and got into the car. Luis took the opposite side, and the two doors thumped closed as the policemen moved to the front. Immediately, I began to feel constricted. This car was not as fragrant as most, but it was still deeply unpleasant, redolent of plastic, hot metal, unwashed flesh, and old food. I studied the interior door. There were no release handles; however,

I comforted myself that this would hardly slow either of us down, should we choose to leave. Earth Wardens are not easily caged; Djinn, no matter how humiliated and cast out, even less so. But there are disadvantages to having such powers; for one thing, one cannot always find a useful way to apply them.

As now.

The policemen entered the car. It was warm inside, though not oppressively so; still, I felt stifled, and panic rose inside me. I closed my eyes tightly and concentrated on breathing, pushing air in and out of my fragile lungs, trying not to imagine what it might be like to be robbed of air, of breath.

"Hey, what's wrong with your friend?" the smaller detective asked. I didn't open my eyes. "You ain't gonna puke, are you? If you do, you're cleaning it up."

"She doesn't like cars," Luis said. "Especially ones that stink like last night's drunk tank. Now that we're away from prying ears, what the hell do you want?"

The larger detective turned around, arm over the back of the seat, and said, "You're an Earth Warden, right?"

I opened my eyes for that. Luis didn't react in the slightest, not even by a change in his heart rate or respiration. "No idea what you're talking about," he said. "I do environmental work. Big business these days, you know? Thinking green and all that."

"Don't bullshit me. You're a Warden."

Luis didn't say anything, just watched him. The big man finally sighed and ran a square hand over his face.

"I know all about it," he said. "Shit, you people made a big freaking splash all over the television, remember?

Besides, my sister-in-law's one of them Weather Wardens. Beatrice Halley. Works out of Chicago, does stuff with the lakes up there."

Luis sat back a little. "I know Bea Halley," he said. "You must be Frank Halley. She said her brother-in-law was a cop."

"Yeah, well, she don't like me much, and the feeling's mutual, but whatever. This ain't about that."

"So what is it about?"

"I got a job for you," Halley said. "Sick kid."

A shadow passed over Luis's face. I knew he hated saying no to people, but at the same time, Earth Wardens didn't normally agree to healing for the general public. It was harsh, but necessary; if word got out about what they could do, it would bring an endless stream of sufferers to their doorsteps, and it would prevent them from carrying out their larger duties.

"I know it's not normal," Halley said, "but this kid's kind of special. She showed up half starved, dehydrated, with a nasty case of infection; no family, no missing kid bulletin out on her. She's about five years old."

Hope flared hot in Luis's eyes, and I know it must have registered in my expression as well. "No name?"

"She's too sick to talk."

Halley was, I believed, deliberately vague as to details. He was allowing Luis's desperation to fill in information.

I thought I understood why. "This girl," I said. "She is not Isabel Rocha. You wish us to think she could be, to bring Luis face-to-face with her. You believe he could not refuse once he saw her, even if she isn't his niece."

Halley and his partner stared at me. I didn't blink.

"Yeah," Halley finally said. "That's true. Look, the kid's in bad shape. They've tried all the treatments, even the IV antibiotics. She's dying. I figure you're about the only shot she's got left, unless Saint Joseph works a miracle." He paused, studying Luis. "You a religious man?"

"I been to mass a time or two." He was, in fact, much more religious than that; I'd heard him praying, from time to time, that we would find Isabel. Or avenge her. "Why?"

Halley shrugged. "Always wondered is all. You Wardens, you're practically gods, what with all the slinging lightning bolts and healing the sick. Bea ain't religious. So I just wondered."

"We're not any kind of gods, big *G* or small," Luis said. "Ain't even angels, man. We're just people. Smart Wardens know that better than anybody. You play God, people die."

Halley looked like he wanted to keep on talking, but I broke in to say, "If the girl is as sick as you say, we shouldn't waste time."

Both policemen looked startled, although they covered it quickly. "So you'll go?" Halley asked, and started the car's engine.

"Of course he'll go," I said, without so much as a glance at Luis. The bond between us was strong enough that I had no doubts of it; I wouldn't have doubted it in any case, because it was exactly the sort of thing Luis would do, whether or not it was wise. "You should have just asked."

Halley rolled his eyes. "Yeah. Shoulda thought of that."

* * *

The girl was in the hospital. I had never visited one before, although of course I knew the theory; there had been no need, when Manny and Angela were shot, because their wounds had been immediately fatal. If they had been taken to the hospital—and I supposed that they might have been—they would not have been placed in one of these complicated beds, hooked to machines, reduced to a limp, suffering sack of dying meat.

I did not like the hospital.

The child was so *small*. Smaller than Isabel, and nothing at all like her in coloring: blond, rosy pink skin, a delicate rosebud mouth. I could not see the color of her eyes; she was deeply unconscious.

Parts of her body were deeply discolored and bruised. The infection Detective Halley had mentioned, but not a violent attack. This child was thin, ill-looked-after, but her fight was against a much more ruthless enemy.

The room stank of death. I paused at the door, swallowing convulsively, and Halley came to a stop with me.

"Sad," he said. "Right?"

I didn't answer. I watched Luis. He entered the sterile room in slow, deliberate steps, as if he was afraid he might frighten the child, who surely could not have known he was there. He was, by contrast to her tiny body, a large man, well muscled, heavily tattooed, and it struck me as I watched that a human chancing on this scene would have assumed Luis to be a criminal, intent on harming the child.

Until they saw his face, his eyes, the heartbreakingly gentle way he laid the back of his hand on the girl's forehead and settled his weight on the bed beside her. He had large hands, but his fingers stroked gently through her hair, as if she might feel the comfort he offered.

"Cass," he said. "I need you."

He looked up into my eyes, and I felt it like a physical shock—a demand, but a kind one, with good intention behind it.

And more. More than that. A complicated mixture of need and desire, dread and worry. For a disorienting moment, I saw myself through his eyes: tall, pale, expressionless, and apparently free of all connection to the human world.

Apparently.

I was abruptly conscious of my body, all the complex and fascinating parts of it; I felt the chilled air of the room moving over my skin, and felt gooseflesh gather. My heart pounded harder, altering its rhythm. My mouth felt dry, and without conscious decision, I stepped forward, first one foot, then another, until I was standing across the child's bed from Luis Rocha.

He held out his right hand, keeping his left in gentle contact with the girl's forehead. My fingers closed over his, and the raw tactile pleasure of it took my breath away. I felt a tingle of power pulse through the link between us, and then through him. I touched the wellspring of power hidden deep in the Earth herself—slow, silent, strong power. The feel of it coursing through my nerves, through Luis's, was enough to send my memories sparking to other times, other places, other lives. I had never been human, but I had been Djinn a very, very long time, and this, this feeling of touching the eternal . . .

I let out a shaky sigh, almost a moan, and began to

refine the power, shape it, form it into a golden flood that Luis used his human expertise to direct into the child's fragile body. This was a thing some Djinn could do, and others could not; I had never been very interested in healing, but I found myself fascinated with the gentle precision with which he worked. It was all out of proportion to his physical appearance, his intimidating aspect.

I found that pleasing.

Luis worked with great concentration, and it took a very long time—hours, in fact. The policemen left, returned, and left again. Doctors and nurses came and went, but no one bothered us; I wondered why, until I realized that there must have been some common consent that this last effort would be tolerated. There was no harm in it.

The mottled stains beneath her skin gradually began to fade. Luis stopped for a few moments then, gasping for breath, and I poured him a glass of water from the carafe standing next to the bed. He drank it in two convulsive gulps, and I realized that his shirt was dark with sweat, and his hair was dripping with it. His muscles trembled with the strain.

I put a pale, dry hand on his moist arm, over the flame-shaped tattoo, and said, "It's enough."

"No," Luis said, and held out his glass for another pour from the carafe. "It's still in her blood. Tough little buggers, but I'm getting them. I've got her major organs cleaned, but if I don't kill it in her bloodstream, she'll reinfect." He paused to drink again—three gulps, this time. "You got enough to keep going?"

Did I? The question surprised me, and I quickly

turned my appraisal back on myself. I was unused, still, to human limits, but he was right; my body was trembling, robbed of energy, and I was burningly thirsty.

I took the glass from him, refilled it, and downed it in two convulsive swallows. "I'm fine," I said.

He took the carafe, shook it, and then shrugged and upended it to drink the last few mouthfuls, depositing it back on the table, empty. "Then let's do it."

I held on to his arm. "Luis." I didn't need to say more, and he didn't need to do more than shake his head to reject my concern. "Very well," I said.

My fingers felt burned when they left his skin; he was warm, so warm it felt wrong to me. Effort and power, consuming him from within.

He would not stop. I understood that very well.

It took the rest of the afternoon, and the sun was slipping below the horizon when Luis finally sighed, removed his hand from the girl's forehead, and tried to get up. Tried, and failed. I grabbed his arm as he began to slide off the bed; I couldn't hold him, but I broke his momentum from a fall to a controlled slide to a sitting position on the floor. Someone had refilled the water pitcher, and I grabbed it and moved around the bed toward him. My legs trembled violently, and I had to stop and brace myself against the wall for a moment as dark spots swam and drifted in my eyes. I then summoned up all the energy left in me to drop down next to Luis's side.

I didn't spill the water.

"You okay?" he asked me in a faint, rough voice. I handed him the carafe, and he guzzled down more than half its contents without a pause. "We need food. Protein and carbs, the more the better."

I took the water from him and finished it before asking, in a voice I hardly recognized as my own, "The girl?"

Luis gave me a slow, exhausted smile. "She'll be okay," he said. The smile, warm and sweet, faded too quickly. "Physically, anyway. No idea what happened to bring her to this. Could be too bad to get over it as easily as this."

If *this* had been easy, I could not imagine hard. I started to get up, but my legs wouldn't respond. Luis took my hand.

I tried to pull away, but even in his weakened state, Luis was a strong man. "No," I said. "You've spent too much power already."

"You need it more than I do right now." His last reserves of power cascaded into me, flooding warm through my nerves, sparking waves of pleasure as it passed. An echo only—he had little to give me, but it was enough to sustain me for another day, perhaps two, until he recovered.

If I didn't use my power recklessly.

I didn't mean to do it, but my hand seemed to move of its own volition, breaking away from his grip and moving up to touch his face.

Luis's eyes widened, and for an instant we were staring at each other with all the doors open, all the walls thrown down.

Then I dropped my hand, dragged myself to my feet, and walked off in search of the proteins and carbohydrates his body so desperately needed to replace. I met Detective Halley in the hall heading toward the room, laden with a tray full of food. Hamburgers, hot dogs, some sort of stew in a bowl.

"She going to make it?" Halley asked, holding on to the tray.

"Are you withholding food from us if she doesn't?"

He blinked, shook his head, and handed the food to me. "You tried. Can't ask more than that, I guess."

"Then I am pleased to tell you that Luis believes she will recover." I started to take the food into the room, then turned back to him and asked, "How did you know?"

"Know what?"

"That we would need this."

He shrugged. "I asked my sister-in-law. She said if you made it through, you'd be hungry as a cloud of locusts."

Halley, I decided, would be allowed to live after all.

The girl woke up after a deep, but natural, sleep. That was not significant.

What was significant was *how* she woke up . . . crying, screaming, panicked, and desperate.

Her distress set the room on fire.

It happened very quickly—one moment the child was shrieking in terror, and the next, the bedding around her burst into hot orange flames. So did the cushions on the chairs nearby, and the cheerful yellow curtains draping the windows. Colorful characters charred on the walls.

This was the worst thing that could happen. Luis's powers were focused around Earth; a Weather Warden could have found ways to shut down this sort of event, but for an Earth Warden it was much more difficult.

My powers were limited by Luis's, though I could wield them more creatively; I quickly altered the composition of our skin and lungs to make us fire-resistant, though making us fireproof was beyond my capabilities. It was good that I did this, because Luis plunged into the flames, grabbed the child, and pulled her off the bed and into his arms. If he'd been a normal human, he would have sustained terrible burns.

The moment the girl was in Luis's arms, the flames began to die away, hissing and sputtering into nothing an instant before the overhead fire-suppression system began raining and sounding its alarm. I cut the flow of power, and Luis's body and mine reverted to their normal states.

"What the hell . . . ?" A crowd of people had formed in the doorway to the room, but two broke away from the pack to rush inside, looking very much in command. One, dressed in a white coat, I assumed was a doctor; the other was, of course, Detective Halley. It was Halley who'd spoken. "What happened in here?"

The doctor ignored such concerns and moved to take the girl from Luis's arms. "No," Luis said. "Not a good idea."

"I need to examine her for burns!"

"She's not hurt. She's just scared."

"And dangerous," I said. "And wrong."

Luis's gaze brushed mine. He knew what was wrong with her her, just as I did; the child's powers should have been dormant until her body had time to grow the channels through which they would run. She was too young—*far* too young—to bear this kind of burden. It would be difficult enough at adolescence, with the sort of raw ability she had just demonstrated.

"How did this happen?" I asked him quietly. Luis cradled the child in his arms, and she clung to him with her small arms around his neck, blue eyes wide and terrified. I retrieved a thick, nubby blanket from the closet, which was the only place in the room that had been protected from both the flames and water dousing, and took it to Luis. He wrapped it tight around the girl.

"I didn't mean to," she whispered, very seriously. "I really didn't."

"I know, *mija*," he said. "Don't you worry, nobody blames you. I'm Luis. What's your name?"

She considered the question very seriously before answering, "Pammy."

"Pammy, what's your last name?"

"What's yours?" she asked. Luis smiled.

"Rocha."

"That's a funny name."

"Maybe so. It's Spanish. Is yours funny?"

"Gegenwaller," she said, very proudly. "It's *German.*"

Luis shot a glance toward Detective Halley, who nodded and pushed his way out of the crowd in the doorway. He had the information he needed, and he would begin his search. "Pammy Gegenwaller," he said, "where are your parents?"

Her face just shut down, becoming a still, empty mask far too old and experienced for her few years. "They're not important," she said. "The lady said so."

"The lady," I said. "Who is the lady?"

Pammy turned her face away, pressing it against Luis's neck.

"Hey," he said, and jiggled her gently in his arms. "That's Cassiel. She's nice. She won't hurt you."

"She will," Pammy said. "Just like the lady."

Some of the paralysis among the medical staff finally

broke, and as if by common consent, a swarm of them broke the invisible barrier at the threshold and surged around us. A nurse plucked Pammy from Luis's arms, and as she yelled in protest I saw a flash of pain and fear go across his face. "Wait!" he snapped. The nurse paused, frowning, struggling to hold the flailing child. Luis put a hand on Pammy's forehead and murmured, "Sleep now, sweetheart. You're safe. You have to trust these people, they want to make you better. Okay?"

He was using his powers in a strong but subtle way, a kind of sedation that swept over the girl and relaxed her body. Her eyes drifted closed, and she rested her head on the nurse's shoulder.

Luis removed his hand. "She should stay asleep for a while," he said. "Keep someone with her. I left a suggestion with her that she'll trust you, but if she gets frightened that could change. Keep her calm and you shouldn't have any trouble. Don't leave her alone." He reached in his pocket, took out a small notepad and scribbled down a note, which he handed to the woman. "Call that number. It's the Warden hotline, they'll assign someone with the right power profile to come help. If nobody's available, I'll come back. My number's on there too."

"All right, let's move her to a fresh room. Somebody get maintenance in here! And call the fire department—they have to sign off on this!" the head doctor bellowed. The nurse took Pammy away, heading from the room. Luis and I followed, but he stopped once we were in the hallway. The air reeked less of smoke and melted plastic, and I took several grateful breaths.

"You understand what she said?" he asked. "What just happened?"

"The child was a latent Warden," I said. "Someone woke her powers, far too early for safety. Someone female. Someone like me."

"A Djinn," Luis agreed. "And I think we both know who that would be."

Pearl.

Pammy had been at the Ranch, where Pearl trained her captured Warden children—but trained them for what? To do what? "She was rejected," I said. We had seen other examples of it—children who had been brought to Pearl for evaluation or training, but had failed whatever obscure standard she had applied. Many had been used as perimeter guards for the Ranch, where the group kept a stronghold.

Pammy had either escaped, or been returned because she had become uselessly sick. "Pearl had to change her location," I said. "Perhaps she's changed tactics as well." We had found her stronghold in Colorado, and by the time we had assembled sufficient strength to try to take it, it had been destroyed, only her expendable human allies left behind. She'd taken the children with her.

We had spent weeks trying to find any sign of where she might have gone.

"Maybe," Luis said, "and maybe this *is* her goal—maybe Pammy didn't fail. Maybe she's exactly what Pearl wants her to be: a child time bomb."

I considered it, then slowly shook my head. "No. Pearl is not interested in random destruction. She has a purpose, though the purpose is not yet clear. But if she returned this child, Pammy fell short of her expectations."

That put a bleak light in Luis's eyes. "Christ," he said.

"The kid could probably blow up the hospital if she got angry enough. That's not enough power?"

"Not for Pearl," I said. "Not yet."

He sighed. "I need three shots of whiskey and about a day and a half of sleep. We can't keep going like this. Time to stand down for a while."

I didn't want to, but I also felt the drag of exhaustion, and the faint, fine trembling in my muscles. My flagging brain interpreted sights and sounds as too slow, too fast, too bright, too loud; I did need rest, and if I needed it, Luis *desperately* needed it.

"Home?" I asked.

"Home," he said. "Now."

Chapter 2

HOME FOR LUIS was his brother's home, which he had decided to keep after Manny and Angela's death. Partly this had been to allow little Isabel some continuity and familiarity in her life, although expecting her to return was less logic than sheer, bloody-minded determination. Partly it was convenience. Luis had moved from Florida, and had not yet rented an apartment before the murders.

I had an apartment, but it was not a home—merely a way station where I kept my few belongings, slept, and cleaned my body.

The Rocha home was . . . more.

"I should take you back to your place," Luis said as he unlocked the front door of the small, neat house; that took a while, because he had installed new locks and an alarm system. His words lacked conviction, and I ignored them, moving through the opened doorway into the familiar living room. It was comfortably furnished, with things that did not quite match—the sign of people who had bought their possessions over time, and because of love, not fashion. Unlike his brother and sister-in-law, Luis kept it very neat, but there was a sense of peace in it. Order. Love. Some sadness.

It eased some anxious, tired knot in my soul.

I locked the door behind me and sat down on the couch. Luis glanced at me without speaking and went into the kitchen. He came out again with two glasses—both decorated with colorful cartoon characters—and a bottle of amber liquid, which he set on the coffee table before sinking down next to me with a sigh that spoke of utter weariness. "Drink?" he asked.

"I don't know," I said. "Do I?"

He poured me a thin line of liquor and handed it to me. "Try."

I sipped carefully and made a startled, strangled sound as the fiery, smoky flavor coated my tongue and throat. Luis leaned forward and tipped a much more generous portion into his own glass, lifted it vaguely in my direction, and said, "*Salud,*" before downing the liquid in two heavy gulps. I took a larger sip. It didn't burn as much the second time, and had more flavor.

Luis refilled his glass. I drained mine in three more slow sips, feeling an odd calm begin to work through me. Distilled chemical sedation. I began to understand why people sometimes pursued this course of action.

Luis put his glass down empty, refilled mine, and poured himself a third helping. "Last call," he said, and capped the bottle. "How is it?"

"Interesting," I said. I wasn't quite sure I approved of the changes in my metabolism, but somehow that disapproval remained theoretical, and far away from the warmth that coursed through my body. I felt looser now, less on guard.

Less constrained. It sparked dangerous memories of being free, powerful, utterly different than what I was now.

Luis watched me over the rim of his glass as he drank—this time, much slower, almost matching my careful sips. "You were good today," he said. "*We* were good today."

It wasn't often the case. Luis and I didn't know each other as well as Manny and I had; I had been comfortable with Manny, and I had understood the dynamics of our relationship, which were almost all professional in nature.

Luis was . . . complicated. I responded to him more strongly, both in terms of the power passed between us, and in purely physical ways. Since becoming human, my flesh had surprised me more than once, and continued to act in mysterious ways that seemed divorced from the cold logic of my thoughts. I was not sure how humans combined these things. Or Djinn, for that matter; I had never been one of those who enjoyed assuming human form and playing at being mortal. Some, like David, almost *were* human. Others, like Ashan, wore flesh as a skin-deep suit, nothing more.

I wasn't sure which more accurately described me; it seemed to be a shifting question.

I sighed and leaned my head back against the couch cushions. "Do you think she will recover?" I asked, cradling the glass between my long white fingers. Luis finished his last sip of whiskey.

"It's not a matter of recovery," he said. "She'll learn to live with it, or she'll become more and more unpredictable and unstable. If that happens, the Wardens will have to remove her powers. God help whoever gets that job. It's risky enough with an adult."

There was a small, elite force of Wardens devoted to

tracking down those who were, or became, dangerous and bringing them back for that process, which was a kind of psychic surgery performed only by the most expert Earth Wardens. There was every chance of leaving someone scarred, psychically crippled, insane, or dead.

Yet some Wardens actually chose to take the risk, rather than continue as they were.

And some had to be treated by force.

"I hope that will not be necessary," I said. I put the glass on the coffee table and felt my whole body relax as I curled in on the couch, knees up, body turned toward him. My head rested against the cushions.

"Yeah," Luis agreed. He hesitated, then leaned over and put his own glass down. "You want another shot?"

I glanced at the bottle. "No," I said. "Do you?"

"Can't," he said. "I set my limits, and I stick to them."

Limits. That was a concept unfamiliar to most Djinn; we had few limits, and those few were imposed on us by the immutable laws of the universe. Still, I understood him; I had imposed rules on myself here, in this place, simply by agreeing to live as a human instead of perishing as an outcast Djinn.

Some of the limits were even my own choice.

I realized that I hadn't spoken, and Luis had fallen silent, and we were still looking at each other. I had noticed that humans did not typically gaze steadily at each other, unless they were seeking confrontation; glances were more common, polite and fleeting.

This was different. Luis watched me as if he had forgotten how to blink. There were thoughts behind this, thoughts I could not understand easily, having little experience of the human condition.

I understood my reaction, however. Deep within my body, warmth was blooming, spreading, and my blood was moving faster through my body. My breathing had deepened. My pupils, I suspected, had widened.

Arousal—deep, violent, and primal.

And hotly enjoyable.

"I should get you home," he said, finally. His voice sounded different—deeper, slightly rougher, as if he had to force the words out.

"You can't drive," I said, and looked at the bottle on the table. "Three drinks would be too many, correct?" Except that as an Earth Warden he could easily control that; he could dismiss the alcohol from his system with a simple pulse of power, or at least minimize its effects.

If he wished.

"That's true," he said, in a neutral voice. "I should probably wait a while." He picked up the bottle and looked at it with dark, narrowed eyes, then slowly uncapped it and tipped another splash of amber into his glass, then my own. He didn't speak. I didn't either. We sipped the whiskey, intensely aware of each other's presence, and when I had finished the glass I felt stickily warm, impulsive, aware of every nerve in my body.

I sat up abruptly and stripped off the pale leather jacket, dropping it onto a nearby chair with a heavy thump. Beneath it I wore a thin pale pink cotton top, sleeveless. I had not bothered with the inconvenience of a bra; my body was not built in such a way as to make it structurally necessary, although I sometimes wore one for comfort, or to satisfy societal expectations.

But not today.

As I sank down on the couch again, skin lightly flushed and damp, Luis looked sideways toward me. Not toward my face. Toward the thin cotton fabric, where my nipples were hardening in reaction to the cooler air, and responding to his rapt attention.

Still, I said nothing. Neither did he. He raised his eyebrows and took a last sip of his drink, then put the glass down.

"Cass," he said then, very softly. "I'm not sure we ought to be doing this."

"Why?" I asked. I angled my body sideways on the soft cushions, and met his eyes directly. "You want me to be human. Yet you resist when I try."

Luis let out a shaky laugh. "Yeah, I'm resisting all over the place, here. Lady, if I was resisting, I would have stopped at half a glass of whiskey and booted you the hell out of my house."

I frowned, trying to work it out through the warm hazy pleasure that was coursing through my body. "But you didn't."

"You noticed."

"But you are not sure—"

"Indecision. It's the human condition, Cass. Get used to it. Although they're going to kick me the fuck out of the Guy Club if I go all virtuous right now, with a drunk hot woman trying to get in my pants."

He said *woman,* not *Djinn.* That was somehow significant to me. Some barrier between us that I'd barely been aware of had fallen away, and I didn't know why. It could have been the alcohol, of course, but I didn't think so. It might have equally been the extreme focus of the two of us working to save the small child in the hospital . . . or, simply, that we had both been thinking of this moment for some time, and denying it was so.

I slid off of the couch again, shoved the coffee table back so violently that the open bottle of whiskey tee-tered in an unsteady dance on its surface, and I reached out to catch it and center it before it could tip. Then I lifted it to my lips and tilted it, my gaze still hard-locked with Luis's. Silky, liquid heat poured into my mouth, and I held it for a moment in savor before swallowing.

Then I put the bottle down and knelt astride Luis on the couch. My weight came down on his tensed body, and I settled against him in intimate contact—closer than I had ever been to him, in fact.

He made a startled sound, low in his throat, and I felt his muscles go tight all over his body, as if he was fight-ing his own impulses at a well-nigh-cellular level.

"If you don't find me attractive," I said, "tell me to go."

It was patently evident that he found me attractive. With my weight pressed hard against his hips, it was very difficult to argue the point.

He closed his eyes and pulled in a deep breath. I could feel his heart pounding. I could see the pulse throbbing in his temple. A drop of sweat slid down the gleaming flesh of his throat, and I watched its glide with single-minded intensity. I strongly considered licking it.

"It's the whiskey talking," he said. "You're going to hate us both tomorrow."

I laughed softly. "I don't need whiskey to make me hate anyone," I said. "It is my natural state. As you very well know."

Luis pounded his head backwards against the soft

cushions of the couch, twice, then opened his eyes to look at me. The distance between us seemed to contract, even though neither of us moved.

"I wanted to hate you right back," he said. "I tried. When Manny died—"

He'd been right to loathe me. I had seen Manny and Angela fall, fatally wounded, and instead of leaping to save their lives as Luis had done, I ran after those who had harmed my friends. I had selected vengeance over mercy. That was Djinn instinct, and it was still a raw wound inside of me.

But complicating that pain was the knowledge that even had I done as Luis had, even had I applied all my skill and power to my two fallen friends, they would almost certainly still have died. And Luis knew that as well.

"I wanted to hate you," he continued softly, "but I couldn't. You're just . . . baffling."

"Baffling," I repeated. I rather enjoyed that description. "How so? I try to speak my mind."

"No shit." He pulled in a breath as I circled my hips on his. "Holy crap, don't do that."

"Is it because I wish to touch you? To remove your clothes and touch you everywhere, to know you completely?" I was not certain of human protocols in these matters, but Luis didn't seem offended. I leaned closer, slowly, and settled my arms around his neck. His skin felt hot and firm. "Because I wish to feel your body on mine? Your needs pounding through your veins?"

"Cass," he said faintly, and then took a deep breath and said, in an entirely different tone, "Oh, what the hell, anyway."

And he kissed me.

I didn't know what I'd expected from this meeting of skins, but my body clearly did. In an instant, my mind blazed white, and I thought of nothing, nothing but the warm, damp glide of his lips, his hands gripping my waist and pulling me hard against him. It was challenge. It was surrender. It was an intoxicating brew of instinct and need and emotion, and I shuddered and opened my lips to the stroke of his tongue. One of his hands stroked slowly up the bumps of my spine, brushed the tender skin at the base of my neck, and cradled the back of my head in primal warmth.

I had been holding myself suspended, just a little, above his body, but now my knees seemed to spread of their own accord, lowering me the last half inch. He groaned breathlessly into my mouth, and I moved my hips back and forth against his. Pure, wild instinct, springing from the body I wore, from a hundred thousand years of human coupling hardwired into my DNA.

It took my breath away, as well.

The kiss deepened, and time stretched, measured in racing heartbeats. He was flesh and bone and muscle, all of it suddenly, insanely new to me. My hands stroked over him, sensing where he was hotter, colder, softer, firmer. I explored the long sweep of his arms, feeling the knotted cords of muscles moving beneath.

I felt an alien heat moving through me now, something coming not from my own waking human desires, but from his, bleeding over through the link that sustained my life and power. Coursing through the white-hot network of nerves, pooling and triggering pleasures that made me moan into his mouth, lost and only half-aware. The bliss was extreme, and dangerous—not because Luis's Earth-based powers were in any sense overwhelming me, but because I felt his own precise control eroding.

"Is it always like this?" I asked him, between gasps. It took him a long time to form words for an answer.

"Sometimes," he managed to reply. "Between—really strong Wardens—but different."

That was nondescriptive, but interesting to me. I traced a fingertip over the strong muscles of his shoulders, and I actually *saw* power moving between us, strong enough to manifest in a golden afterimage where I touched.

I laughed, took hold of his shirt collar, and pulled the knitted fabric over his head to bare his chest to me. The color of his skin was like the darkest honey, the muscles strong and tensed beneath. He had more tattoos than those on his arms, I discovered, though the tribal symbols meant little to me except in sharp indigo contrast to the rest of him.

I felt his hands on me now, restlessly moving, finally coming to rest around my waist on either side.

Moving up and in, to cover my small breasts in warmth through the thin material of the shirt.

Without breaking his intense, dark gaze, I pulled the shirt from my body and dropped it on the floor to mix with his. The difference in our skin tones was startling, and beautiful to me . . . my milk to his honey, and mine was beginning to pulse with opalescent colors that I was not sure really existed in the human realm. He looked down to the place where his hands now cupped my breasts. His thumbs stroked over the hardened tips, bringing a shudder through me that started from somewhere deeper than I could explain.

Bodies. Instincts. It was all frighteningly uncontrollable.

"Cass," he whispered. I sensed the fight in his voice, the struggle to contain the same instincts that haunted me. "Cassiel—"

I kissed him, and we melted together, one constant ecstasy of light and sound, power and bodies, and yet I knew there was more to this; my body craved it, demanded it, screamed for it.

Luis twisted and took me down to the couch in one swift, almost violent movement. My hands struggled to reach the fastenings of my pants, because I knew only one thing now, and that was how much I wanted to feel his skin everywhere, hot and damp against mine.

The air around us suddenly chilled, and I felt a crackle of energy that pierced even the fog of desire around us as heat was forcibly ripped from the air and coalesced together. I felt it before Luis, and I was able to shove him bodily out of the way of the strike, rolling him up and over the top of the couch.

He yelled in surprise. Before his body hit the floor on the other side, I was rolling the other direction, off the couch and to the floor, shoving the coffee table as I did. The bottle of whiskey tipped and spilled.

Lightning tore through the room, exploding from every electrical socket, stabbing toward a central point— the couch. It was a one-shot attack; the forces channeled through the lines overloaded the fuses almost instantly, but the convergence of the four-direction attack left deep, smoldering burns the length of the sofa.

Before the blue-white afterimages faded, I rolled to my feet, glanced at the burning couch, and reached down for my shirt. I pulled it on, then yanked on the leather jacket as Luis scrambled up on the other side, breathing hard, eyes wide with surprise.

"Someone just tried to kill us," I said.

"No shit. Really?" He came around the couch, took up his own shirt, and tugged it over his head. "Weather Warden, right?"

"Most likely."

"That won't be their only shot." He looked at the couch, charred and smoking, and then at the blackened outlets on the walls. The power was out in the house, of course. "Fuck, there goes my insurance premiums. You got any direction on this asshole?"

We had effortlessly shifted from intimacy to professional alertness, and I felt Luis burning the intoxication out of his blood, then out of mine, ensuring we were both perfectly prepared for battle. I crossed to the window, but I saw nothing amiss on the street outside; Luis launched his awareness out of his body and into the next plane of reality, which both the Wardens and the Djinn call the aetheric. Because I was linked to him, I was able to follow, and I did, rising up into a realm of existence that was less rooted in physical reality, and more in the reality of power. All things in the human world are invested, to some extent, with power; whether it is a faint spark or a flood depends strongly on its history and heritage. Humans tend to manifest strongly in the aetheric; after all, they come from long, long lines of ancestors, many wielding extraordinary energies, whether they know it or not. They also manifest themselves unconsciously, so what is seen on the aetheric tends to be more revealing than their physical forms.

Luis showed himself not too differently from his

usual physical body, but the flame tattoos on his arms glowed red, and moved like real fires. It struck me that on the aetheric, he looked very much like a Djinn; there was a sense of power and purpose about him that was startling. He had gained in strength recently, though whether that was because of his association with me or his personal tragedies, I could not say.

As a Djinn, I had a less obvious presence on the aetheric, but anchored as I was now in human flesh, I had a form of some kind. I couldn't see it for myself, and there were no mirrors in this plane, but I assumed it was fairly close to the shape I had donned in the human world. After all, this form had been—on some level— my own choice.

Luis and I hovered close together, and his wraith form took the hand of mine. I felt the indefinable click of power cementing into place, and then we rose together—up, far up, to dizzying heights. Beneath us, Albuquerque spread out into a map, but it glowed not with physical lights, but aetheric energy. History pooled and glowed in the older buildings, violet and green. Old battles and crimes stained the map in angry reds. But what we were looking for was easy to spot, even among the confusion . . . a spark of power like no other color showing. A Warden, moving among the streets. I saw the white flare of our own two presences as well. The attacking Warden was close, but not close enough to be within our physical line of sight. Weather Wardens did not need to be.

As we watched, the Warden reached out for power, gathered it in like a black vortex from the world around him, and flung it out in a focused, cohesive blow. It was not aimed for the house in which our physical forms stood.

It was aimed up, at the warm, stable weather systems covering the city. There was little for the Warden to work with, but all clouds contain stored energy, and there were enough to make a difference.

The Warden slammed together a storm, working in a crude, brute-force way that spoke of little training. This was odd, because in general the Weather Wardens were among the most precise; they had to be when working with such massive and volatile forces, which could so quickly spin out of even a gifted user's control.

Luis silently noted the Warden's location, and the two of us plummeted down through the shimmering layers of force and color, back in a dizzying fall to our bodies. I felt a second's disorientation, and then grounded myself in my flesh and whirled to run with Luis to the back door of the small house. He hit it first, slamming it open and leaving it to swing on its hinges, and jumped down the three shallow concrete steps that led down to the packed earth and sparse grass of the backyard. The back fence was sagging chain link, and beyond it we saw a figure in a black coat, running.

Overhead, clouds swirled, gray and troubled. Lightning flashed within them, still randomly aggressive but building up to a level that could become dangerous. I noted the risk, but we had little choice; a Weather Warden could rip the house down around us with surgical precision, and there would be very little we could do to stop it. Luis's powers were primarily those of stability, of life, of healing; there would be little overlap to cancel the more ephemeral, destructive powers of air and water.

There was a gate in the back, locked with a padlock. Luis reached out and snapped it off with barely an effort, turning the metal brittle and fragile with a pulse of power, and then we were out into the alley. It was piled with trash—boxes, cans, and plastic bags awaiting pickup by the city. The stench was horrifying, and after the first choking gasp I vowed to stop breathing until I was out of this miasma. A useless vow, of course, but it made me feel better.

Luis was a powerful runner, and he quickly pulled ahead of me as he dodged the trash and occasional stinking puddle in the alleyway. I gritted my teeth and forced my body to greater effort; my long legs ate up the distance between us, and I drew level with him just as we reached the end of the alleyway. My held breath exploded out, and I gasped in sweet, untainted air as we both scanned the street for the Warden we'd been pursuing.

He was standing about a block away, stock-still, staring upward. As I touched Luis's arm to alert him, the Warden reached up a commanding hand to the heavens, and lightning leapt from the low, gray clouds in a furious pink-tinted rush, grounded in the Warden's left palm, and exited from his right . . . straight at us.

"Down!" Luis shouted, and we both dove for the pavement as the energy sizzled toward us. One point was in our favor: The Warden seemed to have little fine control, though an overabundance of power. He was not able to redirect the strike toward us when we fell. Instead, it hit and charred a metal storage shed behind us, melting a wide, smoking hole in the side.

Luis slammed his open palm down on the sidewalk

next to his head, eyes focused on the Warden, and a line of force ripped through the ground, rising and falling like an ocean swell, cracking pavement and shoving aside everything in its path. It hit the pavement on which the Warden stood, tossing him off his feet and rolling him onto the thin grass of someone's yard. The grass was little to work with—thin, brittle, ill-watered—but I poured energy into it, forcing it to grow in long, rubbery runners that wound around the Warden's thrashing legs. It wouldn't hold him, but it would slow him down.

Luis softened the ground into mire, sinking the Warden's legs but leaving his upper body supported to prevent smothering. In seconds, the Warden was mired as his feet and lower legs sank into the soft mud, and were trapped as it hardened.

Luis offered his hand to help me to my feet, and we walked across the street to where the Weather Warden lay panting and helpless, locked into the earth.

He could not have been more than twelve years old.

Luis and I exchanged looks; I do not know what mine said, but his was appalled. *Just a boy,* it said.

A boy who'd tried twice to kill us. I was less appalled, and more interested in why.

I sank down to a crouch beside the boy, and examined him more closely. He was typical for the age, I supposed: a defiant glare, a childish, undefined face. Black eyes, black hair, coloring much like Luis's. "Your name," I said. "Give it."

He responded in Spanish. It was easy enough to guess the content of it, especially when accompanied by an aggressive hand gesture. I felt him gathering power again from the clouds overhead.

I reached out, thumped a forefinger against his forehead, and disrupted his concentration. The power fell into chaos, and the child blinked at me, startled.

"Name," I said again.

"Candelario," he said. "*Puta.*"

I raised my eyebrows. "Candelario," I repeated. "I assume that other was not your last name."

Luis said, from behind me, "Not unless his name translates to *whore.*"

I thumped the child-Warden's head again. "Stop. I can kill you if I wish, you know that?"

His concentration faded, and I felt him let the powers he'd been gathering up fade along with it. "So?" he challenged me. "You kill me, it don't matter. You're messing with *her.*"

I knew exactly who he meant. *Pearl.* My sister Djinn, once. My enemy. My conquest, or so I'd thought.

Pearl, insane and predatory, who had wiped an entire race of protohumans from the face of the planet once, in her jealousy and madness. She should by all rights have been destroyed, long gone from this Earth; I had seen to that. But instead she lived on, drawing strength and power in steady, parasitic increments from these hijacked Wardens.

These *children.*

Candelario was like Pammy—a victim, although it was likely he didn't know this, and would never accept it. He almost certainly believed that he was chosen, special, a trusted soldier in a war against evil. Pearl had convinced many. It was a signal weakness of the human condition, to be so easily swayed by those who wished them ill. To be rotted from within by their own belief in their virtue.

"Where is she?" I asked the boy. He spat at me. "She is using you. She is not your protector."

"You don't know anything!" he shot back. "Let me go or she'll kill you all!"

"I doubt that," I said. "Or she'd already have done so."

Something shifted inside the boy—a change so basic that it seemed that the bones inside of him moved along with it. His face seemed to grow sharper, more adult. More like . . . someone else.

"Do you?" An entirely different voice than the boy's, although using his vocal cords. "Really, do you doubt it, my sister? I thought you knew me better."

Pearl. Pearl was speaking through this boy. I caught my breath. I felt Luis's warm hand grip my shoulder, and I put a palm down flat on the warm ground, taking in power and feeding it through the cycle between us. Preparing for the strike, if it would come.

The boy's eyes were still black, but now it wasn't adolescent anger in them, it was something worse. Focused malice. Real evil.

"You send out your troops ill-prepared," I told her. "His attack was crude, you know."

"I'm not interested in subtlety," Pearl said. "You should know that about me, Cassiel."

Oh, I did. All too well. "Then why not come to me directly? I'm your enemy. Not this one."

"You're wrong," she said, and there was such deep, ancient anger in it that even I shuddered. "I have nothing *but* enemies. Doubt me not, sister mine. I will destroy this world and everything living on it. You're a fool if you believe otherwise."

With that, she was gone. Just . . . gone, leaving no clues, no comfort. She did not explain herself. She never had, and never would; I would have to guess at the dark motives behind her plans. But it would have to do with hatred and jealousy, just as it had before.

We had all felt it, when she had struck in those long-ago mists of time. Almost a million thinking beings killed in an instant, a mass murder on the scale of a god, a million souls screaming in pain and confusion. It had destroyed Pearl's mind, or what remained of it; in response, she had begun to rip at the universe around us, damaging things that should never have suffered injury. Things that lacked the capacity to heal.

I had destroyed Pearl, or I thought I had. I was the original murderer, among the Djinn. The first of us to kill one of our own.

Ironic, that some seed of her had survived, had somehow cast down roots among the new species that filled the emptiness she'd left on the planet with her crimes. Humanity was where Pearl hid. Humanity was where her power lay.

And so Ashan, the leader of the True Djinn, had ordered me to repeat not *my* crime, but Pearl's. By ending humanity, I would also, once and for all, end Pearl. So he believed, and it was likely true.

If I acted, I would become a monster. If I failed to act, Pearl would use the power she sucked from these humans to destroy my people.

Choices.

Candelario resurfaced, still glaring. I could see that he had no idea of what he had said—or what she said, using him as her remote tool. She hid within him, within all of them, like a virus.

This was, I realized, not a serious attack at all. Candelario was a crude instrument, powerful and poorly trained. A failure, she would classify him. Expendable. She sent him to me expecting him to be destroyed.

I exchanged a look with Luis, and then cupped a hand behind the boy's head. Bravado or not, he was sweating; I felt the clammy moisture against my fingers.

"Sleep," I said, and took a small measure of Luis's power to course through Candelario's nerves. The boy went limp, head gone heavy against my hand, and Luis softened the ground around his feet while I pulled him free. The grass was tenacious where it had twisted around his legs, but I finally convinced it to withdraw. I eased the boy to his back on the grass and looked up at Luis. "What now?"

He would be a bad enemy to leave at our backs; he might not be clever, but I sensed that he would be implacable. If he couldn't hurt us, he could threaten those around us, innocents caught in the crossfire of powers that they couldn't understand.

Luis was quiet for a moment; then he said, "I'll call Marion." Marion Bearheart, I understood this to mean; she was a powerful Warden in her own right, and she had been left here to oversee the skeleton crew of adepts remaining in the country while the majority of the Wardens were off chasing some other threat—what, I did not know and did not care. It was none of my concern.

Marion Bearheart was also the head of a division of

the Wardens which concerned itself with policing those with powers. They were police, judge, jury, and executioner when required.

We had little choice but to involve her. Only her resources could deal with this boy in anything other than a fatal manner.

Luis turned away to make the call on his cell phone, and I considered the boy on the ground. He looked thin, but not unhealthy. No scars or bruises that I could see. He had not been abused, or at least not in a way that left marks. Still, there clung to him an aura of desperation, of darkness, and I wondered if, on some level, his subconscious mind understood how little he meant to the one he followed so ardently.

I dug into his coat pockets, turning up the detritus of a young life—sticks of gum, a small cellular phone, a bus pass which showed he had arrived in town recently, coming to Albuquerque from Los Angeles, which I remembered was in the state of California. Many hours away. In another pocket I found a thin wallet, quite new, which contained only a library card for a place called San Diego, and some thin green sheets of money—not many. None of the other things that men like Luis normally carried in their wallets—no plastic cards, no slips of paper, no receipts for purchases. Only the cash, and the one simple card.

I held the card up to Luis as he finished up his phone call. He frowned as he read it. "San Diego?"

"What's in San Diego?" I asked.

"Awesome shoreline, big naval base, great weather. Apart from that, I have no idea." He handed it back. "Marion's dispatching a team to take the kid into custody while they see what's been done to him. Twelve is too young for anyone to be using the kind of power he did today. It could hurt him."

Regardless of whether or not it hurt *him,* it would certainly, inevitably bring tragedy to those around him. Candelario was too powerful, and had none of the training and balance of an adult Warden. (Though I wondered, from time to time, how much difference that made with many of the Wardens, who had a tendency to act like spoiled children in their own right.)

"How long before they arrive?"

"You're kidding, right? We're short-staffed everywhere. She's got to send a team out from Los Angeles. They'll fly in, but it'll still be tomorrow before they get here. We need to keep him on ice until then."

I didn't understand *on ice* until I framed it in the context of his words. *Keep him controlled and unconscious,* I interpreted. "Is that not kidnapping?"

"Sure," Luis agreed. "If anybody is missing the kid. Which they might be, but we can't give him back like this. He's been brainwashed, like the rest of Pearl's kids. Maybe Marion's people can deprogram him and de-activate his powers until he's old enough to grow into them."

That was a positive interpretation. The other side— the likely side—was that the Wardens would be forced to remove Candelario's powers completely, to ensure he didn't harm himself or others.

But neither of us could afford to take a personal interest in the child's rehabilitation. *Isabel,* I reminded myself. *Isabel must be saved.* Manny and Angela's child, Luis's niece. And something—though I hated to admit it—something to me as well. I dared not define it more than a simple admission that I had a connection to the child.

More than that implied threads which bound me into this half-life of human existence, and I was not yet ready to truly explore the depth of these connections.

None of which solved the problem of the boy lying at my feet. "What do we do with him?"

Luis shrugged. "Take him back to the house, I guess," he said. "Can you shield us?" He meant, from prying eyes—a thing which, in fact, I had already done when I realized how this might look to the random humans in the area. It was not invisibility, but it was similar; they would see us, but their brains would attach no significance to it. No memories would capture us.

Luis, on my nod, picked up the limp body of the boy in his arms, and we walked calmly across the street, down the alley (where I, at least, held my breath), and into the backyard of Luis's house. I refastened the lock on the gate, repairing the damage, and followed Luis inside.

He took the boy to Isabel's room, still furnished with all her little treasures and brightly colored toys, and stretched him out on a bedspread covered with cartoon characters. In a curiously kind gesture, he removed the boy's shoes and put them beside the bed, then touched his fingertips to the child's forehead. I sensed the sleep I'd given grow deeper.

He wouldn't wake for hours. "Unless you are planning to be here when he comes out of it, we should restrain him," I said.

"Great. Kidnapping *and* restraining. I guess we have to tack assault on to that, since we knocked him down."

"He was trying to kill us." I glanced toward the living room. "Also, he burned your couch."

"Well, that makes it all okay." Luis sighed and sat down on a delicate white stool decorated with tiny pink flowers, which did not seem at all suitable. "Seriously, Cass, we're in weird territory here. This kid could make a case that we abducted him, drugged him, tied him up. We could look at major prison time for this if we're not careful."

"He attacked *us.*"

"And you seriously think anybody's going to believe that? Anybody who wasn't there, I mean?" He shook his head. "We need him out of here before he wakes up."

"And how do we do that if the Wardens can't send someone until tomorrow?"

"Meet them halfway," he said. "We stick him in the backseat of a car, put a blanket over him, and drive. I've got a real bad feeling that if we don't, we're going to be sweating in a cell by nightfall."

I didn't really see the danger; with the power we had at our disposal, a jail could hardly hold us—at least, not a jail the way normal, nongifted humans constructed them. Holding any kind of Warden was extremely difficult, but Earth Wardens were by far the worst. Jails were made of metal, of stone, of wood—materials worked from the Earth and connected to her by chains of history.

If he was not unconscious, or drugged, Luis could make short work of most locks and stone walls. So could I, through him.

"You're not worried about escaping," I realized. He grunted.

"Thing is, I'm not exactly tops on the Good Citizen

list. They're going to come for me guns blazing, and there are a lot more of them than there are of us." Interesting that he was now automatically classifying the two of us as facing adversity together. "Trust me, it's better if we don't get into a fight. Not that we can't win it, but we shouldn't have to try. People will get hurt."

It wasn't the nature of the Djinn to be so prudent, but I saw his point, and I nodded. "What do you want me to do?"

"Manny's van is in the garage," Luis said. "Get it started, I'll get the kid. If you could tint the windows a little darker . . ."

Child's play. I went to the garage and did as he asked, and before long, Luis appeared in the door of the garage with the slight burden of the child in his arms. I opened the back sliding door, and we settled the boy across the bench seat in the back, sleeping quietly and wrapped in a colorful blanket from Isabel's closet. He looked even younger now than before, and much more helpless. I saw Luis touch his fingers gently to the boy's forehead, both in gentle affirmation and to ensure the deep sleep continued uninterrupted. I took the passenger seat up front, and Luis closed the back and entered the driver's side.

"You ready?" he asked. I shrugged. "Yeah, me neither. Here, take my phone. You make arrangements with the Wardens. Shoot for someplace halfway."

He backed the van out of the garage and into the street. The day remained quiet and sunny, few people around to see us leave. Manny and Angela's home— Luis's home, now—looked small and abandoned, and it was quickly left behind us as we made the twists and turns to lead us to the freeway.

The Wardens' central hotline connected me directly to Marion Bearheart. I knew her by reputation, as I knew most of the prominent Wardens; she had been well thought of by many of the Djinn, although that had never extended to me. She knew of me—that was certain—because I sensed the guarded tension in her low voice.

"We need a meeting place," I told her, without introduction; there was no need, as she would have been brought up to date by her staff or by Luis in any case. "Halfway between Albuquerque and your team's starting point. We can't wait here."

"You're sure? Crossing state lines with that boy is a federal offense."

"I'm fairly certain that we've already crossed that line," I told her, "and in any case, if we stay we're likely to be betrayed before they can reach us. We need to move."

She didn't argue the point, which was a pleasant surprise. "I'll send the team to Las Vegas," she said. "It'll be about a six-hour drive from where you are, and they can get a short-hop flight. Go to the casino with the pyramid, and ask for Charles Ashworth. I'll alert him that you're coming."

"He is a Warden?"

"Wardens are thin on the ground right now. He's Ma'at."

"And we can trust him?"

"In this, I believe you can." I approved that she limited her trust. Most humans didn't, to their great tragedy. "Call me when you arrive, or if there's any trouble. How powerful is this boy?"

"Very," I said. "Far too powerful for someone his age. He lacks control and focus, but in power I would rank him highly." I paused for a moment, then said, "I believe you will have to remove his powers."

"That's a last resort."

"I believe it will be necessary," I repeated, and shut off the phone. Luis cast me a doubtful look.

"Las Vegas," I told him. "I shall sleep now."

I drifted into darkness, only a little bothered by the noise of the road and the memory of Luis's hands moving on my skin.

When I woke up, it was because the car was skidding violently sideways, heading for an oncoming truck.

Chapter 3

"HOLD ON!" Luis shouted, and wrenched the wheel hard, trying to control our skid. The van jittered, wheels spinning, and finally straightened out. I blinked and grabbed the handle for security as gravity whipped us violently, and cast my senses out to see what had happened.

Ice. The road was covered with it, an impossibility in the current weather conditions. The air was warm, and there had been no freeze, no rain.

And yet the ice was at least an inch thick, slick as glass, and the van was not made for such conditions; its tires spun and slid, trying vainly for traction as our momentum sent us hurtling onward.

Likewise, the truck coming toward us was helpless, driven by its massive kinetic energy. The driver's attempts to steer were creating torque, and the trailer connected to the truck was beginning to slide as well, out of line with the cab.

"Weather Warden," I said. Luis nodded without taking his eyes off the oncoming truck. He looked tense, but unafraid. Timing his actions. With a deep breath, he held out one hand to me, and I took it, feeling the snap of energy between us—complex, deep, and growing intimate.

"Now," he breathed, and sent power out in a tightly focused wave. It plowed through the metal of the tractor trailer, slicing it cleanly in two. The two halves spun away from each other, spiraling outward from the release of energy, and Luis arrowed the van directly into the gap.

As we passed the wounded truck, I glanced over and saw the mangled remains of some large household appliance, which had been sliced in two by Luis's strike.

"Man, I am *hell* on insurance companies today," he said, with a trembling manic edge to his voice that was not quite humor. "Hold on. Could get bumpy."

The ice was already thinning, and a hundred feet on, it ended altogether. The tires bit into asphalt with an almost physical hiss, throwing us to the side.

Luis hit the gas and arrowed us onward. I looked back over my shoulder. The driver of the truck was out, duckwalking cautiously on the ice, shaking his head at the mess that had been made of his load. He probably did not understand in the least what had just happened, which was best for us all, I thought. We drove for a few tense moments.

Nothing else came at us.

"What do you think?" Luis asked. "You think she got ahead of us somehow? Set a trap? You sense anything else?"

"I didn't sense that one," I pointed out. "But somehow—I don't think so. It must have come from . . ."

From the boy. I felt that conviction strike me hard, and quickly twisted over my shoulder.

The boy's eyes were open, wide, and focused darkly on me.

I waited, but he didn't blink. There was an emptiness in his gaze that chilled me.

"Pull over," I said to Luis, as I unbuckled my seat belt. I climbed over the seats to land lightly next to the boy, who still lay bundled in his red-and-yellow blanket. He didn't move, not even to shift his gaze to follow me.

There was a dry flatness to his eyes.

I pressed my fingertips to his neck, feeling for a pulse. Nothing. No spark of life responding to my touch at all.

The boy was empty.

Candelario was *dead.*

Luis bailed out of the driver's side up front, slid the cargo door back and climbed inside the van. I sat back and watched as Luis performed the same search I had, but with more effort, more anxiety. He came to the same result, but he didn't simply accept the fact; he pulled the boy down into the flat open space between the seats and began pressing rhythmically on the unresponsive chest, sharp downward pumps that mimicked the beating of a human heart.

He glared at me. "Breathe for him."

I didn't move. "It's no use."

"Fuck you, Cassiel, just *do it!*"

This time, I didn't answer at all. His look should, by rights, have melted the life from me as well, but then he dismissed me and bent to breathe into the boy's slack mouth himself.

It took a long few moments for him, Earth Warden though he was, to admit what had been obvious to me from the beginning: The boy's life force was not struggling to remain, it was long departed. Destroyed. No matter what efforts were put in, he would not be miraculously waking.

Luis sat back against the metal wall of the van, breathing hard, eyes unfocused, and then pressed the heels of his hands against his eyes. He was trembling. I wanted to reach out to him, but I knew he wouldn't welcome the touch, not at this moment; instead, I reached down and gently closed the boy's open eyes, then lifted his heavy, limp body and put him back on the seat of the van.

When it finally came, Luis's voice was rough and uneven. "What the hell, Cass. What the *hell* is happening?"

"He was expendable," I said. "Pearl didn't get ahead of us; she used him to attack us. When he became of no further use, she used him to power the ice on the roadway; she hoped that you would be unable to avoid a wreck, perhaps fatal. She ripped so much power from him that he couldn't survive it. She killed him to try to get to us."

"I get that," he said raggedly. "But *why* kill him? Why now?"

I shrugged. "She doesn't have the respect for young life that you do," I said. "You are all insects to her, regardless of your circumstances. It means nothing to her to kill. Sometimes, she does it for her own amusement." Or she did, once, in my distant memories.

I had, in thousands of years past, watched Pearl stand at the leading edge of a storm of destruction, tall and wild, only vaguely holding to a shifting human shape that glittered and flowed on the wind. Before her a wide, pleasant valley stretched out, covered in thick yellow flowers. There was a settlement there of creatures who were not humans, as we would later recognize them, but shared most of the same ancestry.

Pearl rode the wave of destruction down the hill, sweeping everything before her in a storm of ashes and death. She was terrible and beautiful, and insane.

It was the last settlement of its kind, and Pearl destroyed every last life in it, erasing the existence of that race of prehumans, erasing any trace that they had ever been. She unmade them, leaving behind the clean, green meadow, the nodding flowers, and an Earth that remained, for a time, the sole province and plaything of the Djinn. Before the rise of humans.

I had watched. Watched, and done nothing. Only later had I acted, when we all realized just what Pearl had become. When her selfish desires no longer ran in concert with our own.

And I had made the fatal mistake of defeating her, but not fully destroying her.

"She isn't at her full strength," I said, almost to myself. The Pearl of that ancient memory was a primal force, a goddess, something that woke shivers in me even now. "If she were, she'd destroy us without a thought. Us, the entire city, the nation. She doesn't understand restraint, and the losses mean nothing."

"Great," Luis said. "And this bitch has Isabel."

"She wants Ibby alive. Ibby could not be in a safer place for now." Far safer than she would be with us, at least until we worked out what it was Pearl was doing. "We should perhaps worry about ourselves."

"Trust me, I'm worried." Luis turned his gaze back, unwillingly, to the boy. "Why didn't she just kill us the way she did him?"

"I don't think she can," I replied. "Yet. The boy must have trained at the Ranch, where she kept the children. It's likely that she has access to those who've surrendered their will to her in ways that she doesn't to others, like us, who resist. But she's powerful, and growing more powerful with every passing day. The more who surrender their wills to her . . ." I shook my head. There was no point in taking it further; he understood my concerns fully.

"If she's killed her only connection to us, maybe we can make it to Las Vegas before she gets another one in position to take us on."

"Maybe," I said slowly. Something did not seem right about that, however, and it dawned on me precisely what it would be. "Luis. We have to leave him."

Silence in the van, deep and weighty. The wind outside rattled sand against the windows, and the metal frame rocked slightly from the pressure. Luis's face was blank, his dark eyes hot.

"I'm going to pretend you didn't just say that."

I raised my eyebrows. "Why?"

"Because if I seriously thought you would dump this poor kid like trash at the side of the road—"

"Luis," I interrupted him. "*Think*. She did not have to kill him. Why would she? He was perfectly placed to destroy us, if we gave him time to recharge, and he is young enough that we would have hesitated to fight him with full strength. It would be a significant advantage. She sacrificed a pawn who was in position to destroy us. *Why?*"

He didn't answer this time. I don't think he understood my point, so I made it clear.

"When we tracked Isabel toward the Ranch where Pearl was keeping her, what did Pearl do?"

He opened his mouth, then shut it, thinking. Then squeezed his eyes shut as if he had a terrible headache. "She whistled up the cops and accused us of kidnapping," he said. "Nothing the cops will respond to faster than an endangered, abducted child."

"And when they arrive," I said softly, "they find a boy dead in the back of our van."

He understood, then, and leaned forward to press both hands to his face. He had a record with the police, the kind of thing that predisposed them to suspicion. His own niece had disappeared.

This would not go well for him.

I continued, only because I felt I had to drive the point home. "She intended this to slow us down, confuse us, delay us. Separate us. As you pointed out before, the police can be defeated, but they are many, and we can't fight them on fair terms. We must run. And we *must* leave the boy behind."

"Wouldn't do any good. Forensics and shit, don't you watch any of those cop shows on television? They'll link the kid to me sooner or later. Hell, the blanket around him is Isabel's. And my DNA's in the system."

I shrugged. "Those things, I can fix. We leave him, and I remove all traces and links to us, both physical and aetheric. But we must do it now, quickly. She won't be waiting to put her plans in motion. All my skill won't help if the police search the van and find him here. I can't credibly hide him from their sight. It's too small an area."

Luis waited a torturously long second, then wiped

a palm over his hand and nodded. He looked ill. I didn't hesitate; I picked up the boy, slid open the door of the van, and jumped down the embankment of the road in a shower of pale dirt, sliding out of sight of the road.

"Wait," Luis said. He'd lunged to the opening in the van, and his knuckles were white where he gripped the door frame. "Don't just—don't just dump him. He meant something to somebody. Like Ibby means something to us. Please. I'm asking you. Treat him—treat him like you care."

That said a great deal about what Luis presumed he knew about me.

I stared at him for a few seconds, saying nothing, and then walked away.

Desert stretched out on all sides, hot and sterile, dotted with the alien shapes of the only plants that could fight the harsh conditions. But the desert was far from empty; no, it throbbed with life, from the busy burrowing insects to the running rabbits to the cunning, coiled snakes.

It was a hard place to leave a child.

I let the sense of bruised hurt fade, and focused on my task. I balanced my burden—suddenly much heavier than its mere physical weight—and set off at a steady run, heading far from the road.

I didn't look back, but I heard Luis say, very quietly, "I'm sorry." I didn't know if he meant it for the boy, or for me.

I made the boy a grave on a hillside, near an overhanging fragrant bush that offered a little shade. It overlooked a valley lush with the rainbow of the desert—russets, ochers, and tans, dotted with vivid greens and the occasional struggling flower. It had a kind of empty, wild beauty. It was all I could offer as apology, as acknowledgment of what Luis had said—that somewhere in the world, someone was missing this boy.

I stripped away the blanket and carefully, using bursts of Luis's power, removed any traces that might link the boy back to us before wrapping it tightly around him again, in an obscure wish to give comfort. Conscious of the press of time, I knew I couldn't hesitate, yet something made me do just that.

I looked down on the boy's silent, empty face before covering it, and said, "Be at peace, child. I will stop those who hurt you."

Then I leaped out of the grave and triggered a heavy landslide of dirt to cover him. The earth flowed and shifted, thumping heavily down, and I felt myself flinch from the sound. Not a Djinn reaction, a human one, a primal recognition of what it meant to be beneath the ground. To be gone from the world.

I sent out a thought that might have, in a human, been a prayer, as the earth settled in place above him.

I felt the Mother stir slowly and quietly beneath my feet, a sense gifted to me through my connection to Luis—although even Luis rarely felt *Her* presence so clearly. A tendril only, a whisper, questioning, like a murmur in sleep. This borrowed touch, fleeting and faint, made me drop to my knees and press my hands flat into the sand. I gasped in ragged breaths, begging with all my soul for the blessing of her awareness, of her embrace.

I had forgotten how alone I was, until for a single, shining instant, I was found.

Then sense faded, and I was alone, lost, and afraid once more.

Human, again.

I rose, still breathing hard, and wiped the tears from my dusty face before heading back to the van.

"Here they come," Luis said, less than half an hour later, glancing in the rearview mirror. "You know the drill, Cass. Stay cool."

I nodded. The van was completely empty of any trace of the boy. No doubt there would have been witnesses that saw the boy back near the Rocha house, but one thing I had quickly learned about Luis's neighbors: They were not eager to help the police.

It was highly doubtful any of them would talk.

I looked in the mirror on the passenger side and saw the lurid red and blue lights, and heard the rising wail of a siren. Luis immediately slowed the van, pulling off to the gravel shoulder of the road.

The police car pulled in behind.

It went as Luis had no doubt assumed it would; we were ordered to get out of the van and lean against the hot metal of the vehicle. The policemen—two large men who kept their ready hands near the butts of their guns—searched the van, then each of us. Luis stayed bland and calm. If I fumed at the casual way that they dared to touch me, I kept the reactions carefully hidden. That was one thing that Detective Halley had done for me; he had taught me to handle these official invasions with some semblance of control.

All licenses and registrations were current, and, as I had expected, the police had nothing but an anonymous report on which to question us. Without some physical evidence, they were forced to let us go.

I didn't imagine for a moment that they were happy about it.

Luis let out a slow breath as the police car, its lights still flashing, disappeared behind us. He kept the van to a careful speed, mindful of all road laws, and at the next turning pulled off in the parking lot of a diner that advertised HOME COOKING. It smelled like grease, even from where I sat a hundred feet away.

"Are we turning around?" I asked. I sincerely hoped we weren't stopping for food. Not here.

"I was thinking about it," Luis admitted, then shook his head. "No, it's no good. We need information, and we're not going to get it sitting around waiting for Pearl to send another kid after us. The Ma'at know things we don't. Let's see what we can get out of them."

Activity. I felt a slow smile spread across my face, warm and genuine. "Sounds like fun."

"Your definition of fun sometimes worries me." Dark eyes examined me for a moment. "You want something to eat?"

I shuddered. "Not here."

"You're sure."

"Yes."

"Not even pie?"

I did love pie. I turned my gaze to the diner, and said, "Not here."

"You're too picky."

"Perhaps," I said. "Perhaps I have a better-developed sense of self-preservation than you do."

He frowned. "You just got no appreciation for the little things."

I continued to smile as the hot breeze blew in through the open window, washing away the stench of burning food. "Then how is it that I like pie?" I asked him. "Or that I like you?"

"Hey, I'm not a *little* thing. Don't you go spreading that rumor."

"Everything is small," I said, and my smile faded. "Everything. Even me." The memory of that brush of the Mother's touch ached inside me, woke needs that had slept since I'd been cast down into human flesh. I wanted, needed . . .

Luis took my hand in his, a human touch that was irrationally comforting. "Stay with me, Cass. We're going to find a way out of this."

I knew the way out. I kept my gaze trained on the desert as it swept by outside my passenger window, and I tried not to think about how much destruction lay along that path to victory.

I would lose him.

I would lose them all in winning, and it would be such a fierce, cold victory. A world empty, new, swept clean of the complications of humanity. The way Pearl had swept the world clean, once. For the good of the Djinn, or so we had pretended.

It had not been worth it then. I was far from sure that it would be worth it now.

*   *   *

Las Vegas was a dizzying wonderland of lights that reminded me of nothing so much as the aetheric. It was filled with spinning, brilliant colors that seemed to blend one into another, too many for the eye to take in. It seemed to burst out of the ground in fantastic shapes, more a defiance of nature than its product. Where Albuquerque often seemed shaped by its environment, Las Vegas seemed to deliberately ignore the land upon which it sat.

There was a certain magnificent idiocy in that, a denial of all the reality so evident around us. Humans. I would never truly understand them, even if I survived in this body a hundred years. That made me wonder ... would I grow old? Develop infirmities and diseases? Could I actually create life, the way humans did, to live on after my time on the Earth?

The thought made me involuntarily look at Luis, who was navigating the van through traffic with the ease of someone who was a frequent visitor to this town. He glanced back. "What are you thinking?" he asked.

"I don't think you would want to know," I said, very truthfully. I couldn't imagine Luis would find it comforting to consider the prospect of a child, much less being the father of *my* child.

Although, if the earlier events had been at all indicative of his feelings, and not simply raw physical needs let loose by the whiskey, then ... perhaps. But it seemed not to be the time to pursue the thought.

"Okay," he said. "So we're going to meet with the head guy for the Ma'at. You're going to mind your manners, right?"

"Of course."

From the rude noise he made, Luis evidently did not believe me. That was, perhaps, appropriate. "Just try not to destroy anything. Or make enemies out of the only real allies I've been able to scrounge up. It's not like we're neck deep in people willing to help us, you know."

The Ma'at, from all I knew of them, were not the strongest allies that might be had in any case, and I was far from certain they were really interested in helping us. They were people who, though having some tendency toward wielding the same powers as the Wardens, had been disqualified for admission into their ranks— usually because their powers were not deemed significant enough to matter. In some cases, though, they were powerful indeed, and had somehow managed to slip through the complex net that identified potential Wardens as young adults, which meant they lived a furtive double life, and were jealous of their secrets.

The Ma'at were unique in that they had set out from the beginning to work with the Djinn—not to hold them as slaves, as the Wardens did, but to seek out those who were free and might be interested in an alliance. There were few of these, and almost all were New Djinn, not the elders like me. In fact, I knew of only one of the True Djinn who had taken such a direct interest in humanity: Venna, who often presented herself as a child when in human form. Venna was ancient and extraordinarily powerful. I suspected the child-form to be a complex sort of joke I did not fully understand.

Las Vegas burned in alien colors as we entered the main part of the city—brilliant greens, acid yellows, burning reds and pinks. The patterns and hues rippled and changed in brilliant, mesmerizing patterns, and I

stared at them without blinking, fascinated by this manifestation in the physical world of what I so loved about
the realms available to the Djinn. Crude it might be, but
the fact that humans found this mesmerizing as well
showed a connection between humanity and the Djinn
that I'd never really considered.

I hardly noticed the crush of strangers passing on the
streets, or the river of wheeled metal rushing around us;
I hardly even noticed the stench of exhaust and rubber
that never seemed far absent from these clusterings of
humanity. That was a measure of how delighted I was by
the triumphant blaze of light around us.

And then, quite suddenly, we were facing something
that I recognized with an almost physical shock—a
shock that quickly faded, because the familiarity was
only a surface impression. This was not the magnificent
carved Sphinx, nor the towering majesty of a pyramid;
these were modern reproductions, lacking in the so-
phistication of those long-dead artisans, or the sanctity
with which those works of religious fervor had been
imbued.

These were cheap copies, packaged and sold as mere
entertainment, and just for a moment the glitter of the
place fell away, and I grew angry. Angry that humans
valued their history so little. Angry that even their great-
est achievements could be made so commonplace.

I wondered what would happen if I melted the false
Sphinx into a messy heap of painted slag, and then
remembered—regretfully—that I had promised Luis
not to destroy anything.

Still. There was provocation. I could claim self-
defense, in a way.

"Right," he said, parking the van in one empty space in a vast field of concrete covered with neatly ordered glittering vehicles. "Please do me a favor. Keep quiet and follow my lead. And don't start anything."

I glared at the Sphinx. In my opinion, something had already been started.

It stared serenely past me, toward the distant horizon. That, at least, it had in common with its ancient cousin.

The lobby of the hotel was cavernous, dark, and—like the exterior—a cheap exhibition that had little to do with the history it claimed to honor. A constant chatter of chimes, coins, and voices set my nerves trembling with the need to make them all fall silent and leave me in peace, but I gritted my teeth and held on to the promise I had made to Luis. *They will help,* I told myself a little desperately. *They will help us find Isabel.*

The carpeting was thick and plush underfoot, and it had soaked up a million spilled drinks. The entire room reeked of desperation, old liquor, and cleaning fluids, although most humans wouldn't have noticed anything at all. I tried to breathe shallowly, and balled my hands into fists. I must have seemed angry, because I noticed uniformed security men and women turning to watch our progress through the room. One lifted a small device to his lips and spoke.

Luis went to a simple phone set into an alcove; the label above it said PRIVATE USE ONLY. There were no buttons, only the handset and cradle. He picked it up, put it to his ear, and said, "Luis Rocha and Cassiel to see Charles Ashworth. We're expected."

Before he'd replaced the handset, one of the security

men was behind us, hemming us into the alcove. Not aggressively, which was all that saved him, but certainly with unmistakable purpose.

"Please wait," he said, and set his feet in such a way that I could tell he would not be moving without orders. Or, of course, without the application of appropriate force. But a glance at Luis told me that this was still not the time, nor the place, for that kind of action.

Someone not far away screamed—not in fear or pain, but in some kind of joy. I heard a sustained clatter of coins, and a flashing yellow light began to pulse about fifty yards distant, among the ranks of quietly chiming machines.

"Man," Luis sighed. "Wish I had that kind of luck."

"You're an Earth Warden," I reminded him. "You could bring gold from the ground if you wished it."

"Yeah, I know. But I don't. Because that would be wrong, and besides, it'd attract too much attention from the other Wardens. So no."

"You could simply force the machines to deliver winnings."

He eyed me as if he'd never seen me before. "You want me to cheat in a casino run by the Ma'at? You really think that's any kind of a good idea?"

I shrugged. "I am simply pointing out that you make your own luck. Whether you use it or not is your choice."

"Yeah, well, stop putting bad thoughts in my head already."

"Was I?"

Our eyes locked, and I felt his attention like the heat of a distant fire. "Pretty much all the time."

That made me want to smile, but somehow, I resisted

the urge. I was making a habit of resisting urges. I wondered if that made me virtuous, or merely stupid.

After another few moments, the security man received a message through a tiny speaker tucked inside his ear, and stepped aside. "This way," he said. Polite, but firm. He led us through the rows and rows of casino machines, then off behind a busy, glowing bar with a phalanx of bartenders pouring dozens of drinks. There was a plain, dark wooden door set into the wall, almost invisible in the shadows. A plain gold plate was engraved with the words PRIVATE SALON.

The guard swung the door open and stepped aside to allow us to enter. Beyond, it was just as dimly lit, but much smaller. Dark paneling, discreet inset paintings that I instantly felt were true classics. A heavy desk at the far end of the room, with two substantial armchairs placed at precise angles in front of it. An empty poker table, covered in green felt, sat in the corner, surrounded by comfortable chairs.

Behind the desk at the far end sat a small, neat man. Older, with white hair and a lined, sharp face. His hands were folded together on the empty, clean wooden surface, and he watched us without much of an expression—neither welcoming, nor suspicious.

He didn't rise to greet us. "Rocha," he said, and nodded. "Sorry to hear about your brother and sister-in-law. My condolences."

"Thank you," Luis said, and took one of the chairs angled to face the desk. I wondered for a moment if I should take the other, then decided to stay standing, arms folded, behind Luis's chair. He *had* told me to follow his lead, but I was not entirely comfortable here, in this place. There was something powerful, and it was also something that I did not quite understand.

"You're Cassiel." That pulled my attention back fully onto the old man. "I'm Charles Spencer Ashworth. For now, I'm the head of the Ma'at."

"For now?" Luis asked.

"Let's just say there was some management reorganization. Internal politics, nothing you need to worry about. Coffee?" He didn't wait for a reply, simply pressed a button inset in the top of the desk. "You've got some explaining to do, I think."

He assumed a very clear posture that said he was awaiting our report. Luis took a moment before saying, "I'm not sure I should do my explaining to you. With respect, sir."

Ashworth's thin lips stretched, but I didn't think it could be properly named a smile. "With respect," he said, "I think that if you're standing in my hotel, surrounded by my people, and there's a Djinn standing in the corner ready to enforce my wishes, I really think you should reconsider."

I whirled.

In the darkest corner of the room stood a Djinn— not one of those I felt the most fellowship with, but a New Djinn, one who had been born from human origins. An artificial creation, I had always thought. A pretender.

This one was tall, slender, and the bluish color of smoke even in human flesh. He bowed his head slightly as I met his gaze. His eyes were a bright, liquid violet, and his hair was dusty gold. Beautiful, in a shocking way, although not in a way I had ever seen before.

He was—for a New Djinn—powerful.

"Cassiel," he said, and his voice was magic distilled—soft, warm, deep, comforting. "I've long wanted to meet you—though, I admit, I never wished to face you on the battlefield. You may take that as a sign of respect."

He was gracious in pretending that I was still something a Djinn could truly fear. I nodded unwillingly in return. "Your name?" I could have read it from the air around him, once. Not now.

"Rashid," he said.

I turned back to Ashworth and said, "He belongs to you?" It was a deliberate provocation, and I heard a soft laugh from Rashid—amused, almost mocking, but far from offended. Ashworth smiled again, this time more genuinely.

"No one belongs to anyone," he said. "Tenet of our society. Anyone who joins the Ma'at joins as a volunteer, and they can leave when and if they desire."

"How democratic," I said. I didn't put any special weight on the words, which made them, by default, a touch sarcastic. "I had heard you made use of Djinn when necessary. I see it's true."

"We make use of anyone willing to work. Including you, should the spirit move you, of course."

I shook my head slightly and focused back on Luis. My conversation had given him time to decide what to do, and I could see by the set of his back and shoulders that he was bracing himself for some kind of impact.

"The boy we were trying to save is dead," Luis said.

"We did our best, but whoever sent him drained him in the last attack. We couldn't help him."

Ashworth's thick brows slowly climbed, though his face remained set and still. "Really. I'd heard you were a skilled Earth Warden."

"I am." He glanced at me. "So is she."

"Then I think you'd best explain to me why a child attacked you in the first place, and why you couldn't simply stop him without death entering into it."

Luis did his best, but Ashworth gave no indication, throughout the explanation, as to whether or not he believed a word of it. When Luis came to the point where we'd left the boy's body behind, I heard a soft hiss from Rashid, behind me. I resisted the urge to turn.

"It was not my first choice," I said. "But it was necessary. She intended for us to be caught with the body. She hoped we wouldn't notice his passing until it was too late."

"She," Rashid repeated. "Name this enemy." I didn't. He gave another soft sound of disgust. "There is no great villain in this, Ashworth. Only the twisted desperation of one who was once a queen among our kind. Don't believe her. The humiliation of being cast down into skin has turned her."

"I'll believe what I like, Rashid. Thank you for your input." I'd never heard a human rebuke a Djinn in quite that way, firm and authoritative—not a human who didn't arrogantly assume that owning a Djinn protected them from retribution. The aggression raised fierce, cold instincts in me, even though it was not directed toward me. I wondered what it did to Rashid. "I was at the

Ranch," Ashworth continued. "I understand what you two think you saw."

"We don't think," Luis said. "We know. She exists. We may not be able to find her yet, but we will. And we're going to get my niece back, safe and sound."

Ashworth didn't comment on that. He said, instead, "Not many Wardens left these days. Some are off chasing ghosts, some lying low, the rest just trying to hold things together. A good portion of them died fighting the Djinn in the rebellion. Some say there's still a war going on, one of attrition. Fewer Wardens, stretched thinner. Enemies picking them off, one by one."

"Some say it could benefit the Ma'at," Luis pointed out.

Ashworth's face twisted in a tired grimace. "People talk nonsense most of the time. I have no interest in making the Ma'at any kind of replacement for the Wardens. You should know that, better than most. The world needs Wardens; if she didn't, they wouldn't be here. They're part of the natural order, same as the Djinn. Same as regular human beings, animals, plants, insects, protozoa. Ma'at, boy. Everything in balance. Now. Why are you here? You could've turned around and gone straight back home, nothing to stop you."

"Guess just wanting to visit Vegas isn't a good excuse."

Luis's attempt at humor—never more than half-hearted—fell into a cold silence. Ashworth didn't reply. He shifted his gaze to me. "You really do think this creature's real."

"Yes," I said. "She's real. She's a threat to the Djinn. A genuine threat. And until we can locate her again, we are fighting shadows. She can target us. We can't target her in turn."

Rashid made that sound again. I turned to face him, and he folded his arms across his chest. "Yes?" he asked. "You have something to tell me?"

"Not really," I said. "I presume when you're screaming your last, the way Gallan screamed, you will take my words more seriously."

I left that deliberately ambiguous. He would know of my friend Gallan's death—the death of a Djinn never went unremarked, and Gallan had been no minor power. What Rashid did not know, from the sudden burst of brightness in his eyes, was whether or not I had been the cause of it.

I knew well enough what he suspected.

"I take you seriously now," Rashid said. "Believe it."

"Enough," Ashworth snapped. "The both of you. You'll not be settling any grudges in my office; I just redecorated. Luis, what the hell do you want from me? I can't offer you any real help. And I don't have any real information."

"Then there's one other thing you can do. You can lend me a Djinn," Luis said.

There was a sudden, startling quiet among the four of us; Ashworth's gaze leapt to Rashid, and mine moved to focus on Luis as I struggled to process what he had just said.

He *had* a Djinn. He had *me.* I felt a sudden, baffling surge of rage and confusion, and I wondered if it was … jealousy? Surely not. Surely I had not sunk so low.

Rashid's voice came from behind me. Very close behind, so close that I felt the whisper of air on the back of

my neck. "You must not be performing to his expectations," he said. "How very sad for you."

I turned, slammed the palm of my hand into the flat of
his chest. It should have sent him flying across the room,
splintered paneling, crumbled concrete in his wake.

Instead, Rashid simply stood there, smiling at me
with a terrible bright light in his violet eyes. Then he
took hold of my wrist, and snapped my arm.

I cried out as the bones broke, twisted, and ripped
into muscle. Pain tore through me in a livid white wave,
loosening my knees, and darkness flickered over my
eyes.

"Rashid!" Ashworth shouted, and surged to his feet
behind the desk. Luis, however, was faster. His armchair
tipped over, and before it hit the carpet with a dull thud
he was next to me. He pointed a finger at Rashid, and
for a second I saw—or thought I saw—black flames lick
up and down his arms. I blinked. It was an effect of the
pain, surely.

"You," Luis said. "Let go of her. Now."

Rashid did, still smiling, and stepped back. Luis took
my arm in both his hands, and his touch was extraordinarily gentle and warm. I felt the warmth cascade into
me, power twining in intimate circles around the damage. I swayed closer to him as my strength left me, and
he caught me with one arm around my body, holding the
injury clear as the healing continued.

"Point made," Rashid said, sounding bored and
waspish. "She's no better than a human, is she? Hardly
of much use at all. You *do* need a Djinn. But why, I
wonder?"

"I need one who thinks he's invulnerable," Luis said through gritted teeth. "You'll do fine."

Rashid frowned, and a little of his overwhelming arrogance flickered away. Not enough to matter, however. I found some strength left after all, and pushed away from Luis to stand on my own. My arm felt fragile and barely knitted together, and I knew I shouldn't test it, though the healing was vastly accelerated. Rage had subsided to a low, hot burn deep within me, but I was less pleased with what had replaced it: fear. Was this how humans lived, so afraid of pain, so aware of their fragile and temporary bodies?

I didn't like it. Not at all. "What are you doing?" I asked. Luis sent me a dark, urgent look that almost demanded my silence. He went back to a silent war of stares with Rashid, who, finally, crossed his arms across his chest, lowered his chin, and gave a wolfish smile. "You think you can challenge me with threats of danger? Little man, you don't know what you're talking about."

"Oh, sure, you're a big man, breaking the arms of women without giving them chances to fight back," Luis said. "Big talker. I get that. But what I'm asking is for something that's going to take some balls and some brains. Maybe you should go get somebody, you know, better. I'll wait, man."

Rashid's eyes grew molten, and I thought for a dull, terrible second that he would simply burn Luis down to the ground for that. He was fully capable.

Instead, Ashworth snapped, "Enough, you two. We don't have time or luxury for this. Rocha, tell *me* what you want, and don't be coy about it. Now."

It must have taken a sincere and awesome act of will to turn his back on Rashid, but somehow Luis managed it. For security, I kept an eye on the Djinn. I didn't for even an instant trust him. He was a jackal, sniffing for opportunity, and I had a sudden and sickening experience— for perhaps the first time in my long existence—of being the wounded prey.

"I need a Djinn who can verify where this boy came from," Luis said.

"The dead boy?"

"Yes. Time's critical. Traces fade. I need somebody who's not full of bullshit and bluster." That, of course, was specifically thrown at Rashid, and I watched the Djinn consider, again, whether or not to kill us. If he decided to act, there would be little Ashworth could do to stop him, and while Luis and I would put up a fight, it was a foregone conclusion how it would end.

Wasn't it?

I don't know what expression must have crossed Ashworth's face, as he assessed all these things, plus of course the potentially lethal damage a fight could do inside his dark-paneled sanctum. Finally, he said, with absolutely no emphasis, "I think we could work something out. However, it would have to be done as a strictly voluntary effort on the part of the Djinn. That's our code."

"Of course," Luis said, and hesitated before continuing. "Thing is, from everything we know about this situation, tracing this dead boy back to the ones behind him could be dangerous. Even for a Djinn. I wouldn't want anybody to misunderstand the risks involved."

Rashid was still giving us that unsettling predator's smile. Now he said, "I wouldn't miss it for the world."

Ashworth sighed.

"Then I pronounce you all friends and allies. Mazel tov," he said, in a tone that was weary with disgust. "Now all of you, get the hell out of my office, out of the hotel, and go kill each other someplace where I don't have to worry about cleaning it up."

Chapter 4

I KNEW LITTLE about Rashid. My kind looked on our younger, upstart cousins with little respect, and we'd rarely taken the time to know or acknowledge them individually.

Except, of course, for Jonathan.

Even now, thinking of him, I felt a knot in my chest. Jonathan had come on us like a black storm of power, unlooked-for. He had lived as a mortal man, and he had been the first of all those we now called Wardens; his bond to the Earth was something even those of us who remembered formless voids could not explain, or imagine. His death had woken her to fury and grief, and she had preserved Jonathan's soul by creating a new form around him. A new kind of life.

She had made him a Djinn, by gathering in the dying life force of thousands near him. Not only him—another had been created that day. Jonathan's friend David, who had died with him. The first of many, after them.

But it was Jonathan who had been given the heart of the Mother, and it was Jonathan who, regardless of his human origins, had wielded more power over the Djinn—*all* the Djinn, old and new—than any other, before or since.

We had never accepted him, but all of us, however unwillingly, had obeyed him. For thousands of years, the True Djinn had bent our necks to one we should have, by rights, despised; and some had, though quietly. But there was also respect in even the most militant of us. And yes, love. Jonathan had shone with a kind of purity that I could never understand, nor hope to imitate.

I had even grieved for him when he was lost to us. But there will not be another Jonathan, another New Djinn who can charm and bully us into becoming one people. The True Djinn will always stand apart. We are too arrogant to do anything else.

And that was the gulf that lay between me and Rashid, and always would.

We walked out of Ashworth's office into the chiming dimness of the casino, none of us speaking. Rashid was on one side of me, Luis on the other. People avoided our path, though whether consciously or unconsciously, I don't know. I caught sight of us striding together on a security monitor; Luis looked utterly focused, tall, and dangerous; Rashid had moderated the alien nature of his coloring just enough to keep himself from drawing stares, although in this strange place that probably wasn't necessary.

My pale, severe face, white hair, and pale leathers seemed to glow like a ghost between the two of them.

We looked . . . like nothing any sane human would want to challenge. Heads turned to follow us as we moved through the crowds, and I felt eyes assessing me, measuring, coveting.

It was oddly interesting.

Outside, the hot wind dried a faint trace of sweat

from my face, and Rashid's skin darkened, just a touch, to better absorb the sun's harsh rays. Luis slipped on a pair of sunglasses. We stood in the shadow of the false pyramid, not far from the false Sphinx, and faced each other without speaking.

Then Rashid said, "Take me to where you left the boy."

Luis nodded and led the way to where we had parked the van. He slid open the back and gestured for Rashid to get in, but the Djinn simply stood there, frowning, head cocked.

"You came in this?"

"Yeah, obviously, not up to your standards, I get that. Just get in." Rashid curled his lip and stepped into the van, dropping into the seat with obvious distaste. Luis looked at me and rolled his eyes. "I thought *you* were bad. I see it runs in the Djinn family."

I said—and Rashid said, from within the van—"We are *not* family!"

Luis burst out with a short bark of laughter. "Sounds to me like you are." Before sliding the door shut, though, he fixed Rashid with a long look, and leaned in to say, "You touch Cassiel again, you hurt her again, and you and me, we're going to have a disagreement, Rashid. It'll end in a world of hurt. You understand?"

Rashid turned his eyes straight forward, not even so much as acknowledging the threat. Luis slammed the door, sighed, and said, "Try to get along, okay? This is tough enough without bar brawls with our supposed allies."

Like Rashid, I didn't bother to acknowledge his words, although they were undeniably wise.

I heard Luis say, grumpily, as he rounded the front to climb into the driver's side, "Freaking Djinn."

I smiled. Just a little.

Luis drove us to the approximate location where we'd stopped, and I led the two of them through the sand and scrub out into the wilderness. Luis kept up a steady whisper of curses under his breath as he trudged. He hated the desert, I believe. Certainly he was not in favor of its heat, although Rashid and I both gloried in it; Djinn were creatures of fire, and even as muted and diminished as I was, I could still feel the tingle of ecstasy along my nerves.

Luis sweated.

We arrived at the hillside where I'd buried the boy, with its view of ocher and red gullies and a burning blue sky, and Rashid crouched down, drew thin, clever fingers through the dirt, and looked up at me in surprise. There was something that shone in his eyes, momentarily, like respect. Then it was gone.

"How?" he asked. Luis looked at me, frowning.

"How what?"

"She knows."

I did. he was asking about how I had touched the spirit of the Earth here, in this place.

I shrugged. "She came," I said. "You can't summon her. You know that."

Rashid did, in fact, know. He watched me for another moment, then nodded and raked fingers through the dirt again. "You didn't kill the boy," he said. "I stand corrected."

"I told you we didn't," Luis snapped. "Can you hurry

up and track where he came from? Some of us need shade around here."

For answer, Rashid plunged his hand down into the dirt, all the way to his elbow, and then drew it back out with a sharp twist. He shook the dust from it and nodded, eyes gone bright, but somehow distant. "The trail is clear," he said. "But fading. I will leave you and follow it. It will be faster."

"Rashid," I said. "Don't go too close."

He made an impatient gesture. "I'm not afraid of your phantom enemy."

"Neither was Gallan," I interrupted. "Who is gone, Rashid. I don't like you. But neither do I wish to see you destroyed. I am warning you: *Don't go too close.*"

He heard the urgency of what I said, and finally, unwillingly, nodded. Still, I didn't feel he had truly understood. I stepped forward, touched his hand, and said, while looking directly into his glowing eyes, "She was once one of us. A Djinn. She will kill you if she can."

He shook his head, rejecting the idea—mostly, of course, because it came from me. I controlled a flash of anger and continued. "I would ask another task of you."

That made his eyes widen. He cocked his head, a trace of a frown between his brows. "What?"

"Find the boy's people," I said. "His family. Those who lost him. I would wish—I would wish to return him, if we can."

He stared at me, no expression on his face for a long moment, and then gave a sharp, dry nod.

And then simply . . . faded. Gone. I saw a shimmer on the aetheric as he sped away.

Luis sighed. "So, I'm taking bets. Did we just do something really smart, or really, dramatically stupid?"

"I see nothing to say it can't be both," I said. "There is, after all, an endless supply of stupidity."

We silently gave our respects to the dead child whom we were, once again, abandoning, and returned to the van for the long drive back to Albuquerque.

Before we got there, we ran into a roadblock of flashing lights.

Standing in front of the angled police cars was FBI agent Ben Turner, part-time Fire Warden, looking very grim indeed, and very much as if he had not slept since we'd last seen him. When Luis slowed to a halt and rolled down his window, Turner leaned in, took a quick, comprehensive look around the van, and said, "You both need to come with me. Right now."

Luis and I exchanged a look which clearly said, *This is not good news.* "Why?" Luis asked.

"Not here. Just get out and come with me. Do it now."

Around us, police were quietly drawing their weapons, although thus far, no one was pointing them in our direction. Luis noted it with lightning-fast shifts of his eyes, then focused back on Turner.

"Please," Turner said. His face was a blank mask, but there was tension around his eyes and mouth, and weariness in the slump of his shoulders. "I need your help."

As if that was a magic incantation, Luis nodded to me, and we both left the van to stand on the roadway, facing Turner. Dusk was falling, and so was the temperature, but the asphalt had trapped a great deal of heat during the day. It radiated up through my feet and legs uncomfortably.

Turner motioned to the police, who holstered their guns and got into their cruisers, although they didn't leave their positions.

"I've got an abducted kid," he said. "It fits the pattern you described. Little girl, age eight, got snatched from school. I checked. Her mother washed out of the Warden program."

Luis traded a glance with me. We both remembered the boy we had rescued from captivity at the Ranch: C. T. Styles. His mother had left the Wardens as well. She had held a grudge. "You cleared the mom?" Luis asked.

"She's got nothing to do with it. That lady's practically in ruins. God only knows how she's going to handle it if this turns out badly." Which, from the tense, hard set of his expression, he clearly recognized was a risk. Even a probability.

"What about the father?" I asked.

"He seems okay, too. No connection back to the Wardens, and I'm not turning up anything questionable on him. I think they're both okay."

"Perhaps it isn't related," I said.

"Maybe it's not. But it's still a little girl, missing. I figured you'd want to step in." Turner squared his shoulders and looked first at Luis, then at me. "I could really use your help. If this is connected, it's our freshest lead. It's the best possible place to start."

"We're already—"

"Let me rephrase," Turner said, and this time I saw the flare of banked anger in his eyes. "You're going to help me with this or I'm going to find all kinds of reasons to make you wish you had, starting with dressing funny and ending with suspicion of terrorism, which means you'll end up so deep in a hole you'll never see the sun again. So give the keys to your van to one of the officers; they'll drive it back to your house for you. You're coming with me."

I thought uncomfortably of Rashid, certain to reappear at any time. Luis, I was sure, was thinking the same. He would find us regardless of where we might be, but Rashid had not struck me as someone willing to keep a low profile. He might, in fact, find it amusing to advertise his nature in public. If the police began shooting, we could be injured.

Rashid would probably find that *very* funny.

"Let me make it real easy for you," Turner said. "You have two choices. One, get in my car and drive back to Albuquerque and help me find this girl. Or two, turn around for the cuffs, because I *will* charge you with something."

"With what?"

"You're kidding, right?" he asked. "There are all kinds of ways I can make your life hell, Mr. Rocha. You really don't want to test me. I can be very creative."

I was fairly sure he was serious.

Luis shrugged and tossed the van's keys to a nearby patrolman in a starched khaki uniform, who plucked the jingling metal out of the air. "Insurance and registration is in the glove compartment," he said. "In case you get stopped by even more cops. Oh, and I'll expect it filled up. Washing it wouldn't be out of the question, either."

The officer did not seem amused.

Turner held open the sedan's back door, and Luis and I slid inside. In less than a minute, we were speeding away toward Albuquerque.

It was home, and yet I had the conviction that we were also headed toward a lethal combination of grief and trouble.

Although it seemed trouble was a constant companion, these days.

Ben Turner was a very fast driver, disobeying the posted speed limits with the abandon of a law enforcement man on a mission.

I sat in the back, struggling to control the nausea that roiled within me. Turner's car was not the most pleasant experience—either sensory or psychic—that I had ever encountered. He'd had blood spilled on the seats. Bodily fluids of all sorts. And death. The car reeked of death—perhaps not in a physical sense, but the impression of a bad and lingering agony was embedded into every part of the vehicle. Something terrible had happened here, before. Something that would never completely go away.

I was struggling with the urge to blow the door off its hinges and leap from the car. The only thing that stopped me was the absolute certainty that Luis would suffer for it if I did so.

And then I was distracted.

"Shit!" Turner yelped, and in the same instant hit the brakes. Tires screeched, and Luis and I both reflexively threw out our hands to brace ourselves as the sedan's nose tipped down, fighting its own momentum.

Rashid had appeared in the middle of the road, perhaps five hundred yards away. Arms folded, a shark's smile on his face, watching the car hurtle toward him at killing speed.

Turner, face gone white, fought desperately with the vehicle.

"Just hit him," I said, through gritted teeth. "It serves him right."

Turner paid no attention to my excellent advice. He managed to bring the car to a smoking, sliding halt no more than a foot from Rashid's immobile body.

For a moment, no one moved. White, stinking smoke from the scorched tires blew into my window, and I coughed and choked. The cloud of smoke moved toward Rashid, but he simply waved it away, still smiling.

Ben Turner looked stunned, but in the next flash of a second, his face turned beet red and screwed up in righteously justifiable anger. He opened his car door and got out, yelling, "You *idiot!* You could have gotten us all killed—"

Rashid simply looked at him. To his credit, it didn't take Turner long to realize his mistake, to take in the slightly-off color of the Djinn's skin, the shine of his eyes. He turned to look through the windshield at Luis, then at me. Then back at Rashid. His lips compressed into a thin, angry line.

"Djinn. So I guess he's with you two," Turner said.

Rashid made a rude sound. "Not in any sense, I assure you." On that, we were in complete agreement. He stalked around to the passenger door of the front seat, opened it, and got in. Leaving Turner standing outside, staring in at us.

We all stared back at him.

"Seriously," Turner said. "He's a Djinn."

Rashid reached out and touched a finger to the ignition of the car. It fired to life without benefit of the key, dangling from Turner's shaking fingers. "Yes," he said. "Seriously."

Turner blinked, as if the world had gone out of focus, and shook his head. He slipped back into the driver's seat, looked at the key in his hand, then dropped it into the drink holder next to him. He put the car in drive and accelerated away, fast. I looked behind us and saw the heavy black streaks of skid marks disappearing behind us.

"Didn't really think you'd show up again," Luis said to Rashid.

I turned my head back. "I did."

Rashid was watching me with a predator's hot intensity. Waiting for weakness. Well, I had that in abundance, but I was not willing to demonstrate it on his command. "You found something," I said. "Correct?"

"No, I came back because I find your company so inspirational. Of *course* I found something." His mouth stretched and settled into something that was almost a smile. "I found the boy's bloodline. His sires are gone from the world."

"Siblings?"

"No. Distant branches. Nothing close."

I shook my head and translated that for Luis. "His parents are dead. No brothers, sisters, or cousins."

"Yes," Rashid confirmed. "His father was a Warden, killed in Ashan's uprising. His mother was mere human, dead of disease."

"Orphan," Luis said. "An orphan with latent Warden powers."

Rashid said, "He was listed so on the rolls."

Both Turner and Luis sent him identical looks. "Rolls?" Turner was just a beat faster at the question than my Warden partner. "You mean there's a list?"

Rashid lifted an eyebrow slowly. "You mean you don't keep your own lists? How careless of you. How do you ensure your progeny are trained properly if you don't have a record of their potential?"

Luis's mouth opened, then shut, and he looked at me instead. "Let me get this straight, okay, just so there's no confusion: The Djinn have a record of kids born with Warden powers?"

He was asking me. It was embarrassing, but I had to admit the truth. "I don't know," I said. "If it's done, I had nothing to do with it. I had no interest in Wardens, much less regular humans."

Luis stared for a beat, then went back to Rashid. "Can you get us that list?"

"Why?"

"Because the kids on that list are all at risk. It's our best way to get ahead of this bitch and stop her from taking more kids. If we can lock down all these potential victims . . ."

"You forget," I said. "Some of their parents are willing participants. And we don't have enough Wardens to do this."

"We've got enough FBI. And enough cops," Luis shot back. "To hell with the Wardens, they're not doing squat for us anyway. We work with law enforcement, we got plenty of firepower. And I don't think she'll have planned to fight her way through *that*. She's looking for a magical resistance, not a physical one."

Luis, I had to admit, had a point. But when I glanced at Rashid, I saw that his face was closed and hard. He said nothing.

Luis sighed. "Come on, man. I get it, you're a bastard. You don't care. Fine, whatever. I'll give you all the respect you want, just give me the goddamn list."

"I can't," Rashid said. "Whether I wished to or not, this list isn't mine to give."

"Yeah? Then who the hell do we have to talk to?"

I knew, with an ill feeling, before Rashid said anything. "The Earth Oracle."

Rashid nodded once, sharply. Of course. My last encounter with the Earth Oracle—archangel to the Djinn's angels—had been uncomfortable, and nearly shattering in its intensity. Not by her doing; the Oracle simply *was.* There was no being reachable by the Djinn who was as deeply rooted in the mind and soul of the Mother, not even the Fire Oracle, or the one with dominion over water and air. Each had separate, distinct powers and attitudes, and of all of them, the Earth Oracle was perhaps the most approachable—the most willing to understand and assist us with this matter.

It did not change the fact that she had once been halfling-born—the daughter of the Djinn David and his Warden love, Joanne. Imara, she had been called. And Imara had been a special sort of creation, one with no real place in the natural world until Ashan himself had violated the laws of the Djinn and murdered her within the sacred precincts of the Earth Oracle's temple.

Imara not only had survived, but had become . . . more. Other. She wasn't a half-powered Djinn anymore. She had gone vastly beyond all of that. Yet, some of her human heritage still lingered, and I retained enough of my Djinn snobbery to remain just a touch uncomfortable with that fact.

I wasn't sure Imara had any great and lasting fondness for me, either. The last thing I wanted was another, perhaps less cordial, encounter.

"Get it for us," I told Rashid. He shook his head. "You must be a special pet of hers, if you know of this list at all."

"I know of it because David told me of it, not because I can lay my hands on it."

David. I fumed quietly. He led half the Djinn—the less consequential half, by my reckoning—but he was nothing I wanted to cross. I had no connection to him, not as Rashid did; I would have to rely upon his pure goodwill. He had, however, been kind to me before— had, in fact, helped save my life, when Ashan cast me out. So it was possible. "Then I will ask David for it."

"You could. He might even be inclined to grant it to you, knowing David; he's so *accommodating*." Rashid made a face that implied he did not altogether approve of this trait. "Unfortunately, he cannot be located."

That stopped me, Luis, and even Turner cold for a long, icy second. "You . . . can't find him."

Inconceivable. David was the Conduit of the New Djinn. He was the core and source of their power on Earth and in the aetheric. How could they *not* find him? It was akin to mislaying a part of your own body.

"He's hidden from us," Rashid clarified. "He told us, before he left, that he would be cut off from us."

"Then there must be some replacement. Someone keeping open the Conduit for you."

Rashid inclined his head, but didn't answer.

"Rashid," I said. "My patience is not just thin, it is starving, and moments from death. *Just tell me.*"

Djinn do love their games, but Rashid seemed to understand that I was no longer playing. He turned to face forward, staring out at the road as the car hurtled along its smooth, straight surface, landscape whipping by in a blur of ocher, brown, and green.

"He would have preferred to give the responsibility to Rahel," Rashid said. "But Rahel likewise cannot be reached. He's walled both her and himself off from us, to protect us. There are risks."

I growled softly, and the sound rumbled through the metal of the car. "You're telling me who he did *not* choose. I only need to understand who he *did* choose."

"Only to explain," Rashid said. "Because we all acknowledge that Rahel would have been, in fact, the logical choice. Instead, we are saddled with . . . *Whitney.*"

I was not at all certain I'd heard correctly. "Whitney. Who is Whitney?"

"Our newest Djinn," he said. "And you will be very, very unimpressed. I confess that I am completely baffled by his logic. Perhaps the woman he's consorting with has finally driven him insane." Rashid sounded not just bored, but actively angry. Jealous, I assumed, not very charitably. Rashid did seem to me the type to think he was the natural heir apparent of all the powers in the universe.

Of course, from what I had seen of him so far, he might have been correct to do so.

"I will need to see Whitney, then," I said.

"That might be a problem, since David ordered her not

to leave Jonathan's house." Rashid cast a scornful glance over me. "I doubt *you* can go to her. Not in that form."

He was right. Humans—and undeniably, I was trapped in human form, unable to shift from it without massive expenditure of power, more than I could safely draw from Luis or any other mortal—could not perform the trick of sifting through the planes of existence, like dialing the tumblers of a lock, to reach the nonspace that held the Djinn stronghold . . . a shifting place, out of phase with the rest of the realities. Once inside, Djinn were insulated from most, if not all, dangers outside; it would take the death of the universe itself to destroy Jonathan's house.

And it would destroy a mere mortal to attempt the access. I knew of only one who'd accomplished it—Joanne Baldwin, David's sometimes human, always presumptuous lover. But she'd been a Djinn at the time, so that hardly counted.

I held Rashid's gaze without blinking. "If I can't go to her," I said, "then you must. I need the list. Tell her."

"No," he said. "Ask her yourself. If you can." He bared his teeth. "Or ask the Oracle. She can give you access. Of course, the Oracle's not as tolerant as she once was. She's become . . . more powerful. Less accessible."

That didn't bode well for my chances, but my chances of getting to this *Whitney* were even smaller, considering her location and my human-form disability.

I looked at Luis and said, "I will go to Sedona to see the Oracle."

"Wrong," Agent Turner snapped. "You're going nowhere except where I take you. I told you, I need your help!"

"You need help," Luis agreed. "Tell you what, I'll go with you. Let her do this. She gets her hands on that list of potential targets and we can start preventing this crap before we're chasing after missing kids in trouble, maybe suffering or dying. Yeah?"

Turner didn't like it, I could see that from the stony look on his face. Still, he knew that Luis was right; if there was a way to prevent more missing children, more *dead* children, he would have to risk it.

"Fine," he said. "So how does this work? You just blip out, or . . . ?"

"Like this?" Rashid gave him a vicious smile and disappeared so suddenly that Turner involuntarily veered the car to the right, staring. Air made a small thunderclap of sound rushing in to fill the space he had occupied.

Turner looked at me in the rearview mirror.

"No," I said wearily, and settled back in the seat to close my eyes. "Not like that. Not anymore."

More was the pity.

In Albuquerque, Agent Turner let me off at my apartment, where I had left my motorcycle parked beneath a shaded awning. He was impatient to be gone, but Luis got out with me, walked me around a corner of the building, and turned to me. It was a cool evening, clear and dry, with the smell of sage and pine flavoring the air. The barely seen smudges of the mountain peaks rose up to the north, lifting part of the city out of its bowl. Overhead, stars sparkled cold in a vast, otherwise empty sky.

Beautiful and only lightly tamed, this place—like the man facing me, hair stirring just a bit in the breeze. Artificial lights glinted on his skin, shadows darkened his eyes, and he said, "You be careful. Remember what happened last time."

Last time, Pearl had sent her forces after me on the way back from Sedona. She'd broken my leg. She'd almost killed me—and would have succeeded, if Luis hadn't come to my rescue. As I thought about it, my still-healing arm twinged. The bones were fixed together, bonded and straight, but nerves were still repairing themselves.

I nodded without speaking. I was no longer sure how to speak to him; something had changed between us, something fundamental had shifted beneath our feet. I wasn't sure if I had forced that change, or he had, or if it would have happened no matter what we did.

All I knew was that it felt . . . different. And it hurt to leave him.

Luis lifted his hand and touched the side of my face. The skin of his palm felt warm against my skin, and I closed my eyes in an involuntary spasm of delight. I sensed the power coursing in his veins, natural as the blood that ran with it.

"Take what you need," he said. "I'm not sending you out there unprepared and underpowered."

He didn't know what he was asking. Not really. I pulled in a quick breath and opened my eyes again, meeting his.

"I could hurt you, doing this too quickly," I said. "I don't wish to do that."

Luis laughed, but it was soft and humorless. He shook his head. "You aren't going to hurt me any worse than anybody else has," he said. "I didn't grow up soft, *chica*. I took bullets before, you know. Knives. Took a hell of a beating when I was jumped into the gang. So just do it already, we're burning starlight."

Drawing power was usually a slower process, and I had almost always been careful to draw at levels that didn't risk his comfort, much less his life. But Turner was waiting, and the clock on a child's life was ticking, and we had no time for the niceties even if the FBI agent was inclined to allow us our leisure.

I slowly put my hand over Luis's where it rested on my cheek, feeling the pulse under my fingers race faster.

"I'm sorry," I said. "I will try not to hurt you."

And then I let loose the hunger inside of me. It was not so much a matter of taking from him, as allowing the barriers to drop; the void in me, the cold, hungry vacuum where once the life force of a Djinn had been, sucked power from him in a ravenous stream. *Too much, too much* . . . it felt astonishingly good to me, like being bathed in light, but I also felt the sudden stabbing pain of overloaded nerves. My pain, but also his.

Luis trembled, but he didn't try to pull himself away from me. His eyes continued to focus on mine, dark and drowning, and I forgot how to breathe as he poured life from his body to mine. There was an intimacy to it that went beyond mere bodies, went into realms of spirit, of pure and perfect *life*.

It was so hard to pull away.

I finally sucked in a shaking gasp and slammed shut the barriers between us again. I hadn't felt so powerful, so *alive* in a very long time, and it was so very hard to give that up. Even so, this rich, intense intoxication was only a fraction of what I'd been as a Djinn. I could drain a dozen like Luis, a hundred, without coming near that lost perfection.

That was exactly what Ashan had meant to do to me, in throwing me into human flesh. He didn't need to torment me. He knew that every time I came up against the natural barriers, I would torture myself, thoroughly, with my hunger and possibilities.

It troubled me less than he'd planned, however. I *could* be tempted, but I was also, by nature, a practical sort of predator; draining a hundred Wardens would kill them all in the process, and even then, I would never again be what I had once been. It was easy to forget when I was fighting for survival, subsisting on barely enough energy to live; it was worse still when I had a taste of the power.

Luis was shaking, but he kept his hand on my face until I tightened my pale, thin fingers around his and pulled them away. His pulse was thundering now, and his face had gone starkly pale under its copper. He was not precisely gasping, but his breathing was more ragged, and more rapid, than I would have liked. I reached out to lay my hand flat against his chest, feeling the too-quick laboring of his heart.

"I'm okay," he said before I could speak. He smiled, but I saw the pain underneath it. "Is that better for you now?"

I nodded, unwilling or perhaps unable to speak. My eyes were glowing, I knew it; I'd rarely been able to afford that sort of display, but it was raw nature, and I had no doubt that I looked . . . different just now, as I struggled to manage the power he had given me in such an intensive burst. I could see the change in his expression. I just could not decide what precisely it was that had created such an indescribable tension in his face . . . fear? Or desire? Something of both, perhaps.

He surprised me by saying, in a low, rough voice, "If we didn't have someplace to be right now, I would take you inside and get down to business."

I blinked. "I don't understand."

He took in a deep breath, then let it out, and finally, I recognized the waves of emotion coming off of him, resonating within me. They were just . . . unexpected.

"No," he said. "Don't suppose you would. You watch your back, Cassiel. I mean that."

Our hands were still linked, fingers wound together in pure, primal need.

"And you," I said. I didn't know what else to say. "I will know if you need me." Immediately, I realized that there were several likely interpretations of that, and immediately amended it to, "Need me to help."

He laughed. It was still soft, but this time, it was lightened with considerable humor. "Yeah," he said. "Sure. I'll keep you on the psychic speed dial. What is that, pound 666?"

He raised my hand as if it was the most natural motion in the world, and for an instant I felt the softness of his lips burning against my skin. Then he let go, took a step back, and turned to walk back to Turner's idling sedan.

I pressed my back to the rough, warm wall and breathed, breathed, breathed.

Then I went inside, recovered my helmet, and got on my motorcycle for the trip to Sedona.

Chapter 5

THERE IS NOTHING, in my human experience, as freeing as a fast ride on a powerful motorcycle. It's a great deal like being a Djinn, in certain ways; there is momentum, power, a sense of barely controlled ferocity raging beneath the surface. A connection to all things—to the wind battering and caressing you by turns; to the ground beneath you, coated in a layer of man-made surface that nevertheless contains its own power, its own connections to life.

It is also loud and exhausting, and by the time I finished the long ride following Interstate 40 west to Flagstaff, I had eaten enough grime and dust to last several human lifetimes. It was now deep night, and traffic was almost nonexistent save for some long-distance trucks still plying their trade.

I stopped for a rest. I had human bodily needs; I could go without food, but water was a necessity that I found I needed both to dispose of and take in. Restrooms at gas stations were an unpleasant and shocking surprise; I had never considered the serious drawbacks of such lazily-cleaned rooms. I was completely unable to ignore the filth, and wasted a burst of power to turn the sinks, floors and porcelain toilet into sparkling, clean examples of their kind before using the facility. I felt that was a much less judgmental response than simply blowing the place off the face of the Earth, which was also a distinct temptation, especially when the storekeeper overcharged me for a bottle of cold water. I paid without complaint, however. I had learned from our earlier problems with law enforcement. Although I could easily overpower, or at least evade, it would be much easier to simply avoid being noticed at all.

That ship quickly sailed, however.

Outside, a whole noisy, thundering fleet of motorcycles pulled in, blocking my own vehicle against the building. Where I was wearing pale pink leather, these other riders were in battered blacks, studded with metal. Their vehicles were better kept than their persons, which were scruffy, badly washed, and—from their expressions—not especially friendly. Big, bulky men, for the most part; those who were smaller or thinner seemed even harder by contrast.

They surrounded my Victory in a ring of metal and bodies.

They were silent when I exited the store, downing the last of my water. I paid them no attention and threaded my way between the bikes until I reached my Victory, which was a calm, gleaming island in the sea of chrome and attitude.

There was no chance, once they saw me, that this was going to end well. I saw it in the predatory smiles, the shift in body language, the gleam of their eyes.

End well for *them,* of course.

I straddled the motorcycle, tossed the empty bottle

effortlessly in the trash twenty feet away, and said, simply, "Move."

They laughed.

"That's a whole lot of bike for you, lady," one of them said. "You sure you can handle it?" That woke suggestions from several about what else I could handle, or might want to.

For answer, I gave the speaker a brilliant, false smile. "Your bike is also nice," I said. "Is it a ten speed?"

This was an insult that someone had offered me once, which I had of course ignored; Luis had been the one to explain the pointed joke to me, after the fact. Intellectually I understood why a prideful human might be offended by such a comparison, but it still meant nothing to me, really.

However, it *did* mean something to this man, whose entire self-image was bound up with his motorcycle, his image, and his pride.

"What'd you say, bitch?"

"I believe I said *move*." Perhaps I should have added, *please.* I wasn't much in the mood.

The man who'd spoken got off his motorcycle and came to walk around mine, and me. I didn't bother to turn my head to watch him as he went behind my back; better to appear completely relaxed and unconcerned than to show an instant's doubt with a pack like this. "I didn't diss your bike, bitch. Why you got to go insult mine? That's a Harley Softail Superglide, not a goddamn Schwinn. You're riding, what, a Victory? That shit ain't even been on the road ten years yet. This Harley's been riding longer than you've been alive."

That made me smile. "Oh, I doubt that," I said, and

looked him squarely in the face. "Are you going to fight with me now?"

They laughed. It was spontaneous and genuine, but there was also an edge of menace to it that might have raised hackles on anyone else.

"Oh, baby, you don't want to go there," he said. "You really don't."

I smiled.

"If you're not man enough to fight," I said, "I think you should get on your bike and pedal away."

The laughter faded. The smiles died. And what was left was cold, hard, and intense as the night sky overhead.

The leader said, in a low voice, "You are a piece of work, bitch. I ought to smack the living shit out of you. Teach you not to talk back."

I raised my eyebrows. "Are you trying to frighten me?" I asked. When he didn't immediately answer, I said, helpfully, "I'm only trying to understand what you want. If you're hoping to frighten me and make yourself feel mightier, then I'm afraid we're both wasting time. And I can't afford that. I'm in a hurry. If I have to kill you, I'd like to do it quickly."

He stared at me hard for a few seconds, and then one of the other men nudged him and jerked his chin up at the eaves of the store. There was a security camera there, which I already knew. The leader stared at it, then turned back to me. "You know what? You're fucking brain damaged. Better run on to your crystals and moonbeams and pyramids and stop messing with the real world before you get what you're asking for." He smiled, entirely falsely. "Have a nice fucking day."

Silence. The desert air blew cool over my skin and

tossed my pale, pale hair around my face, but I didn't blink. Neither did the biker standing across from me.

These men had not survived to reach the status of roaming predators by accident. Some sense warned him that I was deadly serious, that I was not someone to toy with idly. Between that, and the silent witness of the camera, they would either let it go, or bide their time.

He looked at his friends, shrugged, and gave a sharp nod. Those blocking my motorcycle backed their vehicles away, a complicated maneuvering done in close quarters, accomplished with skill, grace and efficiency. They left me a clear path from my front tire to the highway.

"Thank you," I said. I had promised Luis to try to use that phrase more often, and this seemed an appropriate moment. I kicked the Victory to life, donned my helmet, and eased out onto the road, opening up the throttle once I'd gained an opening.

I heard a full-throated roar behind me, and looked in my side mirror to see the entire pack of black-clad bikers spilling out into formation behind me, following.

So. They had been biding their time, after all. Well, it was their choice. I had been very clear about the fact that I was in no mood to play games to enhance their egos. I considered the best way to disable their Harleys without undue violence; I could easily shred their tires, for instance. I could soften the metal of the frames, breaking the bikes apart under their own torque. I could simply disengage a few critical connection points to force them out of control.

I was spoiled for choices, and spent a few empty miles considering which of them might result in the least amount of injuries. They pulled steadily closer.

The leader yelled something at me, and I felt a raw, wild excitement in his voice. He meant to take his power back, redeem himself in front of his men.

He meant to fight.

I was not necessarily opposed to obliging him . . . and then I felt a raw surge around me. Wild energy, sweeping through the aetheric and down into the real world like an invisible tornado.

"Get away from me!" I shouted to the bikers, who had closed in around me, engines roaring. The leader leered at me. He thought I was *afraid*. Idiot. "Get out of here or you'll be killed!"

For answer, he pulled a pistol from under his leather vest and pointed it at me. "Don't threaten me, bitch."

I hadn't been. I'd been warning him.

It happened before either of us had a chance to make our next moves in this pointless chess game. I felt heat, unnatural heat, emanating from the gas tank of the Victory, and realized my time was up. I couldn't stop combustion, but the gasoline was a product of the Earth, and subject to Luis's Warden powers. It took only a minor adjustment to render it inert within the tank of my motorcycle, a second of concentration, and I felt the Victory lurch as the inert fuel fouled the engine. It coughed, sputtered, and died.

The biker riding close on my right wasn't as lucky. His motorcycle simply exploded. Fragments blew out in a terrifyingly beautiful ball, like a flower with a heart of fire blooming lethal, twisted petals. The man riding it simply . . . ceased, as a coherent presence. I felt the psychic blow as the impact rippled the air, but I couldn't note it in any significant way. I didn't have the time. I

dived off the wobbling Victory just as the other motorcycle exploded and flattened myself; heat rippled over
me, and an expanding wave of concussion pressed me
into the pavement for an instant, then passed. I had two
pieces of luck—first, the Victory took the brunt of the
shrapnel. Flying metal shredded the beautiful form of
my bike, mutilating it, but it protected me from the worst
of it for a critical instant as it was blown out, over me,
and spun end over end to crash into the ditch on the side
of the road. I curled into a ball, well aware of the danger
as the bikers lost control all around me; one thick wheel
came within a half inch of my face, but somehow missed
doing worse than laying greasy road marks on the edge
of my sleeve. Metal shrieked and crashed, men yelled,
and I smelled burning rubber even over the stench of
burning human flesh.

Another gas tank exploded. Screaming erupted.

I rolled clear, moving fast, and dropped into the ditch
where my Victory had landed in a sad and twisted heap.
It was good that I did, as more explosions sounded, fling-
ing lethal shrapnel—including human bones—through
the air above me.

Someone else landed in the ditch with me . . . the
leader of the bikers, his leather vest shredded and torn,
skin shimmering with blood, eyes wide and dazed. Not
dead, surprisingly. Not even badly wounded, beneath
the splatter of blood. Unlike some of his fellows, he still
had all his limbs.

"Jesus," he panted, and crawled to put his back to
the raw earth of the ditch. "Jesus, Jesus, Jesus! What the
fuck?"

"They're not after you," I told him, and got a blank,

uncomprehending look from him. "I told you to leave me alone."

"Fucking hell, lady, who'd you piss off, the fucking Marines?"

"I wish," I said. I'd learned the expression from Luis, but from the man's look, I wasn't sure I had delivered it properly. "Stay down."

"Like hell I will. Those are my brothers up there!"

I didn't know if he meant literally, as in blood relations, or figuratively; it was difficult to determine human relationships at the best of times for me. "Stay down!" I almost snarled it this time, and grabbed him bodily by the shredded leather vest as he tried to put his head up above the road level. "This isn't your fight!"

It was, however, mine. I looked down at the mournful remains of my beautiful Victory, sighed, and bent my knees to jump up and out of the ditch.

The biker hit me in a flying tackle from the side, taking me completely by surprise. He slammed me down into the packed dirt and scratchy weeds an instant before another motorcycle skidded drunkenly off the road and crashed down right where I had been standing. It had been blown over by another explosion, which hit my ears with a dull *crump* of sound that told me my hearing had already begun to shut itself off in trauma.

The Harley was undamaged, except for some superficial dents and splatters. I stared at it, then shoved the biker off of me without much regard for his shouted concerns. I turned back to reach into the waistband of his blue jeans and pull out a semiautomatic pistol from a holster he'd concealed there. I checked the magazine—

full, and stocked with hollow points—and slammed it home before removing the safety catch.

"Stay. Down," I said, soft and precise, and straddled the Harley, which was still somehow running. The vibration of the engine sent waves of heat through my body, almost sexual in its intensity, and I took a deep breath before backing the Harley out of the ditch, up the other side, and back another few feet.

The road was carnage. Broken bodies, some weakly moving still. Shattered vehicles. Blood and bone.

And nothing else. No enemy. No face to put to my would-be killer.

Without the anchor of Luis's presence, it was very hard for me to view things on the aetheric plane, where the reality of mere physics took on different aspects; it was like trying to fly while holding a concrete block. I managed it for only a few long seconds, overlaying the burning wreckage and bodies and serene moonlit desert with the floods and flows of intention, power, and truth.

Most of those lying on the road did not benefit from the illumination of their souls; their crimes had warped them into hideous shapes, disfigured their faces beyond recognition. I didn't linger on their self-mutilations. Energy rose up from the destroyed motorcycles in shimmers of gauzy color, but there was something more.

The hot, glowing presence of two Wardens, drawing power.

I saw something lance at me across the aetheric, straight and intense as it cut through everything in its path. It was narrow, and it looked exactly like a laser beam, save that its lurid red color didn't exist at all in the real, physical world.

I pulled broken metal up from the road in a rush, building a steel shield between me and the beam rushing toward me. It hit my improvised defense and blasted it to even smaller component pieces, but the shield had taken the energy and dissipated it into a splash that only melted and seared the remains into a ball of slag.

I snarled and throttled the borrowed Harley into a full scream of power. Tires dug sand, then gravel, and then I was airborne as momentum carried me forward over the ditch and onto the surface of the road. I avoided the worst of the wreckage and aimed the motorcycle for the spot where the beam of power had originated.

This time, the Warden was an adult—young, but fully a man, probably only a few years younger than Luis. He looked scared, but determined, and as I came for him, he readied his defenses.

I didn't hold back. I slammed him backward, off his feet, and the ground opened beneath him. He dropped dozens of feet, and as he fell, the sides of the pit caved in over him. Burying him alive. Pinning him down with tons of crushing weight.

Destroying him.

It took fully a minute for him to die, smothered beneath the sand, but I didn't wait to watch. This was war, and the Djinn in me had come forth, the part that cared little for the disposable lives of humans.

I went after the second glowing spot of power.

A figure dressed in dull brown started out of concealment behind a low jut of rock, illuminated by the fires glowing behind me. For a frozen moment, as I closed the distance, I felt recognition strike me. It was too far to see her face, but I felt the familiar aetheric sense of her, a warm connection I hadn't known I'd missed until it returned, overwhelming in its relief.

That was Isabel. Ibby. Manny and Angela's child.

My child, something in me whispered.

Ibby was no longer the sweet, smiling girl I remembered, or even the traumatized one who'd seen her parents die as she shivered and wept in my arms. She looked older than five now, although physically her body hadn't matured unnaturally; there was something within her that had warped, bringing an adult, cold distance in her expression. A precision to her movements. Confidence, and calculation, although she was afraid.

But she still *looked* like Isabel.

Pearl. Pearl had done this to her. Rage swept through me, turning fear to ash, and in that moment I really *would* have destroyed the human world for what Pearl had done—except that it would have meant destroying Isabel, as well.

I let off the throttle of the motorcycle. Ibby was standing by the side of the road, watching me, body tensed. Ready to attack. Ready to run.

Why? Why was she *here?*

Pearl, again. Pearl was training Ibby as a weapon. How better to use her, than to use her against me?

Oh, Ibby. But she had not led the attack. She'd been here either as hostage, or apprentice, but she was not ready to fight someone like me. She was so young. Too young.

It reduced me to fury and grief.

"Ibby," I said. I had no doubt she could hear me, even over the throbbing growl of the Harley. "Ibby, it's me. It's Cassiel."

It was a ridiculous thing to say. She knew who I was. I

could see that in her face, in the caution and tension, the fear. It shattered my heart to see her fear me; she had always been so accepting of me, so . . . loving.

I kicked the stand of the motorcycle and eased off the bike, walking toward her. I must have looked frightening—stained with smoke and blood, a memory of that terrible day when she'd lost her parents.

She didn't react, other than to narrow her eyes.

"Ibby," I murmured. I came closer, moving slowly. "Oh, my girl."

Her dull brown clothing was a kind of camouflage, a soldier's gear cut down to fit a child. It should have looked ridiculous, like some sort of costume; instead, she filled it with deadly confidence.

She is only five years old. I felt that strike me hard as a fist, and I ached to stop time, reverse the hurts that had been done to her, take her in my arms and rock away the anguish.

Even if the anguish was only my own.

"I can help you," I told her softly. I took another step on the gravel, and I saw her tense, readying herself. I stopped and made sure my hands were loose and unthreatening at my sides. I attempted a smile. "I want to help you, Ibby. Don't you believe that?"

I felt a slight whisper in the aetheric, a brush of power. She was *reading* me. That was . . . impossible. Isabel was a mere child, nowhere near old enough—even should she have the inborn ability—to wield those kinds of powers, never mind with such utter precision. Reading the truth was an Earth power, like healing.

I also sensed another power in her, jittering and familiar. Fire.

Five years old, and already burdened with two kinds of Warden powers. It would shatter her like glass, or worse, warp her into an unrecognizable, twisted mockery with no hope of returning to the person she was meant to become.

In that instant, I hated Pearl, with such a pure and burning passion, such an utterly *impotent* passion that it made me tremble and close my eyes to hold it inside. *Please,* I thought. *Please let me find a way to destroy her, to wipe her from the Earth. She destroys everything she touches.*

Ibby chose that moment to respond. "My mommy wants me to do this," she said. She sounded utterly certain.

My eyes flew open, and I felt the breath congeal in my lungs. "What?" I whispered.

"Mommy says I have to be stronger now," Isabel said. "Or the bad people will win. The bad people who hurt her, like you." Something flashed in her dark, wide eyes, something awful. "I won't let you hurt my mommy again, Cassie. I *won't.*"

The realization almost drove me to my knees. *Pearl, what have you done?* Whether it was the strain of such unnatural power already pulling Isabel apart, or Pearl's vile manipulations, I couldn't tell, but I realized with a wrench that Isabel thought she was *protecting her dead mother.* A mother that, impossibly, she thought was still alive. And no child would flinch from that. Certainly not the child of warriors like Manny and Angela.

I spread my arms wide to my sides and lowered myself to my knees on the filthy road. A warm burst of wind blew out of the desert, stinging my eyes with dirt, but I kept my gaze on hers.

"You can kill me," I told her. "Ibby, if you really think I would ever hurt you, hurt your mother, hurt your father—then you *should* kill me. But I wouldn't. I won't ever do that." Nor could I. Manny and Angela were both well beyond any pain I could bring to them.

She was still reading me. I felt the subtle, golden touch around me, and knew she could feel the truth of my words. The anguish behind them, and the righteous rage I couldn't altogether control.

"Someone is lying to you," I told her. "It isn't me. Please think about that."

She considered me in silence for a long few seconds, then tilted her head to one side and extended a chubby little hand.

"Sleep," she said, and darkness hit me like a falling anvil. I fought it, reaching for my own power, but as I did, I realized that she was trying to show me mercy. If I fought it, she'd use other means, and then I'd have to kill or be killed.

Better to lose. Much better.

As I was driven beneath the surface of the darkness, I thought about Luis, about what he might think when I failed to keep my promise and come back.

And I mourned not for myself, but for him.

When I woke up, I was on the gravel at the side of the road, and Isabel was gone. There was no sign of her anywhere. I tore myself out of anchoring flesh to look for her on the aetheric, but I found no trace at all, not even a lingering shadow of her presence.

I wrapped my arms around my aching chest, where emptiness and confusion burned like a heavy weight. *So close, I'd been so close. I'd seen her. I might have saved her.*

Or killed her. The odds had been far too uncertain.

Not much time had passed—moments, perhaps. Stars still glimmered overhead. Fires still burned. Men still moaned and cried out for help.

A low wail of a police siren was sounding in the distance, no doubt drawn by the death, smoke, and flames still raging on the road behind me. How was I ever going to explain this? I felt a surge of frustrated helplessness, and dragged myself to my feet by main strength.

A motorcycle roared up out of the ditch. The leader of the bikers, leaving behind his fallen comrades, opened the throttles and blazed past me in a blur of metal and leather, not even pausing to kill me, although he no doubt dearly wished to. I wouldn't have blamed him if he'd made the attempt.

He had found another undamaged bike. The one I had salvaged still stood leaning on its kickstand in the middle of the road a hundred feet away, idling. I walked to it, mounted, and raised the stand to balance the heavy weight at its equilibrium point, then gunned the engine. It wasn't like the Victory; the Harley growled in a completely different tune, throbbed at a lower range as its engine cycled. I'd lost my helmet, but that didn't matter now. What mattered was not spending the rest of my day—or all my days—in an interrogation room answering the questions of the police.

I had to get to Sedona.

I aimed the Harley where it needed to go, and let it loose to fly, chasing the taillights of the biker ahead of me as we both, for different reasons, fled the law.

*   *   *

Riding the Harley was a very different sort of experience for me. It was rougher, less forgiving of the sins of the pavement against it—less precise in its handling, although still a very fine machine. It made up for these things in sheer, raw power, and although the traffic began to thicken as I approached Sedona, I had no problem guiding the bike in a fluid, shifting rush around slower-moving cars, trucks, and vans. Sedona's night desert glowed in starlight, a severe and subtle beauty that woke something in me. A hunger for peace. Serenity. Solitude. There was a faint, pink glow on the eastern horizon; the sun was coming. A new day. A fresh day.

A day in which, perhaps, I could find my own brand of redemption.

Not while this abomination goes on, I told myself. The haunting image of Isabel, forced to accept powers beyond her reach, warped by loyalty to a dead mother, made me too sick with rage to consider satisfying that impulse toward retreat.

I will save you, Ibby. I will.

If there was anything of her left to save.

As a Djinn I never considered failure; things either were, or were not, and I had rarely been unable to accomplish what I set out to do. The human condition, though, is a different matter entirely. The potential for failure existed in every heartbeat, every second, every decision I risked.

No. I will not fail. Not in this.

There was nothing but my will to drive me, but I had to believe that would be enough.

I had to believe in myself, as paradoxical as it seemed.

I dodged around a slow-moving RV with Virginia license plates, avoided a head-on collision with a tractor trailer, and after another quarter hour saw the turnoff toward the church. The motor of the Harley left smoke and blatting roars in my wake, somehow indecent in this polite, sleepy town in the predawn dimness, and for a moment I considered spending a few precious drops of power to muffle the noise.

Instead, I spent them on repairing my clothing and cleaning my skin and hair, making myself presentable for a meeting I was already dreading.

The Chapel of the Holy Cross was a popular visitor destination, particularly at dawn. As I parked the Harley in the broad, flat lot, I saw more than a dozen trucks, cars, and, yes, the ever-popular recreational vehicles, all disgorging yawning occupants. Tourists snapping photographs, or pilgrims come to pray and meditate. Their presence would be a bother, but not a deterrent to me.

I left the Harley, stood for a moment to gather my thoughts, and then started up the long path to the chapel. The walk gave me time to think what I might say. I wasn't certain why I was so nervous this time about approaching the Oracle; I had done it before, and she had been, if not warm, at least accepting. What had changed? Rashid's warnings, of course, but it was more than that.

I felt a greater weight on me now.

I knew why, on some level. I was becoming more human, and there was a kind of dread building in me, a kind of instinctual awe that I could not control. I was not even certain if the Oracle would hear me now, and if she would, if she could grant me even the smallest of favors.

But I had no other choice but to try. Lives had already been lost to get me this far.

I was exotically different from the others climbing toward the chapel; that fact became immediately apparent as those nearby cast me a wide variety of glances—admiring, suspicious, scandalized, worried, oddly worshipful. I returned none of them, concentrating on my own journey. Still, I was aware that with my pale skin and hair, my bright eyes, and my aggressive leathers, I was a cat among the walking-shorts-and-tee-shirt-wearing pigeons as the sun began to crest the horizon.

I did not look like either a tourist or a pilgrim.

I looked like trouble.

A priest was taking the air outside the chapel doors, smiling and shaking hands with those entering; he faltered when he saw me, but quickly recovered. He was a man of middle age, neat and trim, only a slight softening of his jawline and a slight drooping of his eyes to disclose that he might be older than he seemed. He radiated energy and a kind of satisfaction that I supposed doubled for purity. I neither liked nor disliked him, but I suspect he disliked me, immediately and without reservation.

He recognized an eldritch spirit when he saw one. No surprise, given the overlapping of sacred ground here; he must have seen the Djinn often, even if he didn't fully comprehend what he was encountering. He gave me a slight nod, but didn't offer his hand.

I didn't deeply care.

Inside, the chapel rose up to a dizzying height, walls

angling in. It was a warm, glowing color that was not quite gold, not quite orange, but something between, with a sheen like living skin. It was a small room dominated by the massive window at the far end that looked out on the majestic vista of the canyon it overlooked. As I studied the view, an eagle glided by in silent grace, wheeled, and began a descent toward its prey. All around me, tourists milled, the penitent prayed, but all were hushed and still in the presence of what felt . . . more than human.

Because it was.

Seated at the far end of a pew near the back was the Oracle. Human eyes skipped over her, but mine focused, and as I watched, she opened her eyes—of no color my mind would recognize—and stared directly at me. No expression on her lovely, still face. Like her Warden mother Joanne Baldwin, the Earth Oracle had a beautiful form, but where Joanne's was animated by a humor and a kind of ruthless determination, Imara was . . . illuminated. She had a kind of peace to her that had its roots in the rocks beneath us, the very spirit of the Earth.

Imara's long, dark hair fell soft and straight around her shoulders, framing her pale face, and she wore a shifting red dress—robe?—that never quite fell into a final shape. It was as if the Oracle dressed in deep red sand, fine as silk, that whispered around her in a constantly moving curtain.

She extended one graceful pale hand and patted the wooden pew next to her.

For a long moment I didn't move, and then, reluctantly, I made my way to the pew and took a seat a bit farther than she had indicated. I bowed my head toward the power in this place. The Djinn understand God in ways that humans do not, but we are not connected to Him by the same strands; all things interweave, but we are the warp, not the weft, of the cloth. Imara, in her role as the Oracle, might have a deeper understanding. She was a nexus at which things crossed. Perhaps she sensed and saw things here I could not.

"Cassiel," Imara said. She sounded relaxed and a bit amused. "Don't be so worried. I won't bite your head off."

Imara had grown much more assured in her role since last I'd seen her. She had, I think, struggled with the complexities of channeling such power, standing in such an awesomely important spot. Now, unexpectedly—and quite different from what Rashid had led me to expect— she treated me almost as a human.

Almost as her mother would, and had.

"Oracle," I said. Around us, the mortals in the room pursued their own blinkered interests. No one seemed to note us at all, not even my sudden absence from their world after standing out so vividly in the crowd. "Thank you for seeing me."

"How could I not see you? You don't exactly blend in." That sounded very *much* like her mother—acidic, funny, yet somehow failing to offend. "I am glad you came to me. I'm sorry I wasn't able to help you as much last time, but things were . . . difficult for me." She started to con- tinue, then stopped and shook her head. Sand shifted and moved on her robes, revealing tiny, pale strips of skin beneath. "Ashan is *really* angry at you, you know. Much more angry than anybody's ever seen him."

My mouth twisted involuntarily. "I'm aware."

"I'll bet. He's ordered all the Djinn he's got power

over to avoid you, and ignore you if you find them. Losing Gallan hurt him. Badly."

I understood that, although I loathed it; Ashan had set me on this murderous path, and now he wouldn't even offer me help. But from his perspective, it was simple logic. I had involved Gallan, and Pearl had destroyed him. Ashan couldn't afford such losses.

"And what of David?" I asked, and risked a glance into those odd, changing eyes. The power in them was so intense that it seemed I was looking into the heart of a nuclear fire, where colors had no meaning anymore. "Can he help me? More to the point, will he?"

"Dad," Imara said, and sighed. She looked away, toward the windows, although I wasn't sure what she was truly seeing. "My father's in a difficult position, like you. I don't know if it's one he can hold for long; being a leader isn't—it's not in his nature. He prefers taking care of those close to him. And I'm not certain that some of the New Djinn truly feel they owe him loyalty. It's hard to know which of them he—or you—could trust."

"What about Rashid?" I asked. "Can I trust him?"

Imara's lips moved into a brief, dark smile. "He's as Djinn as you were," she said. "More than I ever was. He'll do as the Djinn do."

"So the answer is no."

"The answer is the same for any ally you consider. There is no such thing as unlimited trust. At some point, all beings with free will can, and will, betray you when you're no longer pursuing the same goals."

"That's not extremely helpful." I sounded petulant, I realized. I, who had been alive and a power on the Earth long before this *Oracle* had even existed as a possibility, was being schooled by this girl. An extraordinarily powerful girl, perhaps. One with awesome powers. But . . . still. "Pearl has a plan. She is using the children of Wardens to carry it out. I saw—" My voice faltered unexpectedly, and I forced it to continue. "I saw Isabel Rocha on the way here, to you. She—"

"I know," Imara said, very gently. Her hand touched mine, and it was warm and soothing. "I feel her. I feel them all."

"All the children?"

"All the people on this planet," she said, and now the smile was sad. "All those who live, suffer, feel joy, die. Choosing only one out of so many is almost impossible. I'm not that good yet. But I felt what *you* felt. I know how angry you are. How guilty you are."

She didn't tell me not to be angry, not to be guilty. Doubtless, even had she wished to, she knew it wouldn't at all matter.

"You came for something," Imara said then, and her tone had turned eerily like her mother's, like Joanne Baldwin's, with an edge of irony. "It wasn't just for the warm and fuzzies, Cassiel. Tell me." The human term seemed odd, coming from an Oracle, but I supposed that was understandable. Imara was a very odd choice for an Oracle.

I shook myself, trying to regain the focus, the purpose I'd had in coming here. There was something so distracting about her, about the subtle and seductive peace she radiated. About the feeling that here, in this place, I could lay down all my fears and guilt and burdens.

It was illusion. Two steps from her, I would feel it all again. If I didn't, there would be something wrong with me. The kind of peace that Imara represented here, in this place, was for Djinn.

Not for me. Not anymore.

"Rashid told me you have a list," I said. "A roster of human children born with latent powers—the ability to someday become Wardens."

She nodded slowly, but her expression had turned pensive and a little doubtful. "There is a record," she said. "But it's not in a form you can use."

"What do you mean?"

"I mean—" Imara seemed to search for words, then turned on the pew to drape one arm on the back. Sand shivered and whispered into falls of drifting silky waves around her. "I mean it's written in the fabric of the world. I can see it. There is no *written* list as you would understand it."

"Can you make one?"

Imara blinked. I'd surprised an Oracle. That seemed— unusual. "I suppose," she said, and then frowned. "There are risks, you know."

"Risks?"

"Such a list has to be . . . amendable. Flexible. It must reflect reality, if I create it. It's not fixed, at a moment in time; it will change as circumstances change. And it will be subject to . . . interference. Do you understand?"

"It's real-time," I said. "Yes. I understand."

"No, you don't." Imara stopped, and closed her eyes a moment. When she opened them, she said, "You know the Book of the Ancestors?"

It was a codicil of all things Djinn; it was kept by the Oracles, rarely shown in its physical form. But copies had been made, illegal copies, and the consequences of that had been . . . difficult. Almost catastrophic. In the hands of those not meant to have it, works by the Oracles could easily be lethally dangerous.

I saw where she was going. "If you make the list, it will contain its own power."

"It remains linked," she said. "Directly to me. Through me, directly to the fabric of reality. I can't do it any other way. It's not as if I can grab a pen and scribble down the names; there are billions of people on the planet, and even if only a fraction of them are born gifted . . . it is not a static list."

"I understand." I took a deep breath. "How does Pearl know who these children are, if she doesn't have this list?"

"Pearl has become like me," Imara said. "Like an Oracle, although she is not one as we understand it. She is . . . damaged, but she has tapped into something else—a power that is alien to this world, but still a part of it. She is much, much more powerful than a Djinn. She has . . . access to things. We can't stop her. We can't block her without direct confrontation, and if we do, she will do to us what she did to Gallan. She could destroy the Oracles."

Pearl didn't need a list. She, like Imara, could sense children as their potential powers began to form. She could strike anywhere, anytime. And we had no way to predict her moves.

Imara met my eyes fully again. I shuddered.

"Ashan might be right. The only way to stop her may be to remove the foundation of her power. Remove humans from the world. Do you understand me? Remove humans, and the world will recover. Mourn, yes. Create more Djinn. Create more life to replace what was lost, as she has before. But if you remove the *Djinn*, if you remove the *Oracles*, you attack the heart and brain and blood of the Earth. You *destroy* her. And that is what Pearl intends. She intends to be the murderer of this entire world. This has very little to do with the Wardens. It has to do with you, and her, and Ashan. And the Djinn. And hate."

The intensity behind her words was frightening. Imara came from humanity—from a human mother. A Warden mother. And yet there was a dispassionate regret in her that meant she had, in some way, already accepted the loss of humankind as a species.

Even more than I had, with all my supposed detachment.

I sucked in a deep breath. "I won't allow that," I said. "I didn't before. I won't now. I will find a way to stop her."

"Yes, that would certainly be a good idea," Imara said. "But if you do, you must do it soon. If you don't, the Oracles will be forced to act in self-defense. The Earth herself will wake, and humanity will not survive what follows. Do you understand what I am saying to you?"

She was threatening the cataclysm that all Wardens had feared since they'd first begun to know the strength and power of nature around them—a deliberate, considered effort by the forces of the planet to kill the human race, root and branch. An extinction event. If I didn't do it . . . the Oracles were prepared to take that action.

I swallowed. "Will you give me the list?" I asked her. "If I can't find Pearl, I must try to protect the children she's abducting, and disrupt her plans that way. I need the list to do that. You have to give me a chance, Imara. Give *us* a chance. Please."

I got a quick, warm smile from her. "Us," she repeated, and laughed lightly. It transformed her into something so beautiful that I had to squeeze my eyes shut and fight back trembles of ecstasy. "Oh, Cass. Listen to you. How far you've come already." Her tone changed, went solemn. "And how far you have yet to go. You and I, we are alike in that. I've hardly set my feet on the path."

But the light faded out of her, leaving her silent and serious again, and I felt a shiver of true fear go through me as she stared into my eyes. "If I do this," she said, "I am giving you something that wasn't meant for human hands. Something that is too powerful even for a Djinn. You understand? Once it's out of my keeping, it represents a wild power loose in the Earth. Those kinds of things can destroy, Cassiel. Even with the best of intentions."

I swallowed. "It's the only way to find these children."

"Then you must be responsible for it," she said. "And be careful of it. Using it opens you to attack as well as me."

"Then how do I use it?"

"The list will give you names and locations," she said. "Don't touch the surface of the scroll unless you must. That links you to the flow of events. Do you understand? Touching the words makes you vulnerable."

I nodded.

"And on your life, Cassiel, *on your life,* don't let anyone else have the list. Destroy it before that happens."

There was a rustle of sand, a sense of motion. I opened my eyes again, startled, and saw that she was gone from beside me on the pew. It had been a second, maybe less, and save for a few reddish grains of sand on the wood there was no sign she had ever been there.

Except that she now stood in front of the windows at the far end of the chapel. The tourists unconsciously moved away from her, heading back out all in a group. Not afraid, just ... determined to be elsewhere, suddenly. In seconds, the chapel was empty of everyone but me and Imara, who spread her arms wide.

Sand spiraled out from her body in a thick red smoke, veiling and then revealing the pale, perfect skin beneath. Her long, dark hair flowed out on an invisible wind, and her face turned up toward the rising sun. The glow seemed to soak into her and then reflect from her skin, turning it from pale to golden to a bright, burning fire of energy.

The sand suddenly blew out in a puffball explosion, and I ducked as grit spattered against me. For a second Imara stood there, naked and glowing, and then she slowly folded down to her knees, clasped her hands together, and then moved them apart as if unrolling something.

And a scroll appeared between her hands, a long page of pure white, unspooling. I saw fine black script on it, and then it snapped shut in her left hand, and a case formed around it. There was an airless sense of pressure in the room suddenly, of some massive expenditure of power, and then, with the next breath, it was gone.

Imara knelt with the scroll pressed close to her body. She stayed frozen that way for a moment, then closed her blazing eyes, and the sand rushed in again from all corners of the church, spiraled around her, and settled into moving, shifting folds of silk.

It was as if the entire world took a breath, then.

Imara rose to her feet, but didn't come to me. I understood that I would have to come to her instead, and rose to walk those few feet down the aisle.

It seemed . . . harder than it should have been, as if I was moving through levels on the aetheric plane, although in my current shape I couldn't possibly have been doing so. Imara held the scroll out in both hands, and when I finally stood before her, I found myself going to one knee as I reached for it.

Ceremony. It was important to the Djinn, possibly even more important than it was to humans.

The warm weight of the scroll touched my palms, and I felt a flash of almost unbearable heat go through me, a wave of something like a compulsion, but formless in its intensity. My fingers closed around the scroll's hard casing in a galvanic reaction, and I trembled.

Imara let go, and I heard her give a long, unsteady sigh. I looked up to see that she was staring down, eyes gone dim and almost human.

She touched my face with her fingers, a parting caress, and then . . . dissolved into dust, spiraling away.

Gone.

I was alone in the chapel.

I stayed on one knee, holding the scroll in my shaking hands, and then finally stood up. I opened the case and unrolled it, the first inch or so, and saw that there were dense lines of names written there, along with locations. I touched one. It glowed, and immediately, I understood how to find the child. It wasn't that I thought about this process; it simply *was*.

When I took my finger away, the glow died, and the knowledge left me.

She'd warned me, but the reality of it was stunning. This was more than just a list. It was a connection to a level of reality that even as a Djinn, I had never touched. A shortcut to the world of the Oracles.

I wondered, very seriously, if what I had just done was a good thing, or if I had just introduced something new and extremely risky to the balance of the world.

I turned to leave the chapel. At the back of the church stood the priest, trim and neat in his black jacket, pants, and clerical collar.

He looked at me as if I was something unholy.

Which, to be fair, I most likely was.

"Thank you," I said, and walked past him. "It's a blessed place."

He said nothing, but I had the distinct impression he felt it was more blessed in my absence.

Chapter 6

IMARA HADN'T STRESSED IT, but I clearly understood now that the scroll I carried was not merely the best intelligence we could hope for, but also the most dangerous. She had entrusted something to me that was far more precious than even the most valuable human treasure.

I wasn't sure that I could protect it alone.

As I raced along the highway on my newly inherited Harley, I used a steady trickle of power to veil me from prying eyes. It wouldn't be enough to stop a Djinn, but it would keep me hidden from any merely human agents Pearl chose to employ. I wasn't certain about her Warden child acolytes, however. Their powers didn't seem to be limited in the way I would have expected. It was entirely possible that they would be able to see and detect me, whatever measures I took to stop them.

It was also possible that the measures I would have to take against them would be . . . extreme. Not a prospect I faced with any sort of pleasure.

I took a less direct route away from Sedona than I had getting to it, traveling back roads and deserted, lonely stretches with only lizards and coyotes as rapidly passing company. I had no desire to run afoul of the law, even accidentally; last night's events had taught me the value of anonymity, at least. The morning grew bright, edging toward noon, with the fierce amber bead of the sun the only flaw in a featureless sky. I breathed in the smell of the arid, perfect land, feeling freedom here in the emptiness.

And then my cell phone rang, vibrating against my skin. I had tucked it in the bodice of my vest, to ensure that I could detect it over the roar of the engine; even so, I only noticed because it was such a localized buzz, as opposed to the shaking my entire body received from the bike.

I pulled over to the side of the road, coasting to a gravel-crunching stop, and shut off the engine. In its absence, the day was heavy with heat, filled with birds calling and insects droning. I could almost hear the land baking beneath the sun.

I flipped open the phone and held it to my ear. "Yes," I said.

"Try hello," Luis said. "Would it kill you?"

"It might," I replied. "I am trying to minimize risk."

He sighed. "Did you get it?"

"Yes," I said. "The girl?"

"I'm going to need you with me. It doesn't look good." He paused for a few seconds, then said, with a cautious note in his voice, "Everything okay? You have any trouble?"

With a pang, I thought of the death and destruction I'd left in my wake. Of the ruined Victory, too, although I felt that perhaps I shouldn't rate a machine so highly as the lives that had been lost.

Then again, it had been a *very* nice motorcycle.

"A little," I said.

"How little?"

"I have a Harley now."

Luis knew me well enough, it seemed. "Holy crap," he said. "What blew up?"

"Many things," I said. "But I am alive."

"I have *got* to stop letting you off on your own."

His protectiveness made me smile, if a little bitterly. "If you hadn't, you might be dead now."

"*Chica,* you assume a whole lot of helplessness on my part. Check your program. I'm not the damsel in distress."

I considered that. "Next time," I said, "I will let you fight the battles." Then, with a sudden shock, I remembered Isabel's chubby, pretty face, and the unnatural focus in her eyes. "Luis."

"Yeah, still me," he said. "What?"

I didn't want to tell him, but somehow I found the words. "I saw Isabel," I said. "She was here. She was with one of Pearl's agents who attacked me."

For a freezing-cold second, Luis didn't say anything at all. When he did, it was very soft. Deadly in its intensity. "Tell me you didn't hit back at her."

"No," I said. "I didn't hurt her. But—"

"Ah, God, what? *What?*"

It was my turn to pause, to search for words. "Pearl is using her," I said finally. "She's too young. It will harm her, whatever I do. I don't wish this, Luis. Please believe me. I want to spare her all pain, but I'm not certain I can. Or that anyone can."

"*Fuck,*" Luis spat, and then launched into a fluid

course of Spanish curses, liquid fire in words. "You *saw* her. And you *let her go*? What the hell is wrong with you?"

"I did not have a choice," I said. "I'm sorry." It was hard to not feel defensive. It was also very difficult not to feel guilty. "I did not hurt her."

He was silent for so long I wondered if he had simply put down the phone and walked away. Then he said, flatly, "Did you get what you went for or not?"

"Yes."

"Then get your ass here fast, you hear me? Fast."

I kicked the Harley to growling, rumbling life. "I am coming," I said, hung up, and shoved the phone back in the bodice of my vest. This time, when I opened the throttle, I backed it with bursts of power, pushing the machine to its limits.

By the time I reached Albuquerque, both I and the motorcycle were exhausted. I slowed, because even with the clouding veil I maintained, the simple mechanics of navigating through traffic required me to be more cautious, even though I had ceased to fear attracting the attention of the police.

I pulled out the phone and dialed one-handed to shout, "I'm here. Where are you?"

"Christ, what are you riding, a tank? Just come to the house."

The house was far from safe, but he knew that. Maybe he was actively hoping for another attack. Spoiling for it. As angry as I sensed he was, that was not beyond the realm of possibility.

"On my way," I said, and hung up. It was a relatively

simple matter to guide the big bike through the night
traffic, under the glare of sodium-yellow and tungsten-
white streetlights, to the quiet street that held Manny
and Angela's—now Luis's—home. I cut the engine and
coasted to a stop at the curb, dismounted, and was halfway up the walk with the scroll before the kickstand actually hit the concrete.

Luis had already opened the door. He looked me
swiftly up and down, and I was warmed by the flash
of concern in his eyes, however brief. Then he nodded
and stepped aside to let me in, locking the door behind
me.

On the worn, comfortable couch sat Agent Ben
Turner, looking very tired. He was holding a mug that
steamed with what must have been coffee, from the
smell of it spicing the air. Luis likewise had a mug sitting on the coffee table, and a third had been poured
already for me. I took it and sat on the opposite end of
the couch, and gratefully drank. The caffeine would help
mask my physical needs, if not those of the languishing
Djinn within.

"You said you saw Ibby," Luis said, and his dark eyes
were fixed and intent on my face. "What happened? Tell
me everything."

I glanced at Agent Turner. "Everything?"

Turner sighed. "Don't hold back on my account. I'm
in the shit now, sure as death and taxes."

"You can refuse to pay taxes," I said. "Death rarely
asks."

Luis made an impatient sound, and I raised a hand
to slow him down. "I know," I said. "I will tell you." It
wasn't comforting to either of us, but I told the story, and

he heard it. Turner choked on his coffee when he heard of the carnage among the bikers, but said nothing.

Luis pushed the issue. "You got a problem?" he asked.

"You mean, do I have to do anything about it? No," Turner said. "It's local business, not federal. Until it becomes federal, I'm just . . . an interested bystander."

"Even if it's criminal behavior?"

"Criminal like what? Like getting out alive, after being jumped by a gang and threatened with a gun?" He shook his head. "Not my business. I'm fine with it."

I hadn't been particularly worried, either way, but Luis clearly had been, and now he sat back in the threadbare armchair and relaxed, sipping coffee. "But she seemed okay," he said to me. "Ibby. Physically?" He was searching for any hope to cling to, and I gave it freely.

"She looked healthy," I said. "She wasn't injured."

I couldn't tell him, I realized, about Isabel's words about her mother. That would hurt him far more than necessary; there was nothing he could do, at this moment, to relieve Ibby of that burden. Or himself.

So I would carry it for him, a little longer.

"You said you've got this thing you went out there for," Turner said, and sat his coffee cup down on the table to lean forward, elbows on the wrinkled knees of his suit pants. "The list?"

"I do." I didn't move to produce it, however. Before I did that, I anchored myself quickly to Luis's warm, steady presence, and rose into the aetheric, focusing on Turner.

It was not that I had a reason to distrust him. Quite the contrary. But something the Oracle had said stuck with me—that no trust could be absolute.

Overlying the vague outlines of his physical form lay his aetheric one, driven by subconscious desires and needs in his mind and soul. Some humans had radically different aetheric forms. Some were monstrous and twisted, the way some of the bikers had been who'd perished on the road.

Agent Turner's spiritual self was merely . . . routine. He seemed much the same, though possibly taller and broader, more powerful in his spirit than in his body. Like most Wardens, he radiated waves of energy, though his were weak in comparison to the rich, lustrous radiance of Luis's form.

I watched carefully. Sometimes, in the aetheric, one could detect lies, and deception, and fears. But I saw nothing.

Agent Turner simply seemed . . . tired.

I dropped down into my flesh again, stretched a little, and then nodded to Luis. I reached inside my heavy leather jacket and took the warm weight of the scroll case from the interior pocket.

"That's it?" Turner leaned forward even more, chest almost pressed to his knees, trying to peer at the list in my hands. "That's a list of all the kids with Warden powers?"

"Yes," I said. "Worldwide. Constantly updated." He held out his hand for it. "No. No one touches it but me."

He frowned, and I thought for a moment he'd order me to hand it over—which would have been ineffective, at best—then shrugged and settled back in his chair. "Look up the kid we're looking for right now, the latest disappearance," he said. "Gloria Jensen."

I opened the scroll and rolled it until I reached the

middle of the alphabetical list. There were two Gloria Jensens. "California?" I asked. Turner shook his head. "New Jersey?"

His face took on a pinched look. "That all you've got?"

"Yes," I said, and allowed the roll to slide closed. "Two of that name, one in California, one in New Jersey."

"This one was taken from her home right here. New Mexico."

Luis said, "Wait. Does the list show where they're *from*, or where they *are*?"

It was an excellent, startling question, the answer to which Imara had never made clear to me. "I don't know."

"Then what the hell good is it?" Turner snapped.

There was a way I could know for certain, but Imara had cautioned me—strongly—that it made me vulnerable. Still, I saw no real option, if this list was to be of any practical use to us at all. I took a deep breath, opened the list again, and brushed my fingertip over the name of the first Gloria Jensen.

She was in a school auditorium, wearing a cheerleading uniform, screaming as a basketball soared through the air toward a hoop; I saw it clearly, experienced an echo of her youthful excitement and joy. "It's not this one," I said. "Not New Jersey."

I slid my finger down to the second name.

Darkness. Fear. Pain.

I gasped and wrenched my finger away, involuntarily raising it to my mouth as if I had burned it. My heart began to pound in startled reaction, and I felt a visceral impulse to throw down the scroll, to never feel *that* again.

"Cass?" Luis's hands came down on my shoulders, strong and steadying. "You all right?"

I nodded, still breathing too fast, and unrolled the scroll again.

Darkness. Fear. Pain. Alone. The rumble of an engine, a constant bouncing vibration. The smells of rust and oil. "She's in a car," I said. "In the trunk. The car is in California. This is the one who was abducted."

"Where?" Turner's voice, sharp with urgency. "I need exact details, dammit!"

"I know," I whispered, and mimed a pen, writing. Luis's presence removed itself, returned a moment later. He pressed a pen into my right hand, while my left forefinger kept the connection to Gloria Jensen open. I scratched down the information that poured into my consciousness, without understanding where it was coming from, or how. The wildly out-of-control feeling of it made it seem as if I had grabbed hold of the tail of a tornado, something insanely beyond my power to control.

I wanted, desperately, to back away, but I forced myself to stay focused. Stay connected. The pen scratched, moving without my conscious direction, and then stopped. As the pen slipped from my fingers, my finger jerked away from the scroll. I couldn't force myself to stay in contact with the child, not even for another moment.

"I can't *help her*," I heard myself say, numbly. "I can only feel. Only feel." My fingers felt scorched, but it was only an impression, the only way my nerves could interpret the kind of psychic pain that I had inflicted upon myself. Something inside of me was wailing in terror, still. Was this what the Oracle felt? Imara had said she felt them all . . . all their joy, their pain, their fear. This, times a billion. Times *six* billion.

I could not even stand to feel such things from *one*. The prospect of the job of an Oracle made me aware, for the first time, of the awesome scope and responsibility of such a thing. The strength of character it required.

Luis slid the piece of paper out from beneath my trembling hand and read it. Turner rose and looked over his shoulder. "La Jolla," Luis said. "These are a list of cross streets, it gives us a direction."

"Can you give me a type of car?" Turner asked, already reaching for his cell phone. I shook my head. "But it has a trunk. How big?"

"Small," I said. The child had been cramped, struggling for breath. Hot and sweating, terrified. Injured. "She has a broken arm."

"Christ," Luis said. "Get Rashid. Maybe he can—"

"Can what?" Rashid was, without any warning, sitting behind us, crouched against the wall, skin gone from smoke to indigo in the artificial light. He looked wrong and very, very beautiful. There was a silvery shimmer under the surface of his skin, a glow that seemed to echo moonlight. "Help you? I might. What are you offering?"

Turner flinched, but to his credit, he didn't back down. "That all depends. What do you want?"

Rashid's lips parted in a genial sort of smile. "For rescuing a Warden child from her tormentor? Or for bringing you the tormentor in one piece and alive?"

"Both," Turner and Luis said, at once. I said nothing, watching Rashid with wary intensity. The two men exchanged a look, and Turner continued. "Not worth much unless you do it fast. I'm going to have cops all over it in ten minutes."

"But it is ten minutes of pain and fear that you might spare her," Rashid said, with a kind of horrible satisfaction. "And so much can happen in ten minutes, yes? I have crippled a human in less than a second. Imagine what *he* might be able to do, with such a rich span of possibilities available to him. Especially were he warned you were . . . coming."

Time slowed to an icy crawl, and I felt every slow beat of my heart as my focus narrowed in on him. On this Djinn who dared to say such things.

So you would have, once, I heard a whisper say, deep in my mind. *So you might have done, at any rate. Their pain, their weeping, their losses meant nothing to you, all these thousands of years. And now, you know how it feels.*

Yes. But I had been created a Djinn, and I had never come from human stock. Rashid had. Rashid should have known better. I couldn't let that pass.

"If you do that," I whispered, "if you even *consider* it, I will tear you apart. I swear it."

He flashed me a mocking smile, unimpressed. "What is the human phrase . . . ? You and . . . what army?" He quoted the phrase like a visitor unfamiliar not just to the language, but to the planet. Which I supposed he was, in all the ways that might have been relevant to this conversation.

"How about me," Luis said flatly. "How about the Wardens. Every fucking Warden on Earth. You want to go to war with us, Rashid, we'll go right the fuck now. You pull that shit right now, and David won't protect you. No one will. It'll be you, and us. How you like those odds?"

He didn't. He also wasn't so much afraid as cautious, I saw. He was not *certain* that David, in his capacity as Conduit for the New Djinn, wouldn't turn on him for such a thing.

I was. I knew David well enough to know that Rashid's attitude wouldn't go unpunished.

Whatever Rashid assumed about the Djinn, he knew there was no doubt that the Wardens would come after him, for something like this. I could only imagine Lewis Orwell's fury. Or Joanne's.

The odds were not in Rashid's favor.

Rashid, acknowledging this, shrugged. "Only a thought," he said. "A mere hypothetical. If you want me to save the child and stop your villain, then I can do so. For a price. You are free to choose as you like."

"Wait," I said. "How do we know the girl's abductor isn't Pearl's agent? If we act immediately, we could lose any chance of tracing him to his destination."

Luis seemed stunned. "You'd let that kid be *bait?* Jesus, Cass. You're as bad as he is."

That stung. "No," I said. "I simply raise the question." *Like Rashid*, I thought but did not say. "It may be our only chance of finding Ibby and the other children quickly without waiting for another child to be abducted."

"You sure you can't find Ibby or the others through the list?" Luis asked. "Did you try?"

I glanced down at the scroll, and felt that visceral flutter again, that dread. Touching it had torn open something inside of me that I desperately wished to close, a feeling of vulnerability that was anathema to someone like me.

Luis must have seen my worry, or felt it through the connection he held with me. His expression softened, and he leaned closer to say, quietly, "Let me try."

I shook my head. "No. No one else can touch it, especially a human. I'm not sure what the consequences would be. We can't take the risk."

"But we have to *know*. If we can find her this way, we should do it. Right now." Luis sounded tentative, apologetic, but he was also very, very right. We had to know. If I had the ability to end this, I couldn't flinch from it, no matter the pain.

I unrolled the scroll to find Isabel Rocha.

There was no location next to her name. That in itself was odd; adding to the sense of wrongness was the fact that the text of her name pulsed, faded, pulsed, jittered—as if something was struggling to remove it, and failing. For now.

I touched her name with my fingertip, and the glow flared as before, but instead of that immediate knowledge I had felt before—even the knowledge of terror and pain—all I felt from touching Ibby's name was a kind of voracious, hungry darkness. It howled through me like a storm.

Trap. And Imara had warned me. *Touching it will make you vulnerable.* She'd told me that Pearl had become something like a Conduit, like an Oracle, something with power to touch the flow of time and space and reality directly.

With the power to *corrupt* the flow.

I gasped aloud, and tried to pull my hand away from

the scroll, but the darkness surged up through the contact, licking through nerves and veins and flesh. I saw the nail turn black, and then lines of indigo shot up my finger. Quick as a breath they spread into my left hand, a midnight tracery that brought with it an icy, fatal numbness.

Pearl's madness, her power, her furious hunger for revenge, all distilled into a black poison that had been crafted solely for this purpose, for *me*. Imara had known this. She'd known the risk even as she allowed me to take it. She'd tried to warn me how dangerous it could be.

I gritted my teeth and focused, trying to halt the progress of Pearl's invasion within my body. I could feel her black joy, her triumph. It was happening quickly, devastatingly quickly. I distantly heard Luis's sharp intake of breath, and felt him moving toward me as he realized something was wrong. Too late, and there was nothing, absolutely nothing he could do.

Then my hand was knocked away from the scroll, and the paper fell to the floor and rolled away, snapping into that tight, protective casing that looked like polished bone. Featureless and faintly shimmering with power. Turner hesitated, then reached down toward it. "No!" I screamed. "Don't touch it!"

He hesitated, then slowly backed away, leaving it where it had fallen.

I stared down at my limp left hand. It was blackened and numb where it lay in my lap.

Dead.

"Madre," Luis whispered, and shoved me back to kneel in front of me, taking the damaged hand in both

of his. I saw power flare from him, seeking entrance, and felt a tantalizing flicker of heat within the tissues.

Something fought back. I felt the snap of attack, from within my hand to strike at him, and Luis broke off, panting. He gave me a wild look of utter horror. "I can't," he blurted. "It's not—I can't stop it. I can't even touch it. You have to do something. Fast, Cass."

"I can't." My voice sounded level and calm, unnaturally so. "It's inside me now. I can't even keep it contained in my arm much longer. My power is yours; if yours can't stop it, mine can't either. The battle's already lost."

What I meant, what he must have understood, was that I was going to be destroyed. There was nothing to be done, nothing magical that either of us could do or try.

Turner watched, confused and shocked. No help from him. No help possible.

I looked at Rashid.

He smiled, and from his crouch in the corner, said, "For a price, my razor-edged angel. It will cost you."

"What price?" I asked. My mouth was dry, my skin felt tight and clammy. I was afraid, but I also knew the dangers of showing my desperation.

"Do you really have time to bargain?" He cocked his head, just a little, and stared at me with inhuman, unfeeling eyes. "I think you don't. I can stop it. Say yes."

"To what?"

His grin turned feral. "To whatever I want, of course." His tone dripped with all manner of salacious innuendo, but his eyes . . . his eyes flicked toward the scroll, where it sat radiating power. A direct connection to the Oracles.

To the Earth herself, perhaps. Power beyond measure, especially in the hands of a Djinn.

I had promised Imara never to let it out of my hands.

I sucked in a deep, trembling breath. "No," I said. I was not willing to take that particular risk. Not even at the cost of my life. Rashid was a wild, random creature. In his hands, this list could wreak incalculable damage as easily as overwhelming good.

I felt one of the barriers I had built to wall off my poisoned hand break, like a levy under a black tide. More darkness flooded into my hand, and began to spread.

"Yes," Luis said. "Dammit, do it, Rashid. *Do it!* Save her!"

Rashid raised an eyebrow, and didn't move his gaze away from mine. "*She* has to say it," Rashid said. "No one else can answer for her. What say you, Cassiel? Deal?"

I licked my lips. I felt the darkness raging beneath my skin, bubbling like some viscous acid. It didn't hurt, not yet, but that was only because it destroyed physical nerves as it went. It would no doubt be an agony beyond anything I had ever known, when it reached my centers of power. When it consumed and utterly destroyed my soul and unmade me from the world.

And deep within me, the *other* Cassiel stirred. The ice-cold core of me, the inhuman persona who had seen stars burn out, seen death in the billions, witnessed atrocity and miracles with the same utter lack of concern.

That Cassiel knew what to do, where the merely human one failed. I felt her chill in my heart, her clarity in my mind.

I had a choice. It wasn't one my human self could make.

Only a Djinn could make it.

"No," I said again, very precisely. "I do not accept your deal, Rashid. Not for that."

I walked forward and took hold of a bronze sculpture on a side table, a metal representation of two clasped, weathered praying hands. Angela's possession, one dear to her during her life. I felt the whisper of her devotion and passion soaked into the metal. Her history.

Help me be strong, the human side of me whispered. *Help me do the right thing. Help me not be afraid.*

The Djinn part of me had no fear at all, only frozen, emotionless purpose.

I raised power and re-formed the metal. It melted in my right hand into a shimmering pool, then lengthened. Hardened.

Formed itself into a sharp, long-bladed hatchet.

Before either Luis or Ben Turner could stop me, I put my hand and wrist flat on the wooden surface of the dining table, raised the hatchet, and put all my strength into the downward blow. I had to do it in one strike.

To my Djinn mind, it was all angles, force, calculation. An entirely academic exercise.

The human part of me had gone away. That was for the best.

I heard Luis screaming, but it was too late.

Now.

The blade slammed squarely into untainted flesh an inch above where the poison stopped, sliced through flesh, muscle, and through the tough bone. All the way through, burying its edge in the wood below.

Its work done, the Djinn in me faded back into watch-

11

ful silence, satisfied with the precision and power of its work.

The human part of me woke to the horror. I screamed. The pain was tremendous, a hot red storm that threatened to drive me unconscious to the ground; it took all my focus and strength to hold on. Immediately after, shock set in fast, and the flood of bleeding slowed to a sudden, dizzying trickle from the stump. The severed hand took on a strange, disassociated look, as if it had never been a part of me, as if I had only dreamed of ever having such a thing attached to my body.

Rashid had idly noted how many terrible things could happen in a matter of mere seconds.

He was so correct.

"No!" Luis was shouting. He grabbed at me, struck the hatchet from my hands and sent it skittering across the floor, scattering blood drops. "*Dios,* no!" He hissed something else, something I couldn't understand through the hazy fog that descended over my eyes, and took the stump of my arm in a firm grip. Maybe he meant to try to reattach the hand. Earth Wardens had been known to work such miracles, after all.

The hand had other ideas.

My severed hand spasmed, and then it began to *move,* like a separate and living creature. Tentatively at first— stiff little jabs of the blackened fingers—and then it dug its nails into the wood and curled, looking suddenly like nothing so much as a spider preparing to leap.

Rashid, who had not reacted even as I chopped my hand off, suddenly rose to his feet in a smooth, startled motion as my blackened hand began walking across the table toward me.

Rashid reached out, and a broad-bladed knife from the kitchen counter flew through the air to smack into his palm. He advanced with three fast steps, and with a blindingly quick motion, stabbed the knife into the back of my severed, crawling hand, pinning it to the table. It struggled for a few seconds, scrabbling with its black fingernails, and then went still.

Not limp.

Just . . . still. Waiting.

"Holy fucking God," Turner whispered, and then shook himself. "We need to get a tourniquet on her. Fast."

Luis tore his wide gaze from the hand on the table, and I saw him thrust all of it away with an almost physical effort of will. "I've got it," he said. "Cass? You hear me?"

"I hear you," I said distantly.

Luis's face was set and hard, but his eyes were so worried. So vulnerable. "Not going to lie to you, this is going to hurt like hell, so I'm going to turn off your nerves for a second. Hang on, okay?"

I nodded placidly.

Then I was sitting on the floor. I don't know how; it seemed like life had jumped its tracks for a moment, as if a few vital seconds of my life had been erased, crudely and utterly destroyed.

Whatever trauma I had felt, those seconds were gone, utterly vanished. Sometimes the human brain protects itself, creates a fail-safe circuit. That was what Luis had done—triggered that final protection, a kind of static during which the brain resets itself.

I had no memory, because no memory of those moments existed for me. Nor ever would.

There was a towel tied tightly around the end of my arm, which ended abruptly in an empty space. I raised it and stared at it, wondering where my hand had gone. I could still feel it, still feel the phantom muscles flexing. *What happened . . . ?* I knew, but I didn't know. Not really.

My head felt light and vague. I pulled in deep, trembling breaths and felt an arm bracing me across my shoulders. "Easy," Luis said. His voice was wrong, shaking and too high. "Breathe. Come on, breathe."

I *was* breathing, I thought, with a hot flash of annoyance. Even Rashid was watching me with a frown of concentration. Turner and Luis seemed shocked and horrified.

Ah, yes, of course. I had chopped off my hand.

Their reactions made perfect sense, then.

"I'm all right," I said. Indeed, I was. My pain had receded, and the light-headed feeling was going away. The absence of the invading darkness left me feeling unreasonably strong. "Were you able to stop the bleeding?" As if I was inquiring politely about the health of a distant relative, or the weather. Something that had no bearing on my own ability to survive the night.

Luis swallowed. His skin looked cream-pale beneath its burnish of bronze. "It's stopped," he said. "I deadened the nerves and sealed the blood vessels. But it's not good, Cass. Christ, *why?*"

"Pearl," I said. "If I hadn't acted, she'd have destroyed me. It had to be done."

"I could have stopped it," Rashid said. I gave him a long look. "Perhaps."

"It wouldn't matter," I said. "You wanted the list. I

can't give it to you. I couldn't depend on your goodwill, Rashid. Or would you say that you would have acted to save me, regardless?"

He didn't answer. He didn't have to. I'd felt it from him, felt that avarice and pure, selfish desire. I knew him. I had once been Rashid, or very like him.

"It was the only way," I said, and for some reason it came out almost kind. I deliberately hardened my tone. "If you want to make amends, Rashid, you may. The girl, Gloria. Go and get her. There will be no bargain. You will do it because I *tell* you to do it."

Rashid's eyes widened. He looked at the table, where my blackened, severed hand still lay pinned by the knife. Not dead. Quiescent.

"If I save her now," he said, "you will lose your way to the one you seek. I can follow instead, and retrieve the girl before more harm is done."

"She's alone," I said. "She's in pain. She's a child. More harm is done every second. Do this, Rashid. You owe this to me."

He thought about that, and unwillingly inclined his head.

Then he vanished.

In the silent aftermath of his departure, Ben Turner said, "You cut your hand off. Jesus Christ, you cut. Your hand. *Off.*"

"It wasn't my hand," I said. "Not anymore. And it couldn't be saved."

Turner looked a little queasy, and stared hard at the unmoving black thing that sat crouched and nailed to the tabletop. It still didn't look dead. It looked like it was simply waiting for an opening, for a careless moment. I was not entirely certain the knife could hold it, if it truly exerted itself, although Rashid had certainly buried the metal deeply into the wood.

"Yeah," Turner said softly. "I see your point. So . . . what the hell do we do with that now?"

"You are a Fire Warden, aren't you?" I asked. "Burn it. Please."

He sent me a narrow, disbelieving look, then silently asked Luis if he agreed. Luis did, with a bare, silent nod. Turner took in a deep breath, focused his energy, and the wood on the table, for a respectable distance around the severed hand, burst completely into flame.

The hand began to struggle against the knife, jerking, slicing itself blindly as it tried to escape. Luis and I opened the floodgates of power to pour it into the wood the hand was touching. What wasn't yet burning warped, folding over the fingers, trapping it. Fire, metal, earth—it was bound by all the powers, save air, which in this case fed the fire. The hand flopped wildly, trying to pull itself free, and finally, with a crackle of baking bones and sizzling flesh, went completely, utterly limp.

Dead.

A black, viscous liquid flowed from the severed stump of the wrist, turning wood to powdery, rotted ash where it touched, and smothering the flames. But it didn't live long beyond its flesh host, and vanished into black, greasy smoke that faded into nothing on the air.

Turner kept the fire burning hot until my hand was a lacework of bones, bright white and crumbling, and then he let the flames die.

He promptly stumbled to the bathroom and slammed the door. I watched him go without comment. Luis, moving like a man who'd taken a gut wound, let go of me and walked to the kitchen, opened the refrigerator, and took out a beer. He popped the cap from it, still staring into a distance full of horror, then upended the bottle and drank until all that was left was foam. Then he leaned forward and rested the cold empty glass against his forehead.

I stood up, swaying a little from the loss of blood and lingering shock, and retrieved the bronze hatchet from where it lay in a pool of crimson on the floor. I cleaned it carefully against the towel wrapped around my left wrist, then sat down on the sofa and worked the tight knots of cotton twine that bound the towel in place.

"What the hell are you doing?" Luis asked wearily, and tried to stop me. I shoved him away with my good hand and held him there, pulling at the frayed cord with my teeth until it loosened enough for me to slip the towel away.

I had enough control of my body to keep the blood vessels clamped, and the nerves deadened. I wrapped the twine tight again, then contemplated the bronze weapon in my right hand.

"Cass." His voice broke a little. "Cass, what the hell are you doing?" He was afraid, I realized, that I had gone entirely mad. That I was about to start mutilating myself again, to no real purpose.

"Shhhhh," I said, and reached out with power. The metal of the weapon softened, melted, formed itself into a complex and delicate structure. I built it with a Djinn's instinctive understanding of the world, of my own lovely, finely engineered body, the interconnectedness of all things. I think in a way Luis was right—I was quietly, oddly mad. It had seemed completely rational to me to do these things, from the moment I had recognized that I had a choice none of the others—not even Pearl—had foreseen. Sever my hand. Burn the remains.

Now the same ruthless, cold Djinn instinct was telling me to make myself a new hand, out of the weapon that had been my salvation.

I began by building hard metal bones, then overlaying them with fine, strong cables in patterns that mirrored the muscles and tendons of my right hand. Then, over all of that, a light, flexible bronze skin. Fingers. Even delicately etched fingernails, each slightly and sharply pointed, like finely manicured claws.

Then I slipped the complex mechanism over the open stump of my arm and joined up the parts, with little regard to what was metal and what was flesh. It fused together with a hiss and a smell of burning flesh, and I began to move my fingers slowly, one after another, before Luis's wide, disbelieving eyes.

Then I made a fist, with my new bronze hand, and uncurled it to lay it flat in my lap. It was an exact mirror of my right hand, perfect in every visible detail. Even the shine of the metal mimicked living flesh. It was as if I'd dipped my living hand into metal.

I heard the water running in the bathroom, and then the door opened and Turner came out, wiping his mouth with a towel. "We need to get you an ambulance and— what the *hell* is that?" He sounded like a man who'd gone beyond surprise, into weary resignation.

I held up my metal hand and said, "No ambulance. No hospital." I wiggled the fingers to show him that it worked, then lowered it and closed my eyes. "I will sleep now."

I don't know, but I imagined that Turner and Luis exchanged long looks. I simply drifted off into a half-drugged distance of shock, artificial calm, and true, genuine exhaustion.

It felt like I slept only a few minutes before coming awake again, shaking. The calm and shock had left me, the cold Djinn certainty had left me, and there was only the knowledge of what I had done to my fragile human flesh.

Luis was sitting beside me on the couch. I looked mutely at him, my eyes blurring with cold, lost tears, and he put his arm around me, pressed his lips to my temple, and whispered, "Thank God. Thank God you're back."

I was. The person who had been inhabiting my body, from the moment I had realized what my only choice had been, was gone. That Cassiel had once again been banished to the hidden recesses where she lurked.

"That was her, wasn't it?" he asked. "The Cassiel you used to be. The Djinn. The badass you keep telling me about." The one who would make the choice to destroy humanity, if it was necessary.

I nodded, burying my face against his shirt. I couldn't stop shaking. Couldn't stem the tears. His hand stroked my hair over and over, an animal comfort and connection, and I wanted . . . oblivion. Just for a while.

"You were right," he told me. "She's terrifying."

To me, as well.

The next few minutes were long ones, silent ones, filled with the sound of Turner drinking down a glass of water, refilling it, then emptying it again, as if he hoped to wash himself clean from the inside out. I wondered if I should ask for something, but I didn't need to do so; Luis, unasked, brought me a glass and very gently encouraged me to drink.

I hadn't realized how thirsty I was until the water touched my lips, and then I sucked it down gulp after greedy gulp, barely pausing for air until the tumbler was dry. He refilled it, then sat beside me as I drank at a slower pace, stroking my hair with restless fingers.

"It's the power," he said. "It takes a lot out of you, physically. And you—" He glanced down at the metal hand, lying still in my lap. "Yeah. I'm not even sure how you did what you did."

"Which part?" I asked.

"Hell, any of it. I've never seen anything like that before, outside of some big-budget sci-fi movie." He kept watching the hand with guarded fascination. "Are you sure that's not some evil hand or something?"

"Evil?" I raised it in surprise, flexing the metal fingers. "Why would this be evil?"

"You're kidding. I mean, it's a *metal hand.*"

"My flesh hand was much worse, I think." I touched my fingers together. The control was very good, but there was an odd clink as the metal connected.

Luis continued to stare. "Can you feel anything with that?"

"Yes."

"How?"

I raised my eyebrows involuntarily, because it was a question that hadn't rightly occurred to me. I ran the metal fingertips over texture—the sofa, the smooth leather of my jacket, then lightly over Luis's skin.

All different sensations. All exactly as experience had taught me they should feel.

"The metal," I said, surprised. "It's a part of the living Earth. Your powers control metal, so I can interpret the sensations."

"Does it hurt?"

"No," I said, and put my metal palm against his warm cheek. "Does it feel odd?"

He seemed startled, raising his hand to lay it over my bronze one. Before he could answer me, my cell phone began to ring, buzzing against my skin like a trapped insect. I slid it free, flipped it open, and held it to my ear. The screen displayed nothing at all except a random pattern of light.

I put it to my ear.

"Human technology." It was Rashid. He sounded disgusted, and a little smug. "So wasteful, yet so interesting."

"We can't all be you," I said. "Did you get the child?"

"Of course. And before you ask, the man driving the car doesn't yet know that she's gone. I retrieved her when he stopped for a traffic signal."

"Did he see you?"

"Of course not. To all appearances she is still locked in his trunk." Rashid's voice took on a slight edge. "Before you ask, yes, I am following him."

"What about the girl? You're sure she's all right?"

"Did I not say—"

"Yes." I closed my eyes and tried to focus. At Luis's urgent gesture, I put the phone on speaker so the others could hear. "What did you do with her?"

"I am not insensitive; I didn't just abandon her at the side of the road. I found a policeman. I handed her over safely enough."

That eased a weight within me that was staggering once lifted. "Where are you now?"

"In the trunk of his car," Rashid said. "I thought it would be impolite to take one thing from him and leave nothing in return."

"No," Turner snapped. "You need to get out of there. Just get out. If you got the girl, the job's over. Leave it."

"Don't," I said, overriding him. "Stay with him, Rashid. But understand, if he *is* heading toward Pearl, you must know when to let go. You can't allow yourself to get too close. You saw what she can do." He'd knifed the blackened evidence of it on the kitchen table.

"I saw," he agreed. "I will be in contact."

He broke the connection without any sort of good-bye, which was not unexpected. Turner was already dialing his own phone, and turning away to hold a fast, urgent conversation. He was back in just under five minutes, looking immensely relieved beneath his pallor and exhaustion.

"They've got the girl all right," he said. "She's in custody, heading for the hospital with an armed escort. I got a Warden to meet them at the hospital. She'll be watched."

"And her parents?"

"I'm heading over there now," he said. "This kind of good news, I'd rather deliver in person." He picked up his suit jacket, which was as rumpled as his pants and shirt, and shrugged it on, avoiding our eyes. Then he said, "You two want to come along?"

"I'm not sure. She still doesn't look too good," Luis said doubtfully, but I was already moving to stand up. He braced me with one hand under my left elbow, but I felt only a touch of disorientation. The shock was, indeed, passing.

The physical pieces of it, at any rate. I couldn't yet tell what I felt emotionally, or would feel tomorrow. It was entirely new territory for me, to have been so deeply hurt. Especially by my own choice, and my own action.

"I want to go with you," I said. "If you'll allow it."

We all glanced at the burned spot on the table, the soot-blackened knife, and the white exposed bones that were all that was left of my hand. Turner shuddered.

"Yeah," he said. "I guess you've got the right to do whatever you want to right now. Fine."

Luis didn't approve, but he only shook his head and touched my shoulder to turn me toward him. "Hey," he said. "You need more?" More power, he meant. I hadn't dared to check, but now I realized that I was as empty of energy within as I had been parched and thirsty.

I nodded. He sighed and took my right hand in his, facing me. "Ready?" he asked.

I held his gaze and nodded.

His energy flowed into me, a trickle that built to a steady pulse within my veins. It left my skin burning hot, and I felt the interface of metal with my arm grow colder by contrast, like a phantom limb of ice. The power coursed through me, repairing damages, and then pooled deep within. I pulled away then, sending a wordless pulse of gratitude between us, and in an unguarded moment saw the drawn look on his face, and the fierce pain in his eyes.

I was hurting him. He was weary and anguished; he

had seen me do a terrible thing, and had been helpless to stop it, or to save me from the consequences. On top of that, he'd already been through a great deal. Now, I was taking from his precious reserves of strength.

But he didn't hold back. Not at all.

I kissed him. I don't know why; it was wrong, it was the wrong moment, the wrong place. Everything about it was irrational and terribly mistaken, except for the rush of feeling that rose inside me at the soft, and surprised, touch of his lips. At the way his body tensed and leaned toward mine. At the way his hands slipped up my arms and caressed my body.

Luis broke the kiss with a gasp and stepped away, cheeks flaming dark red. His eyes cut toward Turner, who had paused, staring, in the act of turning the knob on the front door.

"What are you looking at?" he demanded. Turner shook his head. "Then get the hell out, man, you never saw people kissing before? Go."

Turner shut his mouth with a snap and left the house. Luis reached down to take my right hand in his left. His forehead leaned to press against mine.

"Hey," he said. "Later, okay? We need to talk about this."

"Yes," I said. "Later."

If there was a later.

I reached for the scroll, sealed in its protective coating of enamel that felt as warm as bone, and slipped it back within my jacket as we left.

The FBI sedan was no more pleasant this time than it had been before, but it was mercifully brief, and I was too tired, too distant to take any notice of, or make any objection to, the various stenches and discomforts. My muscles had begun to ache and throb, complaining of the long day and constant fear. I needed rest, I realized. Sleep. Food. The basics to continue human life.

But first, I needed to see this through. That wasn't logical, but it was necessary.

"Why did she come after you?" Luis asked. "She's doing it more and more, all these little attacks. It's like she's trying to kill you, but not trying too hard."

It was an excellent question. I kept my eyes closed, adjusted my position in the seat to ease an ache in my back, and said, "Have you ever seen a bullfight, Luis?"

"A—hey, man, just because I'm Hispanic doesn't mean—"

"I'm talking about the picadors," I said. "The bull must be angered before the fight. So the picadors torment the beast, stabbing it, arousing its fury until it is willing to charge. It makes a better show."

He was silent for a moment, and I felt his gaze on me. I didn't look.

"I'm the bull," I said. "The sacrifice. She just wants a better fight."

"What about the rest of us? The Wardens?"

I shrugged. "She'll kill anyone who gets in her way," I said. "But her fight isn't really with you. It's with me. With the Djinn."

"I thought you were the bullfighter, *chica*."

I smiled slowly. "Sometimes you're the bullfighter," I said. "And sometimes, you're the bull."

I slept a little during the drive, waking as Turner slowed the car and braked it in front of a house on a

suburban street—a house like many others. Like Luis's own, in fact, if a little older. There were many cars
parked around it—police vehicles and big, industrial
vans bristling with ungainly antennae. There were also
those on foot—simple gawkers, drawn by the mystery
of what was happening, so long as it wasn't happening
to them, of course. Turner's car was waved beyond the
barricades, into a clear space in the driveway.

"Back door," he said. "Follow me. And don't look
over at the crowd. Cameras are filming everything, you'd
be breaking news."

I kept my back to the crowd as strobes flashed, camera lights woke to a bright glare, and questions began to
be shouted in our wake. We walked quickly and quietly
around the corner of the house, leaving the reporters
and onlookers behind, and followed a small brick path
through a neat, small yard to a screen door as the sudden burst of noisy interest faded out in disappointment.

Beyond it, all of the lights were on behind the house,
no doubt to discourage the curious or determined. There
was a girl's bicycle lying on its side on the porch, and a
pair of roller skates, elbow and knee pads, a pink helmet.
A baseball mitt and bat. A soccer ball. Gloria was an ac-
tive child. Turner didn't so much as glance at them, but I
supposed he'd seen it before. Been here before.

Inside, the police paused as Turner came in, turning
expectantly toward him. There were three present, two
of them in plain suits, one in uniform. I didn't recognize
any of them, but they evidently recognized me, and Luis,
with closed expressions and guarded nods.

The two people sitting on the couch, apart but somehow unmistakably together, looked . . . empty. Haunted

and hollowed out by fear and stress. The woman had a glimmer of power around her, only a ghost on the aetheric; she had once tried to be a Warden, I remembered Turner had said. She'd lost whatever power she'd once had, or at least lost the will to use it. She was a thin, middle-aged woman of African descent, with delicate, high cheekbones and skin the color of dark roasted coffee. Beautiful, but drawn and made frail by fear.

The man was taller, a bit lighter in coloring, and his eyes were a striking pale green. He looked at us mutely. Miserably. With, still, a gleam of hope in his expression.

There was an array of photographs on the coffee table in front of them, removed from frames that had been carelessly stacked beneath on the carpet. In each was the image of their child, Gloria—laughing, fearless, strong. A life, laid out in a neatly spaced row.

I remembered the terror and pain in the girl I'd touched, locked in that trunk, and felt another lingering stab of outrage and anger. *This* was Gloria—the confidence, the strength, the possibility. That other should never have been visited on her, not at this age. Not at any age.

A flare of sudden awareness illuminated the woman's dimmed eyes—she'd read something in Turner's body language, or his expression. She came to her feet, suddenly tense, and her husband rose with her more slowly, more carefully, as if he might break if he moved too fast.

"She's alive," Mrs. Jensen said. It wasn't a guess. I watched life spill into her, like water pouring from a broken dam, and she no longer looked frail. No longer tired.

I could now see where Gloria inherited her strength and vivacity. "She's alive!"

She clapped her hands and threw herself into her husband's arms. He continued to stare over her head at Agent Turner, eyes still full of hope and fear, until Turner smiled and said, "She's okay, we've got her. She's on her way to the emergency room in La Jolla. We can have you on a plane in half an hour. You'll see her very soon, I promise you."

The man shuddered and shut his eyes, burying his face in his wife's hair, and the two of them clung together and cried, sinking back down to the couch, weeping in utter relief. There was a feeling in the room as the tension shattered—it reminded me of the clean, crisp air after a storm's passage. A moment of peace.

All things changed, but the moments were what mattered. I had never understood that as a Djinn, where such things were eternal, but now I strove to recognize these moments, cling to them, live in them as fully as I could.

I was happy for these strangers. Just . . . happy.

"I want to introduce you to someone," Turner continued. "This is Luis Rocha, he's a—civilian consultant working with us. And his partner—" He hesitated.

"Leslie," I supplied. "Leslie Raine."

"Yes, of course." He looked briefly embarrassed by the lapse, though he shouldn't have been; I was impressed that he had not automatically called me Cassiel. "They were—instrumental in getting Gloria away safely from the man who took her."

Instrumental. What an odd thing to be, an instrument. But then, I supposed that he was right in labeling me so. I had been used . . . by Ashan, by the Wardens, by Turner himself. In this case, though, perhaps it had been a higher purpose at work.

Still. I did not like being used, not even by God.

Luis glanced down at my left hand, burnished and gleaming; I slid it into the pocket of my jacket before the Jensens could notice and comment on its oddity. Mrs. Jensen sniffled, wiped at her eyes, and forced a smile on her lips as she extended her hand toward me. I shook it gravely, then her husband's. Luis did as well. There was something so vulnerable in their gratitude, so overwhelming, that it was difficult for me to meet their tear-brimmed eyes. I didn't feel worthy of their respect, suddenly. I remembered suggesting that we use their child as bait, and felt suddenly filthy with the memory.

"Did you get him?" Mr. Jensen asked. "The man who took my little girl?"

The police were prepared for the question, I realized; I had not been, and I looked at Luis, who looked in turn at Turner. Turner's expression didn't change. "We're running him down," he said. "He's not going anywhere. We'll have him in custody before your plane touches down in Cali."

"You let me have him," Mr. Jensen said. "You let me have him and you won't have to worry about any of that bullshit. There won't be enough of that bastard to bury, I promise you that."

I knew how he felt. I felt the same, and I wondered, in a strangely disconnected way, if Rashid had also been moved to hatred by holding that little girl in his arms as she wept in pain. If so, Mr. Jensen wouldn't have anything left to punish.

I rather hoped that was the case. It would amuse Rashid, and save Mr. Jensen from any . . . regrets.

"Let's focus on Gloria right now," Turner said, which seemed to distract the parents from their vengeance, at least for now. "Get some things together, and get some of Gloria's as well. That will help her feel more at home in the hospital—clothes, toys, that kind of thing. They're probably going to want to keep her overnight for observation."

They both nodded, eager to have something, anything to do. I felt almost regretful as I said, "Before you go, I need to ask you a question."

The Jensens stopped, still holding on to each other, and both of their gazes fixed on me.

"Have either of you ever been to a place called the Ranch?"

I wasn't so much expecting a straightforward answer to the question as hoping to see, in the aetheric, an indication of surprise. And I got it, from the husband. A faint, but unmistakable, ripple of surprise.

"What kind of ranch?" Mrs. Jensen asked, frowning. "I've got some cousins who own a farm in Indiana—"

I oriented on Mr. Jensen, with his pale green eyes which widened as I captured his gaze. "I think you know what I mean, sir."

He didn't answer. I saw flares of panic in his aetheric presence, bright hot stars exploding and crackling in his aura. It was weirdly beautiful. I felt Luis watching the man, too. And Turner. All of us, using Oversight to lay the aetheric template over the real world and see the changes.

"Mr. Jensen," Turner said. "I need a few words with

you, please. In private. Mrs. Jensen, maybe you can get those things together for me? We need to hurry. I don't want to keep you from your daughter."

Mrs. Jensen clearly knew something was wrong, but she seized the only thing she could from the confusion—the certainty she would see her daughter. Her husband watched her go, looking lost and more than a little afraid.

Turner pointed the way to a small laundry area off to the side of the living room. It was a close fit for the four of us, and it smelled of cleaning products and soothing fragrances. A strange place to accuse someone of collaborating in his daughter's kidnapping.

"The Ranch," Turner said, as soon as he'd closed the door to prying ears. "You recognized the name."

"Maybe I was thinking of something else," Jensen said. I took my left hand out of my pocket and let it hang at my side, bronze and gleaming, clearly alien. His eyes were drawn to it, puzzled, and he cocked his head while he focused on it. "I was wrong. I don't know what you were talking about."

"Don't you?" I asked, and slowly flexed my metal fingers. There was a phantom sense of muscles moving; that was very odd. "You have been there, Mr. Jensen. You took Gloria there, did you not? For evaluation?"

He was sweating now, fine beads of moisture that glimmered on his forehead in the light of the overhead fixture. The air felt close and heavy around us. "It was a camp," he said. "A camp for the gifted and talented. But Gloria didn't like it, so we came back home. That's all there was to it."

"Not all," I corrected. "You saw things, didn't you? Things you couldn't understand or explain."

Mr. Jensen flinched and looked away, and I understood, finally. "She never told him," I said to Turner and to the silently observing Luis, leaning against the built-in sink with his arms folded. "His wife never told him she could have been a Warden. Or that their daughter might inherit those talents. He didn't know what he was seeing. What was happening at the Ranch."

Jensen's eyes blurred with tears. "Is that who took her? Those *people*? But that was last year, it was—it was just a camp, for God's sake, it was one of those kid things. It wasn't—Why? Why would they *do* that?"

Luis and Turner looked at me. All I could find to say was, simply, "Because your daughter has the potential for power. And they want it. You'll have to be on your guard, from now on. Talk with your wife. Tell her you know your daughter has Warden gifts. She has things to tell you in turn."

I was bound to harm these people, by saying these things; they had existed in a false world, but a happy one, and now I was poisoning it. With truth, yes, but nevertheless, there would be no stopping the changes.

Life is change, I thought but did not say, and slowly curled the cold metal fingers of my left hand. The hand I had lost not for their child, but for Ibby. For the child I . . . loved.

Life is change.

"We're going to need you to sit with us," Turner told Mr. Jensen. "Tell us everything, every detail, about how you received the invitation to take your daughter to this camp, where it was located, who you met, what you did. Everything. You understand?"

He nodded, tears streaming down his face now. "I did this," he said. "I put her in danger. I put my little girl in danger from these freaks. Oh my God."

"No," Luis said, speaking up for the first time. "If you didn't take her to them, they would've come into your house and gotten her anyway. It's what they do." A spasm of rage passed through him, registering in harder lines in his face and in red waves on the aetheric. "That's what they did to my niece. Ibby. And they've still got her."

Mr. Jensen wiped at his face with the sleeve of his shirt. "I'm sorry," he said. "Is she okay?"

Luis and I stared at each other for a moment, and he answered, very quietly, "I'm going to do anything I have to do to make sure she gets that way."

Turner let Mr. Jensen rejoin his wife then, leaving the three of us standing in silence in the warm, scented confines of the laundry room. There was a basket of neatly folded clothes sitting on top of the dryer. A young girl's clothes, bright colors, lovingly maintained.

"So," Turner said. "You guys got some place you need to be?"

"Yes," I said. "I believe we will go with you to California."

Turner smiled thinly, unsurprised. "Grab your gear and meet me at the airport."

I was surprised to find that Turner had requisitioned a Warden plane, unmarked save in the aetheric, where Wardens would be able to identify the hidden stylized sun symbol on the tail section. It was a small private plane, sleek and gleaming, holding only a dozen or so people in moderately comfortable surroundings. Turner saw the Jensens settled, their bags stored, before seeing to me and Luis. Not that we needed assistance; we had a small bag each, easily tucked away, and although I was hungry, I didn't feel it was time to eat. Luis asked for a beer. When I raised my eyebrows, he shrugged. "Look, I'm an Earth Warden. I'm not getting drunk. Can't happen unless I let it." He sounded a little defensive. I nodded, closed my eyes, and let my head fall comfortably against the leather pillow behind it. The flight was short and uneventful, for a change—smooth air, no turbulence, no attackers emerging to duel us out from the sky.

Refreshingly different.

I slipped into dreams, of blood and wriggling dark things that scuttled through shadows and clutched at my throat. When I woke I realized that my metallic left hand had clenched tight as a cinched knot. I felt nothing from the metal, only from that phantom, nonexistent hand that still eerily insisted it could feel pain. When I relaxed the metal hand, the pain eased. Phantom or not, it felt . . . real. Pain was, after all, in the mind; if my mind still received messages from nerves no longer there, it didn't matter how the messages arrived. Pain was pain.

Luis was just finishing his beer. He watched me flexing my hand and said, "You still feel it? Your hand?"

His guess was accurate, and startling. I nodded.

"Not all that uncommon," he said. "People who lose limbs in some kind of traumatic accident often talk about still feeling them. Sometimes for years after. Has something to do with the body's perception of itself on the aetheric, I think."

I couldn't see my own body in the aetheric, not in any kind of detail. "How do I look?" I asked him. "In Oversight?" It was a bit of an impolite question, among Wardens; it simply wasn't done to ask directly. But I needed to understand.

His eyes unfocused a bit, and he tapped the bottle against his lips a few times before upending it to capture the last few drops and setting it aside. "You mean your hand? It's still there. Your aetheric self still has it."

"What form do I take?"

Luis smiled, very slightly. "A beautiful one. You glow like a nuclear reactor. The Djinn don't show up that well, you know. You do."

"Because I'm anchored in flesh," I said. "Because I'm not a Djinn any longer."

He tilted his head forward, acknowledging the point. "Not *technically*, no. But you're more than just a Warden. Or a human. Don't kid yourself, Cass."

"Cassiel."

"Cass."

"Stop."

"Make me." His voice had gone lower, more intimate. I found myself captured by the shape of his lips on the words he spoke, not the words themselves, and shook myself from a wave of feelings that were difficult to avoid.

"Wrong place, wrong time," I reminded him. "I doubt Turner would appreciate such a display here, under these circumstances."

That sobered him immediately. "Or the Jensens," he agreed, and put the bottle aside to rest his elbows on his knees, leaning toward me. "Cass, for serious now. Is Ibby all right? I need to know. I need you to tell me exactly what happened out there."

He did, and I hated to tell him, but I sensed the ache in him. He already hurt, infected by his fear and imagination.

"She looked fine," I told him then, looking down at my hands, one bronze, one flesh. The fingers twined together almost naturally. "I saw no signs of mistreatment or hunger."

"But."

I pulled in a deep breath. "But she sounded—not herself. She spoke of her mother, but as if Angela was alive. As if she is doing what she is doing to protect her." A darker thought occurred to me. "Or . . . as if she believes Pearl is her mother." That was chillingly likely.

Luis made a sound deep in his throat, and I saw his head tip forward, hiding his face. He said nothing audible.

"I think—" I hesitated, then plunged ahead. "I do think Pearl is using Angela's image. To make Ibby believe that her mother wishes her to train, to hunt, to kill. To make her do it despite the child's natural gentleness."

Luis raised his face then, and his expression was blank, except for the darkness in his eyes. "That bitch is using a dead woman?" His voice was not his own; it was a low growl, angrier than I'd ever heard it. "Using Angie to get at her own *kid*?"

"I think so," I said. "I think Isabel wants to please

her mother, and she wants her mother back, badly. Pearl would have used that against her. It would have been ... very easy for her."

Luis snarled, and his hands clenched into bone-hard fists. Had I been facing him as an enemy, I would have found an immediate and pressing reason to surrender.

I put my right hand on his clenched fist, making the touch as gentle as I could. "No," I said. "Listen to me. If you fight her directly, Ibby will fight *for* her. She'll have to, to defend her mother. Do you understand? We must go at this another way. A better way."

He shook his head blindly, dark hair whipping, and then buried his face in his hands for a moment. When he finally sat up again and took a deep breath, he had his anger controlled. It was a banked, smoldering fire, but it was under a tight leash. "All right," he said. "You tell me, how the hell do I let that go on? How do I *not* knock that bitch's head off and take Ibby back? Because I'm not really clear on the concept right now."

"Neither am I," I confessed. "But if we face her directly, Ibby will suffer, and we won't accomplish our goal. So please, don't let Pearl use the child to goad you into fighting the battle on her own terms."

He stared at me for a second, then said, "You're talking about tactics now?"

"I'm talking about choices."

"Like the choice you made to chop your own hand off?" He sounded angry, but it wasn't really directed at me. He was simply ... angry. And unable to point it at the person responsible.

"Exactly like that," I said. "Pearl thought she had given me an either/or choice. Die from the poison coming through the link, or accept Rashid's offer. I chose instead to change the game."

Luis blinked. "You think Rashid is in on it with her."

"I think Rashid is a wild Djinn, not a tamed one. I think if he believes that he can gain an advantage, he will have few human scruples about taking the action. He wanted the list. He'll continue to try to find a way to take it, because it represents great power, and the Djinn can never resist that." I felt my lips stretch, unordered, into a smile. "As to cutting off my hand—if I had seen a fourth option, I would have taken it. Believe me."

"So we can't trust Rashid?"

I remembered what the Oracle had said to me. "There is no such thing as unlimited trust," I said. "We can trust him until we can't. Like anyone else."

Luis jerked his chin toward Turner, sitting with the Jensens. "Like him?"

"Anyone," I said. "Even you. Even me. Because if this goes to the endgame, Luis, you won't be able to trust me, either. Or I, you."

He shook his head, as if he couldn't accept that, but I knew he could. He was a pragmatic man, deep down. He knew human nature.

The rest of the trip was spent in pensive silence.

We landed in California in the early-morning hush, although it seemed the human race never stilled itself for long. Lights glimmered; cars moved along roads. Businesses still served, here and there. We grabbed our bags and followed Agent Turner off the airplane, along with the Jensens, to find two black FBI sedans waiting for us. One of the black-suited drivers checked our credentials and loaded the Jensens into the first car, and Agent Turner and the two of us into the second. The FBI car smelled—surprisingly—new, with little olfactory contamination like most other vehicles I'd been inside. I felt less claustrophobic than I usually did. I almost enjoyed the ride.

Almost.

The FBI caravan wound through the sleeping city, and I caught glimpses of the vast, dark ocean, ceaselessly renewing itself with wave upon wave of change. The drive ended at a large, well-lit building, comfortably aged, and Turner said, "Scripps Memorial. Come on, they've got Gloria in a room."

We exited the car and walked toward the hospital entrance; I heard the wail of a siren approaching—an ambulance, carrying a life in crisis to the emergency services at the rear of the building. It was a source of some amazement to me that humans, for all their capacity for—*talent* for—wreaking violence, would also build something so thoughtful as a system to care for their ill and injured, and devote such time and energy to it.

I heard tires suddenly squeal as the ambulance changed direction, and looked around to see the massive metal vehicle plunging over the curb, bouncing wildly, aimed now straight for me, Luis, and Turner as we crossed the parking lot.

I shoved Luis and Turner one direction, hard, and didn't have time to watch where they landed as the ambulance swerved and focused on me. Behind the glass, I saw the driver frantically trying to stop the truck or turn the wheel, but I could tell that it was beyond his control. Like the passenger in the back, and the other paramedic, he was utterly at the mercy of whatever force now had control of his ambulance.

I turned and ran, sprinting across the dark asphalt. Luckily there were no cars in the way, this late at night, and my body was capable—when forced—of speeds that even I found surprising. The ambulance fell behind, but then I heard the engine roar as it picked up speed, eating up ground between us. I heard the dim thunder of the ocean, and the more immediate thudding of my heart, and as I ran I reached back with power and blew out all four rubber-and-metal tires in a tremendous *bang*. The ambulance immediately thumped hard onto bare metal rims as broken rubber flailed in all directions, spun off by the momentum. It lost speed, but I could sense that the one forcing it on wouldn't give up so easily.

Neither would I.

I gained the end of the parking lot. There was a chain-link fence there, at the top of a steep slope covered by ice plants; I charged the ten feet up the hill, leaped onto the fence, and climbed toward the top.

I reached the top just as the ambulance jumped that curb, and its momentum carried it up the slope toward me. But without tires, the metal rims chewed ground, finding no purchase, and it never reached the fence before it began to slide backwards, engine screaming in frustration.

I leaped from the fence to the top of the ambulance. I landed with a hollow, booming *thump,* crouched, and looked from that vantage point out into the night. *You're close,* I whispered. *I know you are.* By making a target of myself, I was hoping to spot the attack before it arrived.

After a split second, I felt power begin to stream

through the aetheric, a red-black pulse heading in my direction, and struggled to identify the type of attack. Not Earth powers, this time.

Fire.

It came as a hot streak of light as large as a man's head, glowing white hot and trailing flames and smoke. I put my right hand down on the ambulance's metal roof and pulled up, willing the metal to flow with me, then jumped down to ground level by the rear doors. As I jumped, the roof ripped free, front to back, peeling like a giant tin of sardines, and hit the ground with a thick, heavy *boom*—arched, still connected to the ambulance at the very top, but extended out like a waterfall of cold steel.

I ducked behind and hardened it just in time for the attacking fireball to strike it squarely in the middle. Ten inches from my face, the metal began to glow a dull, muddy red, and I felt the waves of heat boring through. But I hadn't intended the metal alone to stop it; I heaved up the ground from the other side of the ambulance in a fountain of damp earth and cascaded it overhead, to thump down on the fireball, burying it beneath an organic weight that would not catch fire easily, if at all.

I heard the hiss as the fire began to fail, and the metal in front of me ceased to glow.

I stepped out of the barricade and stared out in the direction from which the attack had come.

There was a shrill, short cry, and then nothing for a long moment before Luis called, "Cass! Got her!"

Her. My heart stuttered in its rhythm, and I spurred

my body back into a run, shattering even the speed at which I'd fled before. *Ibby?*

Luis emerged from the darkness into the glow of a streetlight. There was a child in his arms.

It was not Isabel. It was another girl, dressed in the same dull paramilitary uniform, long golden braids spilling down over Luis's arm and swinging like ropes. I felt my stomach clench, and I slowed to a walk.

I saw the same weary pain in his face. "Had to knock her out," he said. "Same as the other kids. Somebody amped up her powers, big-time. It's burning her out. Goddammit, we have to stop this. How many of these kids does she have?"

"Enough to throw them away on the mere chance of killing us," I said. "You noticed the change?"

He frowned down at the sleeping face of the girl in his arms. "Cleaner," he said. "Healthier. Not dressed in rags and castoffs like the ones in Colorado."

"Uniformed," I said. "And trained. Pearl's army is becoming a reality. I doubt we are the only ones being targeted, if that's the case."

Agent Turner, out of breath, arrived at that moment and heard the last part of my statement. He immediately pulled out his phone and dialed a number, turning away to talk, then back as he finished.

"You're right," he said, folding the phone. "Warden HQ has reports of isolated attacks all over. Kids attacking adult Wardens. The Wardens are off balance, they're not sure what's going on."

"Tell them," I said. "Tell them we have a significant problem, and they should be ready."

"To fight *kids?*"

"To protect themselves," I said. "These children won't hesitate to kill. They've been trained not to flinch. If the Wardens do, they're dead." More of Pearl's games. *Sometimes you're the bull.* She'd use her Warden children as picadors, pricking us, bleeding us, driving us into a fury that she could manipulate.

But perhaps Pearl's control wasn't as perfect as she imagined. Isabel hadn't struck at me with lethal force. She'd knocked me out and retreated instead.

Incomplete training? Or free will?

I could count on neither being true for long.

The next time I faced Ibby . . . I might have to destroy her.

Her, the other children . . . the Wardens . . . the human race.

Destruction radiating out the way the poison from the list had taken my hand.

But if I took that step, that last step, it would not be Pearl making that choice. It would be me, and me alone.

I stared at the blond-haired girl in Luis's arms. She seemed so innocent. So small. Eight or nine years old, no more than that; the age of Gloria Jensen, whom we were here to see. I wondered who had lost this child, and when. And if they even knew of it yet.

Luis said, "I can keep her out. Let's get her in the hospital and make sure she's okay otherwise."

I followed him and Agent Turner to the door as security and medical personnel spilled out, pelting toward the ambulance at the far end of the parking lot. It hadn't crashed, although it had certainly been a rougher ride than necessary; there was that mercy. I hoped that not too much damage had been done to the occupants, but I'd done all I could to safeguard them.

I left it to the more creative among them to explain the missing roof, the metal barricade, and the piled wall of wet earth around the scorches and burns.

I had better things to do.

Chapter 7

GLORIA JENSEN HAD LITTLE TO TELL US, after all. She was drowsy from painkillers, neatly bandaged, with her broken arm set in a plastic brace. Her parents, unaware of the incident down in the parking lot, had already made their ecstatic welcomes, and they sat on either side of her bed, touching her as if they couldn't bear to let her go even for a moment.

Gloria's eyes widened when she saw me. I had come alone; Turner and Luis had stayed behind with our child attacker. Luis was maintaining the artificial sleep that kept the unconscious girl from further destruction, of herself if nothing else; Turner, I think, just wanted to stay out of my way. He was regarding me with more and more caution.

Gloria told me nothing of significance. She'd been taken from school. She'd tried to fight the man who was taking her. He'd broken her arm in the process of subduing her; he'd tied and gagged her, and put her in the trunk of his car.

"Then the other man came, after a really long time," she said. "I don't know how he got in there. He was just there. Then the trunk opened, just enough for me to get out, and he took me to a policeman before he left again. Then they brought mc here."

Rashid. The hushed tone of her voice confirmed that she'd sensed him as being somehow different.

"The first man," I said. "Did you know him? Recognize him? Had you seen him before?"

Gloria nodded, small braids bobbing around her face. "He was at camp, the camp last summer," she said. "His name was Mr. Holden. I didn't like it there, so my dad brought me home. But Brianna stayed."

"Brianna," I said. "She's your friend?"

"Yeah. Her parents travel a lot. She spends a lot of time with me. She liked it there." Gloria made a sleepy face of distaste. "They *seemed* nice, but I could tell they weren't. I told Dad I wanted to leave, and he got me. Bri-Bri wouldn't go."

I took a guess. "Brianna is about your age? With blond hair that she wears in braids on the sides of her head?"

Gloria could not have looked more impressed if I had suddenly waved a magic wand and produced an elephant from thin air. "Yes. That's Bri! How did you know?"

"Magic," I said, straight-faced, and she smiled in delight. "Gloria. I need you to understand something. You, and your parents as well. *You are not safe.* These people could come for you again. I think they will try. You must stay on your guard, all right? And—" Now, I looked at Gloria's mother steadily. "And you must be trained, so you understand what is ahead of you."

Gloria's mother flinched, then nodded. She patted her daughter's shoulder gently. "It's because you're special, sweetie," she said. "Like me. Like I used to be. And you need to understand what that means."

Gloria looked over at her and said, very calmly, "I know already, Mom. I saw the news and stuff. It's magic, right? Like those people who can make rain."

Gloria's mother heaved a sigh. "Yes. Like that. And yes, your powers are probably going to be weather. Like mine were." Another sharp look in my direction. "Will the Wardens protect her?"

"I doubt the Wardens can protect themselves just now," I said. "Look out for your own. That is all I can say."

I started to go, but the pleading look in Gloria Jensen's eyes stopped me, and instead, I took her small hand and said, "You are a fighter, Gloria Jensen. And you won't let this stop you. I know how afraid you were in the car; I could feel that. I know how much pain you were in. But you're strong. I believe you will make a great Warden someday."

"But not right now?"

"No," I said. "Not right now. And you shouldn't let anyone make you try."

I squeezed her fingers and poured some of Luis's healing force through her, which brightened her eyes and damped down some of her lingering pain and fear. Then I nodded to her parents, and took my leave.

Before I did, though, I thought of one more question to ask her father.

The answer, ultimately, did not surprise me.

Brianna was, according to the roll I carefully examined, a girl named Brianna Kirksey. Her location was shown as La Jolla, which was consistent with the hospital in which we stood. When Turner consulted the Warden HQ officials, he found that Brianna's parents were not merely traveling . . . they were dead. Gone in a recent Warden skirmish with something in Florida, whether supernatural in nature or not was unclear. But undoubtedly, both were gone. Their bodies had only recently been recovered.

"Do you think they're killing off the parents?" Luis asked tensely. "To keep the ones they want?" He was doubtless referring to the deaths of Manny and Angela, but I couldn't see how Pearl could have been behind that attack. It had seemed genuinely driven by human motives, not supernatural ones.

"Maybe it's just an accident," Turner said. "Poor kid. She's an orphan and doesn't even know it yet. You think she's been at the Ranch all this time?"

"I doubt it," I said. "Schools would have reported her as missing, unless they had some kind of word that she'd moved. Perhaps someone covered that by telling authorities she was being—what is the term? Homeschooled."

"If they did that, they could have had her the whole time." Turner let out a wordless growl. "Jensen had the chance to take that kid home."

"Not his fault." When the two men looked at me, I shrugged. "She wanted to stay. Mr. Jensen had no legitimate reason not to allow it. It was supposed to be a camp, after all, and she had her parents' permission at the time, I suppose."

"How many?" Luis asked. "How many kids at this camp?"

That was the question I had asked Gloria's father on

my way out of her room. "Hundreds," I said. "And the camp was here, in California. *Not* Colorado." Colorado was where the Ranch had been located when first we'd discovered it, but it had vanished without a trace before the Wardens and the Ma'at could come to finish the job. Pearl had covered her tracks.

I was no longer convinced that there was only *one* location, either. Perhaps there were dozens, scattered throughout the world. Pearl wasn't any longer a physical presence upon the Earth; she was like an Oracle. She could be anywhere. Everywhere. The spider at the center of a dark, delicate web of power.

Brianna had likely been a sort of private joke between us. *Look, I can take a child from your own hometown, corrupt her, send her after you anywhere I wish.* Pearl could have used a resource local to California, after all. She'd made a special point of bringing Brianna here and using her, knowing we would find out who she was.

I had the scroll. I had the means to track the children, but she had set traps for me, too. Each name I touched in hopes of tracing them was a potential opening through which she could attack. Not all, certainly; I thought she could only attack through the connection to the children she controlled. But I had no way of knowing which doors were safe to open, until I had already opened them and been bitten by what lay on the other side. A nice dilemma, one that must have appealed to her sense of irony. I'd outmaneuvered her in gaining the list. She had outmaneuvered me in poisoning its usefulness.

"Hundreds of kids," Turner echoed, appalled. "All Warden kids, you think?"

"Maybe not. It seems likely she would attract other

children, for protective coloring. Possibly to use as distractions for us. Even the children gifted with powers won't be of equal strengths. She'll only keep the ones she thinks are most valuable. The others—the others are expendable." I looked at Brianna, and thought of Ibby, in her miniature uniform with the poisonous darkness in her eyes. *Ibby was expendable?*

No.

"What are you thinking?" Luis asked me. He was touching Brianna's forehead lightly, monitoring her sleep, but he was also reading my expression.

"I am thinking about history," I said. "Your history, not mine. Child soldiers have been used in many eras. They're still being used today, in some parts of your world. They're easily trained, easily replaced. There is little doubt that Pearl would see their value in fighting against humans, but the Djinn . . . the Djinn do not, in general, share the same scruples. Some do, of course, particularly among the New Djinn. But others see all humans, of whatever age, as expendable. A child is no different than an adult, in terms of threat. You see?"

"No," he said.

"The children are weapons against the Wardens," I said. "Not the Djinn. But her fight is with the *Djinn.*"

Luis let out a slow breath. "You mean that she's got something else. Something worse."

"I think," I said, my eyes fixed on Brianna's sleeping, innocent face, "that we must stop this before she can finish with the Wardens and launch her true war, or my choices will become more and more limited."

"To what Ashan wanted you to do in the first place."

"Yes," I said softly. "I feel like an animal in a trap,

Luis. How many parts of myself will I have to cut away to survive?"

His gaze moved involuntarily to my hand, then wrenched away. I closed the metal fingers, and my phantom sensation told me that the metal was cold to the touch. I lifted the fist and opened it. Engraved in delicate etching on the bronze were the lines and whorls of my fingerprints, and the patterns in my palms—ghosts of what had been in flesh. I rubbed the fingertips together, and felt a phantom friction.

"Have the doctors checked her?" I asked. Luis nodded. "Then we need to wake her. Carefully. Can you block her access to power?"

"Maybe," he said. "It depends. I can try."

It was risky, having a Fire Warden in a hospital, with so many delicate and fragile lives that could be put at risk. I knew how he felt. We could counter her, but not completely. Not easily. There were protocols to block and even remove powers, but they were difficult and time-consuming, and extremely delicate. Even with the best of care, a percentage of those so treated were left crippled, mad, or dead.

Doing it to a *child* was beyond insane. I knew Luis would use the least amount of interference necessary to render her quiet, but it was a risk.

Not as much of a risk as letting her strike at will.

I nodded, and Luis removed the blocks that kept Brianna in her artificial sleep. She surfaced quickly, driven by more than a natural desire to wake, and when her eyes flew open they were hard, focused, and not at all confused.

Luis pressed his fingers to her temples on either side

and went very still, head down. Concentrating. Brianna's pupils expanded, and she panted for breath in angry frustration. Her hands convulsively opened and closed, making fists, but she didn't otherwise move.

Couldn't, I sensed.

"Brianna," I said, and sat down on the edge of her small, high bed to look deeply into her eyes. In them, I saw echoes of . . . something else. "Brianna Kirksey. My name is Cassiel. Do you know who I am?"

Without question, she knew me. The hatred in her was astonishing. It twisted her face, arched her body, almost launched her from the bed at me.

"I hate you!" Her scream came shockingly loud, echoing from the stark walls and tile as if a dozen of her were shouting the words. "I *hate you*!"

The bedclothes began to smoke, and Agent Turner stepped up to quell the fire. He likely wasn't anywhere near as strong as young Brianna had been artificially forced to be, but he was capable of counteracting the side effects of her rage. For now.

"I know you hate me," I said. "You hate me because you were told of the terrible things I've done."

"You *killed them!*" she screamed, and writhed under Luis's calming influence, thrashing almost uncontrollably. "You killed my parents! *I saw you do it!*"

Ah. *This* was how Pearl ensured the loyalty of her soldiers, at least the ones aimed at me; she showed them horror, and cast me as the leering villain. In reality, Pearl—or, more likely, one of her trusted subordinates— had killed Brianna's parents, and disguised the killer as me. It was also possible that Brianna had been shown photographs, or video, doctored to place the blame on me. Children believed things in a very literal manner. She'd have no reason to think anyone would lie.

There was absolutely no point in convincing the child—or *attempting* to convince her—that I had not done these things. I abandoned the conversation, looked at Luis and Turner, and said, "I will go." They nodded. Turner looked relieved; Luis looked determined, but then, he was focusing almost all his powers inward, on the girl.

I heard her screaming all the way down the hall, and then I heard her stop. I leaned against the wall, eyes shut, listening to her voice, her tears, her anguish. *I am not your enemy,* I thought to her, although she neither would know nor care. She had been bitterly hurt, if not physically, then emotionally. Her pain was the price of Pearl's determination to remove me from the equation.

I bared my teeth in a silent, fierce grin. *We'll see, sister,* I thought. *We'll see who is left standing in the end.*

I took the scroll from my jacket and held it in my right hand. There was a catch on the hard protective cover, which was surprisingly difficult to work with my prosthetic left fingers; I fumbled it open, took hold of the scroll, and began to scan the list of names. So many names. So many children, and all of them hopelessly at risk.

There must be *something* I could do.

I traced the first name with my metallic fingertip, and felt a distant echo. Not the same intense contact that I had before; this was more of a whisper, something just at the edge of awareness.

The metal was creating a mostly-inert barrier between me and the power of the list. I felt a surge of interest, almost of hope, and controlled it with an effort. *Not proven,* I thought. *Not until Pearl attacks, and fails to reach me.*

I sat down on a nearby bench and tried again, touching first one name, then another. I got a confusing, indistinct jumble of impressions. Normal life, I thought. Nothing I could understand easily. I glided my finger down the list, until I felt something *not* normal.

Intense, fierce emotion. It overwhelmed me for a moment, and then it clarified. Rage. Fear. Terror.

I looked down at the name beneath my finger.

Alex Carter. La Jolla, California.

It was happening here. Right here.

I took a breath and placed my real-flesh right index finger on Alex's name, and shuddered as the emotion rolled through me, flaying my nerves raw. With the fear and pain came knowledge, sure and instinctive.

I knew where he was. And he was not at all far.

I let the scroll snap shut, closed the case, and put it back in my jacket pocket. I could still hear Brianna's sleepy, still-angry voice, punctuated by Luis's, or Turner's.

No, I thought. *This is mine to do. Mine.*

As if on cue, as I headed for the exit, my cell phone rang. I flipped it open without looking at the display and said, "Rashid." No answer. "Rashid, where are you? Are you still following the man who abducted Gloria?"

A burst of static greeted me, and then the Djinn's voice said, "—help—" He was no longer proud. No longer confident. He was afraid. Or at least, he sounded that way.

"Tell me where."

He didn't, not in words. Instead, a burst of data came

across the screen, resolving into a map, with a glowing, pulsing dot.

"I'm coming," I said, and ran out into the darkness. There were a few motorcycles parked in a special area in front of the hospital, locked in place. I snapped one of the chains with a simple jerk of my fingers that ripped the link in half. Then I took the link in my hand, melted it into flowing liquid, and poured it into the ignition, where it hardened into a perfect key.

It was a Harley. That was, apparently, a very popular brand. It was even larger than the last one I'd ridden, all chrome and heavy black leather saddlebags. There was aggression in the lines of it. Anger.

I liked it immediately. It suited my mood.

I opened the throttles and sent the bike roaring from the parking lot in front of Scripps Memorial Hospital, out onto Genesee, heading for Rashid's location as it was marked on the tiny map. Rose Canyon, which was— by no coincidence, I was sure—the same location I had sensed for the Warden child in distress, Alex Carter. I pushed the motorcycle faster, faster still, until the lights around me were a blur, until I was dangerously fast even for Djinn reflexes—which I no longer possessed in full measure. But the fact remained: Rashid was trapped, and the child, Alex Carter, was in pain. In danger. And I might be in time, if I hurried.

I never made it.

I turned down a side street, focused intently on the map, on finding a less obvious way to the goal. Darkened buildings flashed by me in a smear; streetlights blurred together.

And then something hit me from behind, like a massive punch from a giant's fist, throwing me and the motorcycle forward into an uncontrolled slide, and then I felt myself airborne, felt the world spinning sickly around me, and heard the crunch of metal and glass, and saw my own face reflected starkly in a mirror. No, not a mirror, a plate-glass window in a dark building, which I slammed into at almost a hundred miles an hour, fragmenting glass with such force it turned almost to powder where my body impacted it. At the edges, though, it turned lethally sharp, and I felt it rip at me like a shark, only for a single hot instant, and then I was hitting a wall, and falling back, seeing the splash of blood where I had impacted . . .

. . . and then I was down, lying still, staring up at swaying lights.

I heard the crunch of bootheels on glass.

A Djinn looked down at me. *Rashid.* Handsome and exotic and remotely dispassionate. "You're badly wounded," he said. "What will you cut off this time to save yourself, Cassiel? Your head? That would be entertaining."

I rolled slowly to my hands and knees.

Rashid's boot thudded heavily into my back, driving me facedown into the broken glass. I might have cried out. The sight of my blood, again, was disconnecting me from the immediacy of my injury; I felt serene, on some level, and alert.

But I couldn't get up. "Rashid," I said, and turned my face to the side, looking up at him through bloodied pale hair. "You don't seem as if you need help after all." There was something eerie in my voice, as well. Light, unconcerned, almost indifferent. The Djinn in me, rising like a monster from the dark. Rashid gazed down at me, and his eyebrows slowly rose, widening his eyes.

"From you?" he asked, and yawned, showing needle-sharp teeth. "Why ever would I? No. Never."

"Someone called me," I said. "Someone pretending to be you. I was provided with a map. I came to save you."

"Amusing," he said. "But not really important. I'm not so sensitive as all that, to take offense to something not even done to me."

"You should," I said. "If you're not Pearl's creature. She's using you to lure me. Doesn't that offend you?"

The weight of his boot lifted from my back, and Rashid sank into a smooth, almost feline crouch, staring at me with inhuman intensity. "I am no one's creature."

"So I believed," I said. "Yet you just attacked me." And I was hurt, although not devastatingly so. I just didn't allow him to see it. "If you aren't hers, why?"

Rashid shrugged. "I didn't attack you, I just saw your crash. Why would I strike out at you? What does it get me?"

I rolled over on my side in a crunch of broken glass, staring up at him. He cocked an eyebrow.

"Then who was it?"

"You have a truly impressive number of enemies," he said. "I, however, am not necessarily one of them. I came to see if you were dead, that's all. I was curious."

Curious. Of course. I felt a cold, sick wave of anger, and pushed it down; anger wouldn't help me in dealing with Rashid, or any Djinn, unless I was truly in a position to fight. "I thank you for checking," I said, and couldn't keep the sarcasm from the words. "If not you—?"

"Some human." He said it as if they were all inter-changeable. From his perspective, most likely they were.

"Help me stand," I said.

"It will hurt."

"I'm well aware of that, thank you."

He leaned down, hooked a hand under my arm, and hauled me up to a standing position. I braced myself against the wall. Blood sheeted down my sides and pattered on the floor. I concentrated hard on slowing the flow from the wounds—hundreds of them, small and deadly slices that would drain me dry—while at the same time trying to clear my head.

"You're standing," Rashid said. He sounded surprised. I opened my eyes to look at him. "Well, for the moment, perhaps."

"Listen to me," I said. "This war isn't against the humans, do you understand? It's against the Djinn. It's against *you*. Fight now or fight later, when she's much stronger. Your choice."

"You're giving me a choice to fight at your side? Considering how well you're doing so far? I'm flattered." His attention strayed away from me, out to the dark, as if he was listening to something far away. "Something's coming for you. You should leave."

"Rashid," I snarled, "*fight with me, or get the hell out of my way.* The New Djinn must be ashamed to have you among them, running coward that you are."

He froze, face going immobile, eyes blazing, and then I felt a growl echo in the air around me, starting from low in his throat but building in the very bricks and concrete around us. What glass hadn't already shattered did so, with a sharp, concussive *pop*.

Then he turned and put his back to the wall beside me. "If you die," he said, "I will not be overly sorry. But I won't let you survive to tell your lies of my cowardice."

"You may assume that I won't be sorry if you fall as well," I said, and coughed. Blood sprayed the air in a fine mist, but I felt better, after. "Who is it coming for us?"

"Not who," he said. "*What.*"

With a scream of fracturing rock, the street outside erupted, pulping metal and stone in a geyser of smoke and dust, and something . . . stood up from the wreckage.

No. *Built itself* from the wreckage. Piece by piece, stone by stone. A vaguely headlike piece of boulder. Twisted metal for arms, ending in sharp prongs that sparked with random electrical current from the underground power lines. A body amassed of hot asphalt studded with trash, metal, and a single screaming face embedded in the torso, an unfortunate pedestrian caught up in the insanity, frozen in his moment of death.

Another soul on my conscience.

The thing turned its head toward us. As it lumbered for the building, it struck the twisted wreck of the Harley I had been riding, and the frame and tires re-formed and warped, then were sucked into the creature, reinforcing its armored coating.

A golem, straight out of the ancient days. It was held together by a simple, massively effective self-propelling, self-powering seed that had, in its heart, a single purpose. It would rebuild itself, over and over, so long as that core of purpose existed.

Destroy the seed, destroy the golem.

But finding the seed would be like finding a needle in a hurricane of knives.

"That's not good," Rashid said. "You understand how to stop it?"

"In theory."

"Theory is all you have," he said. "It will come for one of us and ignore the other; whichever of us it is focused on, the other must take action. And no more talk of cowardice, O disgraced one, or I will slice off your other hand and feed it to you."

It seemed to me he was quite serious on that point. "If I fall—" I said.

"Then you're dead," he said. "And I am free to leave without incurring any further insults on my courage. So I think it would be advisable for you *not* to die, if you wish to keep me fighting your enemies for you."

I bared bloody teeth at him.

Rashid, for no reason that I could understand, laughed, and then plunged away from me, meeting the oncoming monster head-on. With each step, he gained in size, expanding himself without any regard to human rules of conduct.

By the time he reached the golem, he was almost its equal.

He ducked a sweep of the creature's wicked, jagged talons, put his shoulder against its chest, and shoved, driving it backward with a deafening screech of metal on stone. The golem was still forming itself, still learning its strength and balance, which were shifting as it sucked up new wreckage, new mass from the destroyed street. As it bumped against the slender metal stalk of a streetlight, the light flared, flickered, and the entire structure folded and twisted, wrapping around the golem like a vine. For a second I believed that it was trapped, that Rashid had leashed the thing, but then the golem simply absorbed the metal, ripping the post free of its concrete bolts.

It feinted for Rashid with a deafening crash, like a building coming down, and when he retreated, it turned and came toward me at a ground-shaking run.

I was its true target, after all.

And a golem couldn't be killed.

Rashid had said it: As the target of the golem, my only job was to stay alive. It was Rashid's task to use the single-minded focus of the golem to destroy it. In theory, it should have been a comfort that, even as I ran and fought for my life, there was someone working to ensure my survival.

In practice, that someone was *Rashid,* and I had no real guarantees that he would go at his task wholeheartedly. It did not encourage me to linger.

The typical Earth-based defenses I might have put up to repel an attack would be useless against a golem; whatever I threw at it would simply be absorbed, used to power it even more. So I ran, blowing a hole in the wall at the rear of the wrecked store—a clothing store, I realized belatedly, with the ghostly still shapes of mannequins frozen awkwardly around the edges. I had done considerable damage already, but it was nothing to what the golem was about to do, and there was nothing I could do to prevent it even if I'd wished to do so.

I was dangerously weak now, and I needed healing. The energy I pulled from Luis in a trickle was enough to sustain me under normal circumstances, but these were far from normal. I needed more.

It was going to hurt him, but I had to have it. It was now a matter of survival.

I paused, leaned against a wall, and opened the connection between us, forcing it wider. Power flowed into me, pooling golden in my veins, washing out pain and weariness. Cuts healed, though only enough to stop the blood loss. Scars would have to be dealt with later. I'd escaped any broken bones, but there were some internal injuries. I did what I could, and hoarded the last precious store of energy.

I could feel Luis's pain from what I'd done. *I'm sorry,* I whispered through the link. I'd left him vulnerable, almost damaged.

He had no more to give.

I used another burst of power to blow concrete blocks and debris outward in a hole approximately the size of my body, knocking a door in the back wall, and I plunged through the cloud of choking dust, stumbled on the tumbling bricks, and came out on the other side, in a narrow back alley. The back of the building was featureless, with a scraped and dirty sign naming the business just to the left of a massive, battered metal trash container. I raced down the alley, moving as fast as I could, dodged down another side street into almost total darkness, and continued to run.

Behind me, I heard the grinding crunch of the golem chewing and absorbing its way through everything in its path. The giant metal trash container gave an almost organic shriek as it was ripped and torn, malformed and put to use to build the golem's own body. With every single moment, it was becoming bigger, stronger, heavier, and deadlier—to me, and anything that stood in its way.

There were cars passing on the street ahead, and I ran for the motion and lights, threw myself off of the curb and in front of an oncoming vehicle, a van. It shrieked and shuddered to a halt in a thin veil of white, acrid smoke from its scorched tires, and through the windshield I saw the shocked face of a well-groomed man and a much younger girl who was almost certainly not his wife.

I yanked open the driver's-side door. "Out," I told the man. He gaped at me, started to sputter, and I snapped the seat belt holding him in the car, grabbed him by the collar, and hauled him out to a sitting position on the road. He scrambled up and out of the way, running; the girl in the passenger seat stared after him, then at me, black-rimmed eyes wide.

"You owe me fifty bucks, bitch," she said. "He didn't pay me yet."

"I give you your life," I said. "Consider that a tip you don't deserve."

She bailed out as I slammed the driver's-side door, and before she was a step away I hit the gas, sending the van into a burst of acceleration. I rolled the windows down and watched the rearview mirror. I saw sparks as power lines fell, blue-white flares as transformers exploded behind me.

The golem was a black, lurching shadow against the stars, the more terrifying because it was so featureless.

I wheeled the van into a turn and accelerated again, heading north. Rashid clearly had not been successful yet at his assignment—finding and destroying the seed that powered the golem—so I needed to have some kind of alternate plan. Quickly.

A fresh breeze brought the scent of the ocean with it, and the sound of waves hitting the coast.

Water. Of course.

I wrenched the wheel again, taking the first possible turn west, toward the shoreline. I was close, which was fortunate; glances in the rearview mirror showed me that although the area behind me was hidden in darkness, inky and deep, there was movement there. Glints of metal. And a constant, grinding roar, as if a powerful engine behind me was systematically ripping apart the world.

Rashid suddenly appeared in the passenger seat of the van. I knew he wasn't bound to a physical body, but Djinn sometimes sustained hurts too deep to heal on the aetheric, and those were reflected in any physical form they took.

Rashid looked . . . beaten. There was a long slash across his bare, indigo chest, and blood splashed over his face, hands, arms . . . none of it the golem's. The golem wouldn't bleed.

He sat, limp and gasping for breath, and then leaned his sweat-matted head back against the seat and said, "I can't get to it. It's too strong."

"You're giving up," I said. "You. Rashid the mighty. Rashid the arrogant."

"Save your contempt," he said, and swiped irritably at the blood on his face, then made a disgusted expression and wiped the spilled crimson on the seat of the van. "You have mighty enemies, for one who's already fallen far. Why do they need to kill you so badly?"

"My charm."

"Ah, that *would* explain it." Rashid shuddered a little, and I saw the cut across his chest draw together into an ugly scar. He was healing, but not nearly as quickly as a Djinn should. The damage he'd sustained must have been massive, on the aetheric plane. "You must leave this place. The golem will have a limited range. If you leave—"

"It will just follow, grow larger, and destroy anything it comes against," I said. "I'm not a Djinn. I can't jump from one spot to another to break the trail. It will find me, sooner or later, and the longer it takes to catch up, the larger and stronger it will be."

Rashid closed his eyes for a moment. "Then you can't win."

"I'm not giving up."

"Then how do you plan to—" Rashid fell silent as I wrenched the wheel, tires screaming, and almost crashed the vehicle into the side of a building as I sped down another side road. It was the last of the industrial district. Beyond it was a long stretch of straight asphalt running parallel to the sea. Beyond *that* there were parking lots, metal barriers, and the rocky coast with the heaving dark ocean beyond, glinting with moonlight. "You're not serious."

"Hold on," I told Rashid, and jumped the curb with a hard bang and scraping metal to get into one of the deserted parking areas. There was a sturdy metal barrier between the parking and the walkways, where in sunny weather humans would promenade, enjoying the beautiful views.

I pushed the van's accelerator flat to the floor, picking

up speed as the engine roared. The van hit, bounced up, and its mass and momentum overcame the metal barrier at the end and threw it down. Tires grabbed and propelled us forward, over the mangled steel; I felt one of them shred and blow, but the others held firm.

Behind us, the golem lurched out of the night, huge and inconceivably only a step behind us. It was as tall as a downtown building now, a teetering mass of ripped road surface studded with absorbed wreckage, cars, and unlucky humans who'd wandered in its way. A nightmare, reaching out for the van and slamming down an appendage that was only vaguely hand-shaped.

Metal spikes the size of girders slammed into the roof of the van and drove all the way through, biting into the ground and rock beneath. The van came to a sudden, lurching stop, engine screaming, tires burning, and I realized that it was over.

We weren't going to make it.

"Out!" I screamed at Rashid, and bailed from the door next to me. I didn't wait to see if he'd obeyed; I knew I didn't have time. The golem was a heartbeat away from achieving its goal, and it wouldn't give up. Not now.

A fist made of metal and stone slammed down on the van, drove it all the way to the pavement, and destroyed any sign that it was ever a vehicle at all.

I was five feet from the rocky edge of the cliff. Waves pounded on stone below.

I ran.

The golem crouched, an ever-shifting mass of destruction, and absorbed the wreckage of the van. I didn't see Rashid as the metal, plastic and glass shattered and deformed, as the golem devoured it, but I knew I had no time to gawk. He'd live, or not. I couldn't help him in any way.

I dug deeply for every ounce of strength inside, and sprinted hard for the edge of the cliff. As my feet touched the last of the rock, I let my power explode out, driving me up in a graceful arc toward the moon, a shallow trajectory that rose, hung for a second, and then rapidly slipped down into a dive.

I broke the surface with my outstretched hands, and arrowed deep into the water. The shock of the cold was enough to drive all thoughts from my head for a few seconds, as momentum carried me deeper and pressure built around me. It was so dark beneath the waves that I felt lost, suspended in icy night, and my body began to cry out almost immediately in protest. Too much cold, too much pressure, no air. I was no Weather Warden; this was not my environment, not even a little. There was a vast feeling of *wrongness* to it, of the very primal powers interacting to my detriment.

And then there was a tremendous wave of force that blew through the heavy liquid around me, sending me tumbling, and above I saw a silvery ripple as the surface boiled into a thrash of bubbles.

Something vast and dark began to descend. Curiously, it brought light with it—the headlights of cars, still powered from their batteries, trapped within its vast, sticky body.

Golems are fearfully strong things, and virtually impossible to defeat, but they have a critical weakness.

They really can't swim.

The golem's limbs flailed the water in useless sweeps.

The vast quantity of metal and stone that created and sustained it, that made it so invincible, was nothing but an anchor in the water, and I floated, watching as it fell past me and was pulled down, down, into the depths below me. The car headlights continued to glow, lighting up its struggles as it fell.

I collected myself and began to push for the surface. The icy water was sapping my strength, and lack of oxygen would begin to confuse me soon, and force me to breathe even though there was nothing safe to draw in. The golem was inconvenienced, possibly fatally; if it couldn't get out of the water before the seed at its core was corrupted by the salt water, it would dissolve into a formless mass of junk scattered across the ocean floor for future archaeologists to puzzle over.

But we were close to the shore, and the golem *might* be able to make its way back up, following the ocean floor and climbing the rocks, before the corrosive action of the salt water reached its heart.

A white comet of force streaked through the water, blowing me aside again in an uncoordinated tangle of limbs, and I watched it descend in lazy spirals into the dark, heading for the faint glow of the golem's illumination. I had no idea what it was. I no longer even cared.

My lungs began aching and spasming, hungering for air. I couldn't linger, even if I wished to try. I kicked for the surface, driving hard into the black, but without the turbulence that had briefly turned the upper layers of the water silvery with trapped air, I could see little to guide me. At last I spotted the faint moonlight drifting through the waves, and arrowed for the surface with the last energy of desperation.

I thought I had surfaced, and opened my mouth.

The gasp I took in was equal parts air and water, and I sputtered, choked, coughed, and tried again, knowing that if I failed again, I wouldn't have the strength to stay conscious.

And that would mean death.

Warm, sweet air flooded into my lungs. I floated on the surface, coughing and breathing in uneven gasps. Around me, the water heaved, dark and cold, and there was no sign of the golem. It was gone, as if it had never existed at all. Not even the bubbles remained.

And then, from deep below me, I saw a bright white light that flared out like an explosion—but there was no force to it, only light that lingered, expanded, and faded down to a single hot pinpoint.

It coalesced to a single, bright dot.

A cometary flare, racing upward toward me.

I began swimming hard, all too aware that it was hopeless even as I began the effort; the water would have grounded out my Earth abilities, even if I had still possessed the energy to ready a defense. My speed was merely that of a tired, abused human; I had no chance against anything that might be turned against me, particularly by a Weather Warden, with dominion over the water itself.

The water turned a brilliant aqua blue around me, then a fierce white, as the speeding form came closer. It broke the surface ten feet from me, and the light flared, then faded to a dull glow, then darkness.

Rashid lay floating on the surface of the water, eyes full of moonlight. His skin looked pallid beneath its indigo luster, and there were slashes and cuts on his body that had not healed.

I swam to him, feeling the water and the cold dragging at me like hands. My legs felt rubbery and strengthless, and I was losing all feeling in my arms and hands, which struck the water clumsily, like paddles.

"The creature's dead," Rashid said, and opened his left hand. In it was a glowing metal ball. It had burned his palm in a red circle. "The seed. Must be crushed. Can't be done by a Djinn."

I took it from him, and he gasped in a rushing breath that told me more than his expression what kind of pain holding on to that seed had caused him. His wounds began to slowly knit themselves closed.

The seed felt warm in my hand, and I felt it vibrating, building up its power again. It would only be vulnerable for a precious short time.

I closed my fist around it, and squeezed.

It shattered like glass, spreading something warm and slick, like oil, over my palm. When I opened my fingers again, there was only a faint shimmer of liquid, and a single scrap of oil-soaked paper with a few faint markings.

I took hold of it with two fingers and dipped it into the water. It dissolved almost instantly into foam.

Gone.

I didn't see the destruction of the golem, but that had likely been less than dramatic; the coherence of the thing would have simply . . . stopped, scattering component pieces as gravity willed. It was possible that the central core of the thing remained, stuck and inert, with all the doomed, illuminated vehicles and dead humans trapped inside it. I shuddered a little, thinking of what it meant to have that for a grave, and dipped my whole hand in the water, scrubbing at the oily remains. My teeth were chattering.

"One thing I will say for you," Rashid said, distantly. "You are not the most *boring* human I've ever met."

"I'm not human."

"You grow closer to it every moment," he said, and with a sigh, righted himself in the water. Water cascaded from his skin and hair in silvery threads, emphasizing the flawless shape of his chest, the lines of muscles beneath. For someone so decidedly *not* human, he aped the form very well. "You won't survive long in this water. You're cold."

He was stating the blindingly obvious. I began to swim, heading for the rocky coastline where lights glowed. I was still clumsy, still aching, but I was utterly determined not to allow Rashid the satisfaction of saving me.

After a beat, Rashid followed me, matching me stroke for stroke. The effort warmed my body, cleared my mind, and by the time I crawled up on the stones, battered by waves, I felt I might survive. That conviction quickly faded, though, as my wet clothing clung tightly, leeching the warmth from my skin, and I realized that I had no vehicle. No way to continue to Rose Canyon, where the map had shown me Alex—where I might, *might* find the other children, including Ibby. Where I might prevent more attacks, more deaths. More suffering.

If only I were not so desperately tired.

Rashid climbed up onto the rocks, sinuous as a panther, and looked down at me. So very Djinn. So very beautiful, perfect, arrogant. So curious, in the cock of his head as he watched me.

Then he crouched down and put a hand on my shoulder.

Warmth sheeted over me in a flood, sinking into every tissue, coursing through my nerves and bloodstream. Waking a sleepy satiation in me, and an almost overwhelming sense of exhaustion. I wanted, badly, to lay my head down on the cold rocks and sleep.

I fought it, somehow; simply Djinn stubbornness, my last inheritance from an endless lifetime of never surrendering to weakness. I pulled away from Rashid and stumbled to my feet. My clothes were dry, thanks to his efforts.

I realized, with an appalling sense of horror, that I was going to have to genuinely *thank* him. For saving me. That was very nearly worse than losing to the golem.

Rashid smiled, and whether he meant to or not, he robbed me of the necessity by saying, "The next time you call me a coward, I'll rip your spine out and beat you with it. Just so we are clear on the matter."

I glowered at him. "Go away."

"And you don't need my help."

"No."

"Liar." His eyes were luminous and gleeful. "Where's your human pet? The Warden?"

"Where he's needed. Why do you care?"

"I deeply do not. I was merely curious. You seem ... attached to him." The distaste in his voice made me bristle, again. "It seemed strange to see you here, alone."

"I am not *attached*," I snapped. "I am . . ." I smiled, sharp edged. "Merely curious."

That wiped the smugness from his face, and Rashid stepped away from me. His expression smoothed out into a blank mask, but his eyes continued to burn. "I have not seen a golem walk the Earth in a few thousand years," he said. "Interesting that your enemies have such . . . long memories, don't you think?"

Memories, and powers, I thought, but didn't say. Creation of a golem was nothing that a mere child could come up with, certainly not alone; the Warden children sent against me so far had been powerful, but it was unfocused brute force, not precision. Not the kind of delicate and focused control necessary to create something like a golem. That was a manifestation of Earth powers, but so very specific, so very exacting in its nature that few had ever been able to learn the trick of it. A mere handful of humans, throughout history.

And all of those, so far as I knew, were long dead and gone. There was no one alive today, not even Lewis Orwell, who had the ability to do this sort of thing unaided.

"It's Pearl," I said. "She knows these things. Forgotten talents, forgotten uses, collected for tens of thousands of years. The Wardens of today use powers rooted in science, in their understanding of the world around them. The Wardens of yesterday had no science; their powers had sources in legend, folklore, religion. It is a different thing altogether." The golem was a little of all three. There were others, too. Things that had not been seen on the Earth for hundreds, if not thousands, of years. Giants and monsters. Things the Wardens would be ill-equipped to battle on their own, if Pearl brought them out as weapons. "She's teaching them. These children. Guiding them."

Rashid said nothing to that, but I could see he looked troubled. Like my Djinn friend and sometime lover Gallan, he would not believe me when I warned him of danger. He would have to see it, experience it for himself.

Like Gallan, that would be a fatal error. And I could not stop him from making it.

"You've done enough," I told him, more softly, and stood up. "I will call—" My voice died as I pulled the cell phone from my pocket, flipped it open, and saw a dead screen. Water dripped from the casing in a steady stream.

I *hate* water.

Rashid sighed, reached over, and flicked the phone with a single finger. The flow of water stopped, the phone gave a smug musical chime, and the screen began to glow as it restarted itself.

"I will call Luis," I said, as if I hadn't paused at all, "and we will handle this among the Wardens. Go away, Rashid."

"Say pretty please," he purred. There was a maniacal gleam in his eyes, a Djinn emotion I recognized— *remembered*—all too well.

I simply glared back, unspeaking, until he shrugged, bared pointed teeth, and misted away, leaving me alone on the rocks.

"Hello?" Luis's voice on the phone, small and distant. "Cass? Where the fuck are you?" He sounded anxious. Almost frightened.

"I'm all right," I said, and pulled in a deep breath. The sound of his voice filled some small, dark space inside me that I hadn't realized had gone empty. *Need.* That was a human thing, need. It seemed every moment I lived, I discovered more human feelings inside me.

Curious, how like Djinn feelings they were.

"That was really not my question," Luis snapped. "*Where?*"

"At the shore," I said. "I need you here."

"And I need you *here. Dios,* woman, you don't go racing off by yourself like that, not when we have *kids* here in trouble! What were you thinking?" I recognized the tension in his voice; it had a deadly significance to me, because it was the same tense, furious tone he had used after his brother and sister-in-law had been shot. After I had elected to chase the killers, instead of working to save their lives. "We are Wardens. *We save lives first!* Why is that so damn hard for you to understand?"

"It isn't," I protested. A curl of damp wind blew my hair away from my face, and I looked up at the moon and sighed. "My presence was not a help to you with Brianna. I thought I would do something useful. Such as find Isabel."

He let out a scorching, fluid string of Spanish curses that was as evocative for its fury as its precision. I waited, holding the phone away from my ear, until I heard him pause. "Finished?" I asked him coldly. "Because I will not be talked to in this manner."

"God, sometimes you're exactly like my second-grade teacher!" He almost laughed, but there was no humor in it. "I hated that bitch."

He sounded . . . different. I frowned. "Luis," I said slowly. "*You know* not to talk to me this way."

"Why do I care what you want? You're a leech! You're only hanging around me so you can suck on me anytime you need a fix. You don't care that you just about knocked me down, pulling that much power out of me. You didn't care about Manny and Angela, you don't care about Ibby, about me—" He sounded . . . drunk. Verging on insane. He was raving, I understood that, but it still hurt. Badly. Was this what he thought of me, in the dark, secret recesses of his heart? That I was a mere parasite, pretending to be a part of his world?

It gave rise to a startling, cold question: *Was I?* I had deliberately held myself apart. Deliberately thought of myself as different, better, *more.*

Had that made me less, in the end?

I forced my brain—my very human brain, subject to all these treacherous tides of emotion and pain—to focus. Luis was not a cruel man. I had done nothing to anger him so much; yes, I'd left him, I'd done it without warning, but the reaction was all out of proportion.

I'd left him with Brianna. The little Warden girl, the one that Pearl had so thoroughly corrupted. Another eager little killer, twisted away from her true life and purpose.

Brianna. But Brianna was a Fire Warden, not an Earth Warden; she was capable of incinerating half the hospital, but what I heard in Luis's voice was a very different kind of attack.

One that had insidiously gotten inside of him.

An Earth Warden had created the seed for the golem and called it into being. Set it on my trail.

I had an enemy who had not yet revealed himself. One who was close enough to touch—and twist—Luis. One subtle enough to do it without Luis even noticing.

Turner? But Turner was a Fire Warden. *Only* a Fire Warden? No, it couldn't be Turner. I had looked at him on the aetheric. I had seen his true self. There had been no deception there. Only exhaustion.

Unless he was *very* good. Good enough to fool my admittedly human-limited senses on the aetheric.

With Pearl's help . . .

He'd reached for the case of the list, when it had fallen to the floor. That might have just been reaction.

It might have been a plan. Pearl had sent him to get the list away from me. I'd stopped him. After seeing the lengths I'd been prepared to go to, he hadn't dared make another move, not then.

Luis was still talking, but I was no longer listening. Whether this was real anger, or false, I couldn't know, but I no longer felt that I had left him in safety.

I no longer knew where I could find safety at all.

I climbed from rock to rock, jumped and landed hard on the walkway on the other side of the protective barrier, and ran for the distant headlights moving along a nearby street.

I needed a ride, and I wasn't going to be particular about how I obtained one.

Chapter 8

I CONSIDERED STEALING ANOTHER VEHICLE, but they were all occupied by drivers; I was planning how to force one to stop so that I could remove the driver—without hurting him or her—when, to my surprise, a white sedan glided quietly to a stop at the curb next to me. The tinted window rolled down.

"Hey, is your name Cassiel?"

I looked in, frowning. The driver was no one I knew. "Get in," the man said. The locks clicked open, and he leaned over the seat to shove the door open. "I said get in. Your friends sent me to pick you up."

He was a younger man, probably near Luis's age, although there was something in his eyes that seemed much older. Hard experience, perhaps. The car was clean, neat, and smelled of smoke and narcotics. The man nodded to me as I slipped into the passenger seat and buckled my safety belt, then slammed the door. The window rolled up, sealing me in with the narcotic-flavored smoke. He pulled out into traffic, heading vaguely north.

I watched his profile steadily. "Aren't you going to ask me where I need to go?" I asked him.

"Nope," he said. "Because you're going where I tell

you." He pulled out a knife as long as his forearm from a sheath underneath the driver's seat, and held it casually on his leg. "You just sit there and be quiet, all right? Don't give me no trouble."

"Who sent you?"

"You always ask this many questions when you see a knife? Shut the hell up and hand it over."

"It," I repeated.

"You know what I'm talking about."

The stranger was asking me to hand over the scroll. For a heart-stopping second I remembered the ruined cell phone, dripping water, before Rashid had deigned to repair it. Was the scroll equally damaged? I ignored the man with the knife, although he said something else, probably a threat to emphasize why I had to obey him. I reached into my jacket and pulled out the hard cylinder of the scroll. It looked seamless. No water dripped from it. I traced a finger along the edge, and the casing split, retracted, and the paper beneath was crisp and dry. I let out a relieved, slow breath.

"I *said*," the man driving said, "*hand it over.* I will cut you, bitch. Your choice."

He was jumpy. Unpredictable. His knuckles were white around the knife.

I sealed the scroll, put it back in my jacket with a feeling of cold relief, and sat back against the drug-scented upholstery as he accelerated the car, no doubt to convince me I couldn't safely dive from it.

He lifted the knife threateningly.

I grabbed his hand, twisted, and slammed the blade down into his own right leg.

"Who sent you?" I asked. "Who told you where to

find me? Who told you my name? Who knows I have the scroll? Is it Ben Turner?"

He screamed, face going stark white, and hit the brakes with his left foot, sliding the car to a noisy, jittering stop in the middle of an intersection. Overhead, the swaying traffic signal clicked from green to yellow to red. He whimpered and let go of the knife, staring at it stupidly.

I reached over and pulled it out in one fast, efficient pull. Blood immediately flooded out to soak his jeans. It was deep, but he had missed the larger arteries. Not through any planning on my part.

"You bitch," he said. "You *bitch,* you stabbed me!"

"Technically, I did not. You stabbed yourself." I stared at him without any feeling of empathy at all. Perhaps I was still more Djinn than Rashid thought. "Now, answer my questions. Who sent you?"

"Fuck you."

Luis would have been appalled, but Luis wasn't here. I responded to the man's rudeness by putting a slender bronze fingertip on his wound, and pressing down into it. He whined in the back of his throat and struck out at me, but it was weak, and I easily fended him off as I pushed my finger deeper into the gash.

"Now," I said, in exactly the same tone. "There's another inch before I hit bone. Tell me who sent you."

"Turner!" he screamed. His face had gone the color of spoiled milk. "Ben Turner, okay? I owed him!"

I sat back, wiped the blood from my metal hand onto the upholstery of his car, and considered what he had just said. "He sent you to follow me."

"Yeah." His breath was coming short now. "I was supposed to jack you and get the scroll. Wasn't supposed to be any big deal."

"And how is it now?" Facetious question. I waved it aside. "And how do you know Agent Turner?"

"He busted up a meth lab couple of months ago around here. Told me I'd have to do him a favor to stay out of prison." The man gave a dry, wicked chuckle. "Some favor."

"He didn't warn you about me?"

The man shrugged, both hands now clamped protectively over his bleeding leg. He avoided looking directly at me.

"Ah," I said, light dawning. "You didn't listen. He did warn you, but you thought you could handle me in your own way." I smiled slowly. "How has that worked out for you?"

He was beyond mouthing insults now. I considered leaving him by the side of the road, then reached across him, opened his door, unbuckled his seat belt, and said, "Come around the car to the passenger side."

He stared at me, blue eyes wide and oddly childlike under the baffled rage. "Why?"

"Because I'm going to the hospital to have a talk with Special Agent Turner," I said. "And I might as well take you with me. It seems the least I can do."

I was holding the knife. It seemed that put me in charge. He stared at me for a second, then said, "Don't take my car. I need my car. I got a job and a family and shit."

"Then I feel sorry for your employer and your relatives. Come around before you bleed so much you soak the seat." Because, of course, it would be unpleasant for me—not because I was worried about the man's health. As the thug got out and limped his way around the back of the car, I slid smoothly over into the driver's seat.

I considered driving away. I did. But I waited for him to step-drag his way around the trunk, fumble open the passenger door, and drop inside, sobbing for breath. He'd left a wide, shimmering trail of crimson on the pavement in a semicircle around the car.

"Buckle up," I said, and followed my own advice. He sent me a sweaty, disbelieving look. "It's the law."

He couldn't decide whether to laugh or cry; I could see both in the trembling set of his mouth, the shine of his eyes.

I put the knife flat on my thigh, just as he'd done. My eyes brightened just a little with Djinn fire. I know that, because I saw the reflection in his widening eyes. "Buckle. Up," I said, very precisely.

He jammed the seat belt home with trembling fingers.

I nodded in satisfaction, put the car in gear, and drove, breaking speed limits and ignoring all safety precautions. I sped through red lights, drove down one-way streets, and arrived back at the hospital's emergency entrance in record time, pulling to a halt barely seven minutes after entering the vehicle.

I got out, dumped the bloody knife into the nearest trash can, and walked away into the hospital. I left the driver's-side door open. "Hey!" the man inside the car yelled. "Crazy bitch! You can't just leave like this!"

A nurse on duty at the desk looked up, frowning. I gestured back toward the entrance. "There's a man in the car," I said. "He's bleeding. I think he's been stabbed. Also, I believe he is on drugs. He's not making any sense."

She didn't seem at all surprised. She merely nodded, gestured to a couple of other medical professionals sitting at a table in another room, and the three of them headed out to tend to my new acquaintance.

I didn't even know his name.

That did not really distress me.

I took the stairs up to the room where I'd left Brianna with Luis and Turner.

It was empty.

I broke into a flat run, flying past startled interns and doctors, nurses and technicians, and found my way to the room where we'd left Gloria Jensen and her family as well.

Not there.

All of them—the Jensens, Brianna, Luis, Turner— were gone as if they'd never existed at all.

I grabbed a nurse walking by Gloria's room. "The Jensen girl," I said. "Where was she taken?"

"She was released," the nurse said, frowning, and shook free of my grip. "She's fine."

I sensed something wrong with her. Deeply wrong. When I stared at her in Oversight, I saw damage in her aura, psychic wounds where someone had savagely and swiftly altered her memories. She'd be ill, later— physically first, then mentally, if she couldn't adjust to the invasion.

I couldn't help her. I didn't have time. There was still a chance that I could sense Luis, if he was close, so I spun away from her and focused on my connection to him, my memories of him.

Nothing came to me that could be felt above the spiking sense of urgency I couldn't seem to control.

I leaned against the wall, bowed my head, and tried to remember how it was that Luis, with all his Earth powers, had communicated to me silently. It was not what humans thought of as telepathy; it was an independent manipulation of the ear, re-creating sound patterns precisely, even down to intonation. Advanced work, but fairly common among Earth Wardens.

If Luis could do it . . . so could I. But I had no formal training, no idea how to direct the energy to the person I desired to speak with.

I could only try.

Luis.

Nothing. I concentrated on the aetheric essence of the man, on everything I knew and felt of him. On the connection still stretching between us—power and a growing, steel-core sense of need.

Luis.

Nothing. I felt a wave of frustration and helplessness sweeping over me, and focused even more, willing the world away.

Luis Rocha!

And from a great distance, I felt a whisper return.

Cass?

Relief, brief and sweet, before reality set in again. He sounded dazed, uncertain, and weak. Worse than I had ever heard him. *Cass, be careful, it's not what you think—*

Luis suddenly, invisibly screamed, and I felt the connection shredding apart—not an outside force detecting and destroying it, but his own pain destroying focus.

I opened my eyes, staring blindly at the wall, at the frightened face of the nurse a few feet away, who was gawking at me.

"I'm coming," I told him aloud. "Hold on. Just hold on."

And I ran.

I was spoiled for choices in the parking lot, but instead of a motorcycle I found an ambulance, parked and silent, at the back near a maintenance bay. The paper attached under the windshield noted that all repairs had been completed, but the vehicle wasn't scheduled to be returned to duty until the next day.

I might need medical facilities. And armored transport for several people. The ambulance was a perfect choice, except for the inevitable stew of horror that awaited me on the sensory level. Although it was cleaned, bleached and sanitized, nothing could completely erase the odors—psychic, possibly—of blood, sweat, vomit, and death that lurked in the rear compartment of the vehicle.

Luis had held on to our connection, somehow, but it did not provide much of a sense of direction. He kept up a steady stream of whispers, some bursting wildly into static that told me he was struggling to keep his pain at bay. Twice the connection snapped altogether, leaving me silent and desperate, but he managed to reach out again.

I knew I was his lifeline.

I just didn't know how I would be able to save him.

"I call on the Djinn to bargain," I said. "I will bargain

favors and obligations in return for assistance. I, Cassiel, swear this."

It was a formal call for help, to the Djinn. I had never used it, never in my lifetime; it was an admission of weakness among the Djinn to be forced to bargain with another of equal or greater status, of being unable to charm or trick the service from another.

No one answered.

No one.

I had not expected Ashan to come calling; my Conduit had made himself very clear when he'd cast me out from his ranks that I could not approach him again, save at a crawl, and even then only once I'd fulfilled the mission he'd given me. The other True Djinn would not dare to cross him, except Venna, but Venna had problems of her own, from what I had been told.

But the New Djinn should have been interested enough to at least *ask*.

I had screamed into the darkness, and gotten back nothing. Not even an echo.

And then I felt the weight in the van shift, and looked in the rearview mirror to see that one Djinn had, after all, answered my call.

"Interesting," Rashid's voice said from behind me. "I know that as a human you're required to earn your bread, but surely this seems a strange time to learn a new trade as a physician?"

I looked into the rearview mirror to see that he was sitting on the clean, empty gurney in the back, idly fiddling with medical supplies. He looked better. Still indefinably . . . not quite himself. The battle with the golem had taken something out of him, and it would take time for him to recover. I couldn't give him time.

"Why did *you* respond?" I asked him. "No one else did."

"You mentioned the magic word," he said. "Bargain."

"You're still hurt," I said. It wasn't even a question, and he didn't debate it pointlessly. "What about the other New Djinn?"

"They're not coming."

"Not even one."

"Our new replacement Conduit, Whitney, has allied with Ashan on this. No Djinn will come to your aid, Cassiel. No one." He smiled, briefly, teeth flashing. "Well. One, perhaps. If you make it worth my while."

I stared at him steadily. "Why?"

"Maybe I just like a good fight." His lips twitched, briefly. "I'm not on your side. I'm on no one's side. I simply like mayhem."

"*Rashid.*" I heard the desperation in my own voice, and I know he did as well, though he never looked up from his contemplation of a sealed package of bandage. "Deal with me."

"All right." He sat back, crossed his legs with such fluidity that he might have been a yogi, and leaned against the wall. "Bargain."

"I wish you to direct me to where Luis Rocha is being held—the man named Luis Rocha whom you met, the Warden who is my partner," I quickly clarified. I had been a Djinn once. That would have been the first maliciously exploitable hole I would have seen. "I wish you to fight by my side against whatever comes to save his life, and the lives of the other Wardens and humans we may find. Will you bargain for this?"

Rashid closed his eyes for a moment, then opened them. They blazed with opalescent, changing colors. "If I do," he said, "there's only one thing I will bargain for."

I knew what he wanted. The scroll. I couldn't allow it to leave my hands. I *couldn't.*

"Ask for something else," I said.

Rashid's teeth flashed in a mirthless grin. "I am not extremely prone to being ordered around, you know. What do you offer, then?"

These were not idle discussions, not this time. I had made a formal offer, and now we were dealing . . . and deals, to the Djinn, were extremely important. There was an art to it, of course; the Djinn delighted in finding ways around, under, and through deals to their own advantage, and the disadvantage of those they treated with. A kind of supernatural game of skill and treachery. For all my age, however—and I had been a Djinn far longer than Rashid—it was a game I was not well versed in. I had avoided humankind most of my existence.

Rashid was a veteran of such encounters. There was a very real risk that in this, at least, I was out of my depth.

"Give me a direction to follow before we go any further," I said.

"Why?"

"Because time will be short, and I want to be at least driving in the right direction!"

He accepted that with a placid nod. "Toward Rose Canyon. As you suspected."

I was already headed that way, generally. I felt a tight

knot in my chest loosen enough to allow me to take a steady breath.

"What is your offer?" Rashid asked. I glanced at him again in the rearview, but there was nothing to be read in his expression. His eyes were once again closed, his body relaxed. He could have sat for a thousand years in that position, or that was the strong impression he gave.

"Future favors," I said. "When I regain my position—"

He shook his head. "A stupid bargain. You are very likely to die in flesh, Cassiel. And even if you succeed in returning as a Djinn, the change in form would release you from obligation."

He was right, by the letter of Djinn law; changing from a human to a Djinn—necessary, to regaining my position at all—would mean that I would shed any promises or obligations I vowed in mortal form as well. If I wished to keep them, I could, but it would not be required of me.

A poor bargain for him, indeed. It put him completely at my mercy.

"Then what, as a human, can I offer you that would be of any value?" I snapped. "I'm flesh and bone and blood. I'm *nothing*."

Rashid's eyes opened, and in the same instant, he disappeared from my view. Gone.

No.

I had a fatal second of horror, thinking I had succeeded in destroying the deal with my flash of temper—and then he was back, sitting in the passenger seat next to me, back twisted toward the door to face me. Still cross-legged. I considered ordering him to put on a safety belt, but truly, there was no point.

"Nothing," he repeated. "Is that what you think? That becoming mortal makes you nothing? Then what does that make me? The shadow of nothing? The ghost of nothings past?" I'd sparked a fire in his eyes, orange and red and banked with control. "No wonder the Old Djinn and New Djinn were at war. Djinn have made bargains with mortals for tens of thousands of years. If humans are nothing, what benefit did that have?"

I blinked. I'd been a little prepared for an explosion of fury, not for this precise, reasoned anger. Nor its implications.

"You still don't understand," Rashid continued. "You're *in* human form, but you are *not* human. Perhaps you're getting there; I see signs, here and there. But were you a true human, you would know that what you could offer me is precious. Risk, and chance, and the highest of stakes. A Djinn risks little. A human risks everything in dealing with us."

"You want my life?"

"No," he said, and abruptly his eyes faded to a black so deep it seemed like the heart of night. "I want to *feel* your life. My price is this: Promise to bind yourself to me as a lover. Through this, I will feel mortal things again. Mortal emotions. Mortal joys."

Rashid was *lonely*. It was that simple.

Insane, but simple.

What he was asking was startling, but not unprecedented. There had been human/Djinn lovers before; David and the Warden Joanne were the most visible of these, at the current time. And Rashid was attractive to me; as a Djinn, he could *make* himself attractive to me. Whether he was attracted to my human form, my aetheric presence, or the simple fact that I had been so very powerful, I could not say.

"You can choose any human," I said. "Any one of them would do. There are many who'd leap at the chance to be your lover, you know."

"They're not like you," he said, and that made my breath stop in my lungs. It was a simple admission, but a significant one. As if he sensed this, he turned toward me and said, "It's not human love, Cassiel. It's admiration. You burn. I'm cold. Nothing more."

It was a fair price.

And still, I found myself saying, simply, "No." Nothing else. Nothing more. Just a plain, unemotional denial.

Rashid's eyes stayed black. "I told you, I'm not asking for your love," he said. "I wouldn't even want it."

"And I can't give it. In whatever form." I swallowed hard. "Choose something else."

He was silent. There was a subtle shift in his body; it still *looked* calm and meditative, but I sensed a readiness to move, to act, a restless hunger at odds with his outer stillness. "You're certain. If it's merely a matter of your scruples, I can play the villain. Force you to compliance."

"No," I said flatly. "No bargain."

"Not even for the life of the one you do love?" Rashid knew. He understood why I had refused. Hence, the cold darkness in his eyes. Djinn do not understand rejection. They do not bear it well. "He is suffering now. Greatly. Soon, he will die, and what will your morality matter then? It's a matter of flesh, nothing more."

"If it was nothing more, why would you want it?" I shot back, and saw his face change. His eyes flickered just a little, with hot blue. "Name another price, Rashid. *Anything* else except the scroll, or being your lover."

He shrugged. "Your firstborn."

Surely he was joking. That was an ancient human folktale. Djinn did not collect children; they had no use for them. The idea that Rashid would want to make a pet out of my child—presuming I could even create life within me in that way, which seemed impossible—was ridiculous, and strangely chilling.

"My firstborn," I repeated. "You cannot be serious."

"I am," he said. "Your firstborn child. You will give him to me. Swear this."

"No."

He raised his eyebrows. "Twice you refused me. Once more, and I will go."

"Then *change what you want!*"

"No," he said. "Firstborn. Or I go."

It was a foolish bargain for us both. First, I had no interest in becoming a mother in the primal human way, although I had great fondness for little Ibby. Second, I could not imagine a circumstance under which Rashid would find it desirable to collect on his bargain for a child, no matter what he claimed.

I passed a sign that glowed green and white in the headlights, and announced that I was nearing Rose Canyon. The area seemed deserted, sleeping under the cold moonlight; trees swayed, clouds drifted, nothing else moved.

It was a huge, empty area. Without Rashid's help, I would be too late to find Luis. And too weak to save him.

The fact was that Rashid was the only Djinn still willing to treat with me at all, and by the laws of bargaining, I could only reject his bargains three times before the bargaining ended.

This was my last chance. My very last. And for whatever unfathomable reason, Rashid seemed fixed on his demand.

"Yes," I said. "My firstborn child, offered in exchange for your guidance to Luis Rocha and your aid in this fight to rescue the Wardens and humans. Are we agreed?"

"We are agreed," Rashid said, and a silvery glow slid across his skin, and pooled in his eyes for a moment before he blinked it away. "Go left."

There was a turnoff ahead. I took it, moving from a smooth paved road to one that was still paved, but less smooth—cracked, humped in places, poorly patched. It immediately reminded me of the stillness and isolation of the area of Colorado that Pearl had chosen for her fortress before—something faintly alive about this place, as if the Mother's spirit dwelt a little closer to the world here than in other spots. Maybe it was simply the lack of human presence, the wildness of it.

We drove on, the big ambulance bouncing and creaking as I steered it through narrow, winding turns and across a bridge over an unseen creek. There was little to be seen in detail; the moonlight gave vague outlines of shapes, but the subtlety of that was overridden by the glare of the headlights as we drove. I considered switching them off, and as I reached down for them, they went off without my physical assistance.

Rashid. He was facing forward now, staring intently through the front glass and frowning. I slowed as my eyes fought to adjust to the sudden darkness. He glanced aside at me. "Change places," he said. "I will drive."

I nodded and shifted over; he brushed against me on the way, and his skin felt summer-hot, and less like skin than burnished metal; with a shock, I realized that he felt like my replacement bronze left hand. It felt as if the merest touch of him would leave a burn, and my flesh tingled in passing.

Rashid's lonely need was a physical thing, radiating from him into me.

I tried not to allow that to show.

Rashid pressed the accelerator, and the ambulance leapt forward, tires biting hard and engine growling against the weight it was dragging. He drove too fast for a human, especially in the dark, but Djinn reflexes were supernatural. I was safe enough, so long as he had nothing to gain from causing an accident.

We didn't speak. I focused on Luis again, but though I could hear him breathing in odd, uneven jerks, he didn't try to communicate with me. Not even to scream. Fear tightened in white-hot bands around my stomach and my throat, and I could only wait.

Wait as Rashid reached the end of the paved road, twisted the wheel, and suddenly crashed the ambulance into a boiling green mass of foliage on the right.

It concealed a road. Gravel at first, then raw dirt— neatly maintained, almost flat. The sides were precisely drawn, and there was no grass growing over the lines.

It was a great deal too precise, for nature, and that spoke of Earth Wardens maintaining the landscape. It seemed a foolish waste of power, until I considered that as a training exercise, it would have been useful in itself—teaching acolytes the control and uses of their power. A Warden who could neatly control grass, trees and bushes from encroaching on the road could also do the opposite—block or destroy a road quickly with the same tools.

It meant that we would have a difficult time getting out once they'd been alerted to our presence.

But I already knew that.

The road wound down a steep hill, twisting like a snake through treacherous switchbacks. Rashid flew down it at an insane speed, teeth bared, eyes flaring bright with pure, risk-taking joy.

He lost his smile for a bare instant, and said, "Hold." It was all he had time to say before I saw the ground ahead of us crumble and disappear into a sudden, dramatic sinkhole less than five feet from the hood of the ambulance. The hole was at least twenty feet across, and there was no chance of stopping. Still less chance of a clumsy, non-aerodynamic vehicle like an ambulance somehow jumping the chasm.

But Rashid did both. He stopped the van so abruptly that the momentum pitched the back of the vehicle up in an arc, straight up, flipping the ambulance in a sickening full, whipping revolution *twice*. I clung to the dashboard and the handle above the door, struggling not to lose my grip as gravity's pull tugged one way, then another . . . and then I saw the road coming up at us from below on the last revolution.

We were somehow right side up. The front tires hit first, and Rashid pressed the gas.

The back wheels slipped into the chasm, but the momentum and the front wheels' grip dragged them up with a bump, and then we were flying again, moving so fast that the world passed in a twisting blur.

"Five seconds," he told me. "Be ready." Rashid sounded utterly focused and calm.

I was still openmouthed and amazed that we had survived that impossible maneuver.

You made a good barguin, some part of myself said. It was probably right. My mission would have ended there in that sinkhole if I hadn't swallowed my pride to accept Rashid's help.

I had no idea what we would be coming into in the promised seconds, but the seconds counted down to zero.

Rashid hit the brakes with a violence that threw me forward, then back, and before I could open my passenger door he was out and pulling it open to drag me out. As he did, the ambulance *disappeared*. No, it was still there, but he had successfully hidden it, shifted it between times and realities. It was a rare Djinn skill, one I had never mastered; I hadn't known Rashid was capable of such things.

It was good that he was. In another second, as he pulled me at a run away from the spot where the ambulance had been, a white-hot comet of fire hurtled out of the darkness, growing in size as it went, and detonated on the empty grass where the ambulance had been. It would have been utterly wrecked, and us with it. As it was, I felt the pressure wave and heat on my back, and smelled a faint scorch as the ends of my hair blackened. I stumbled against Rashid, who held me upright and pulled me onward, in a crashing run through underbrush, whipped by branches and slashed by thorns, pursued by something that I sensed coursing darkly through the trees like a bounding black pack of dogs. Our pursuers were silent. I tried to turn to face them, but Rashid wouldn't allow it. Wouldn't let me so much as slow to look.

"Let go!" I hissed at him. He sent me a burning look out of lambent eyes and ignored me. When I stumbled and almost fell, my feet twisted in tangled roots, he hissed, grabbed me, and threw me over one shoulder with his hand gripping the backs of my thighs. It was a ridiculous, helpless posture, but I dared not struggle. He was moving too fast, and with too much purpose. I tried lifting my head to see what was behind us, but between the veil of my blowing hair and the darkness, I could make out nothing.

And then, quite suddenly, Rashid's body tensed, exactly as a human's would have for a great effort, and I felt a tremendous force flow from him to hammer against the ground as he leapt. We rose into the air in a parabolic arc, and below . . . below . . .

Below was a chasm, a deep one, full of sharp rocks and killing drops. Too wide for a human to attempt to jump, no matter how foolhardy. Had I been running on my own, I would have stopped.

Looking down, I saw our pursuers burst out of the scrub into the small clearance between the brush and the cliff. Black as the shadows, vaguely dog-shaped, but with the physiques of bears and the speed of panthers. Nothing natural. Chimeras, forced together by the twisted but powerful skills of an Earth Warden of exceptional talent and madness. Two of them, moving faster than the others, toppled over the edge of the cliff and fell in a shower of stones and dirt to the rocks below—a drama that I watched as the arc of our jump began to decline again, and the far side rushed up at us with frightening speed.

Rashid landed, legs tensed, and barely paused before breaking into a run, again.

He only got a few steps before he stopped and bent to lower me back to the ground. I backed a step away from him, caught between a furious snarl and gratitude, and realized why he'd put me down.

"Well?" He cocked an eyebrow at me. "I'm yours to command, mortal. Temporarily."

From all around us came the metallic clinks of weapons being made ready.

Chapter 9

LIGHTS BLAZED ON, brilliant as morning, illuminating us from two sides, and I saw human shapes stepping out of the trees—dressed in dark trousers, with bulky black vests and dark blue all-weather jackets. Most were armed with assault rifles. Those who weren't were armed with handguns.

All weapons were pointed at the two of us. This didn't pose much of a challenge for Rashid, but for me . . .

Agent Ben Turner stepped out of the shadows. His gun was in his holster. He looked exhausted, hollow-eyed, and *angry.* "You," he said. "Down on the ground, hands behind your heads. Both of you. Do it now!" He speared Rashid with a glare. "I know you probably aren't worried about us, but if you don't comply, she gets shot. Understand?"

Rashid nodded, and without a flicker of his oddly amused smile, lowered himself with Djinn grace to his knees and laced his fingers behind his head.

Then he looked up at me, eyebrows raised.

"Unless you'd prefer to try martyrdom," he said. "Entirely your choice, of course."

I dropped to my knees, turning my glare instead to Agent Turner.

Who had tried to kill me.

I slowly laced my fingers together behind my head—one set flesh, one set metal—and watched as he nodded to his FBI team of agents, who swarmed forward to shove both Rashid and me forward and snap cold steel around our wrists before hauling us both to our feet again.

There was something odd about the handcuffs, and I tested them with a frown.

As I reached for power, a sharp, painful shock went out from the cuffs. "New thing," Agent Turner told me, reading the surprise in my face with eerie accuracy. "We've been developing a few tricks the last few years. Some of us weren't convinced the Wardens were a great thing for this country, what with all the egos and the corruption and unpredictability. We developed some countermeasures. That's one. You try to use your powers, and you get shocked. The bigger the draw, the bigger the shock in reaction. So don't try it. Trust me."

"We," I repeated. "So your loyalty is not with the Wardens."

He shrugged. "Double agent," he said. "I'm spying on the FBI for the Wardens. On the Wardens for the FBI. But only one of those is for real, and that's the FBI side. As far as I'm concerned, if every Warden on Earth disappeared tomorrow, we'd be a hell of a lot better off. Speaking of that—" He reached out, flipped back the leather of my jacket, and found the scroll.

No!

I tried to fight him, but bound as I was, there was nothing I could do. I subsided, panting, as he pulled the case from my pocket. He smiled, and searched for the catch to open it.

There wasn't one. It had sealed itself into a perfect hard shell, like hardened ivory. After a moment of fruitless poking at the thing, Turner put it in an inside pocket of his own jacket. "Something for the techs," he said. "They'll figure out how to crack into it. Once we have the list, we can start to manage this effectively."

"To stop the abductions?"

"For a start," he said. "More than that, we can start managing the Wardens, instead of letting them have an unlimited supply of governmental support and cash."

His problems with the Wardens were, frankly, not my concern. Let Lewis Orwell and Joanne Baldwin deal with the political aspects of their organization; my concerns were much more basic. More personal. "You sent the man after me."

"Him? Oh, Glenn, the guy with the car? Yeah. He was only supposed to tail you, and grab the scroll if he could. I assume, since you still have it, that it didn't work out. Did you kill him?"

"Would you care if I had?"

Turner smiled thinly. "Oddly enough? Yes. I'd like to keep the funeral costs down on this operation if I can. And he was acting on my orders. That means I'm ethically responsible for him."

I shrugged, which wasn't particularly easy with my hands bound so closely behind me. "He shouldn't have tried to threaten me with a knife. Or underestimated me. And your ethics are hardly what I would consider to be spotless." I hardened my gaze and focused in on his face. "Where is Luis?"

"Not here," Turner said. "So don't go nuclear on me.

It wasn't my idea to take him anyway." I didn't blink. "He's safe."

"No," I said. "He's not." I had not heard from him since Rashid and I had been taken prisoner, and although the connection remained, like a hiss of static between us, I thought Luis was unconscious. "He was being hurt."

Turner frowned and said, "No, that's impossible. I know—" He stopped himself, but it was too late; he'd already admitted to me that he knew far too much. I felt a primal growl building in the back of my throat, and I knew that my eyes were growing brighter, creating their own light stronger even than the brilliant halogen spotlights being directed on me. "He's safe. That's all you need to know. The Wardens aren't in charge of this anymore. This is a government matter, and we're taking control."

I barked out a laugh of pure disbelief. "Really."

A hand fell on Turner's shoulder, and another man stepped up, eclipsing him immediately. Not for size; Turner was broader, taller, more physically imposing. This man, however—he was unquestionably in charge. He was small in stature, expensively dressed under his government-issue bulletproof vest and Windbreaker. It was hard to tell his age; anywhere between thirty and fifty, I guessed, but there was no trace of gray in the dark, neatly trimmed hair. Expressive dark eyes that somehow conveyed his regret and command without a word being said. He wore a wedding ring, a pale gold band on his left hand, and a silver ring with a red stone on his right. Like all the agents, he had a communications device curling around his ear.

Unlike most, he had no gun in evidence.

"Ms. Raine," he said. "Or should I call you Cassiel?"

I stared at him without blinking, and didn't answer.

"My name is Adrian Sanders. I'm the special agent in charge of this operation, in cooperation with Homeland Security, the ATF, and several other government agencies. So I've got a lot on my plate right now, not the least of which is that I have to worry about *magic* instead of just good old-fashioned people wanting to blow things up." He sounded faintly disgusted with the idea. "Luis Rocha is in custody at an undisclosed location. He tried to interfere when we took some people in for questioning."

"Children," I said. "You took *children* in for questioning."

Agent Sanders cocked an eyebrow. "Ms. Raine, the way I understand it, our whole problem here is children. So absolutely, I need to question anyone who can help us get to the bottom of things. Including people below voting age."

He seemed so reasonable, but there had been nothing at all reasonable about the pain Luis had been feeling. "I will see Luis Rocha," I said. "Now."

"No," Sanders said in reply, flatly. "You won't. Now sit your ass down on the ground, legs crossed, and don't get up until we tell you. I've got bigger problems than you."

I really doubted that.

Sanders turned away, pulling Turner with him; the two men conferred, backs to me, and Turner set off at a run through the trees with an escort of three others.

"Are you still standing up?" Sanders asked, without

looking over his shoulder at me. "Because one way or another, you're going to be on the ground in about ten seconds."

Impossible to manage all the impulses to violence that erupted inside me; he was angering both my human *and* my Djinn instincts, to deadly effect. I wanted nothing so much as to rip my hands free of these confining restraints and pour power through the man until he was a smoking hole in the ground. The rage was, in fact, frightening in its intensity, all the more so because it was entirely impotent at the moment.

"I'd do as he says," Rashid murmured, and when I looked over, the Djinn was seated calmly on the ground, legs crossed, looking as if he'd chosen the posture for meditation instead of by intimidation. "They'll kill you. They have orders to shoot until you're no longer moving."

The agents around me were aiming their guns, and Rashid was correct; none of them looked in the least like they would hesitate to fire if they felt it necessary.

I sat down next to Rashid, concentrating on regulating my breathing and the impulse to try to use my powers. The handcuffs were delivering stronger and stronger jolts, sensing the energy rising inside me, and my hands and forearms felt burned and tender from the repeated stabs of pain. I stayed perfectly still, eyes closed. Beside me Rashid was as immobile as the mountains.

Waiting.

Luis.

Nothing came back to me, save that wordless static. He was still alive, but incapable of conscious thought.

Drugs, most likely. Or they'd hurt him so badly that his body had, in self-defense, taken away his awareness of the damage. Either way, it was not good news.

Turner had betrayed us, and now there were much greater concerns. Not just Pearl; the *government*. I had no doubts that Agent Sanders thought he was in control of the situation, and the day; he had no idea just how out of his depth he—and all his merely human colleagues—really were.

"This isn't useful," Rashid observed, after at least fifteen minutes of total silence. I pulled myself back from the contemplation of my own, maddening lack of control. "I agreed to help you fight, not help you surrender."

I bit back my first response, which came with another jolt of pain from the controlling handcuffs. "Can you leave?"

"If I wish." He let a beat go by. "It wouldn't negate our agreement. We made a bargain. The fact that it didn't turn out well for you—"

"Is beside the point, *I know*. I wasn't born *human*." I tried to moderate the snarl in my voice. "Could you take me with you?"

"Of course," Rashid said placidly. "The question would be whether or not you'd survive. The odds are not good on that point. I'm not one of those Djinn who can safely convey humans through the aetheric and bring them out alive, and no matter how fast I am, they do have countermeasures."

"Such as?"

"Ma'at," he said. "One or two, not powerful enough to be Wardens, but powerful enough to interfere with you, slow you down. That would be enough to allow bullets to reach you. I believe if I try to take you with me, you'll be dead."

I considered that. My shoulders ached from the restraints, and I was thirsty. Exhausted. I needed sleep. But more than anything else, I needed to know that Luis was all right.

"I know we can't alter the agreement," I said, very carefully. "So I am not attempting to do so. I only say that should you wish to leave this place, no one will be able to stop you. And should you take the scroll from our friend Mr. Turner, I don't suppose anyone can stop you from doing that, either."

"Or destroying him like a small bug," Rashid noted.

"Or that, of course."

He didn't move. I had supposed that a mere mention of the fact that he might lay his hands on the scroll would cause him to flicker out of existence and into Mr. Turner's very nightmares, but instead Rashid sat, patient and silent.

I asked, "Are you waiting for something?"

"No," he said. "But there's no great hurry. I can take the scroll from him anytime I please. He is not the rightful owner. Therefore, it's fair game to take it, so long as I return it to you."

Was it? I didn't know that; I supposed it made sense, by Djinn logic. I was specifically given the list—officially granted it by an Oracle. That meant it was my possession, exclusively, until such time as I voluntarily gave it up. Humans didn't have those types of rules of ownership, which reflected the transfer of power on the aetheric; hence, Turner hadn't thought twice about taking it from me.

But, I realized, the scroll itself wasn't just some mere piece of paper locked in a case. It was *living*.

It was capable of reacting, as it had when it sealed its case shut.

I smiled slowly. "And if you take it into your hands without me granting it to you, it won't open for you, will it?" I asked him. "That's why you wanted to bargain for it, not simply take it from me. I have to give it."

Rashid didn't bother to deny it. "So in liberating it from your friend Mr. Turner, I am only its temporary custodian. Not a thief."

"Not a thief at all," I agreed. "Well then." I felt my smile fading. "While you have it, you'll be a target. Whatever you do, you must not let it be taken by Pearl or those she commands."

"And now you're putting conditions on me," Rashid said, and shook his head. "Cassiel. I'll do as I please, when I please, and you will have to trust that these things will also please you." He looked up at me, and his eyes were bright and direct, entirely inhuman. "Time to go."

He'd sensed something, but I didn't know what. I nodded. That was all the goodbye we said, or needed; Rashid simply melted away, a whisper on the wind, and his empty handcuffs thumped to the ground where he'd been.

That got a reaction from the agents watching us— quick steps in to tighten the cordon, and one small red-haired woman with a pretty, no-nonsense face snapped, "Where is he?"

For all that they'd been briefed on the nature of the Wardens, the nature of the Djinn, the primal terror of a human confronted with the unknown was still there, showing in the tense lines of her body and the flash of disbelief in her blue eyes. She repeated her question, more loudly, pointing her weapon straight at me in unmistakable threat.

I ignored her as I tried to locate what had triggered Rashid's sudden decision to depart. Nothing obvious; the government agents had control of this side of the chasm, separated from Pearl's area by a harsh divide that would be difficult to cross without attracting notice. Likewise, Pearl *could* send her child-soldiers here, but even Pearl had her limits. I didn't imagine she would stage an all-out assault against an armed camp of the FBI. Her followers weren't Djinn; they couldn't travel the aetheric at will. So their approaches would be human in nature—extra-human, possibly, but not Djinn.

I sensed no power stirring in the aetheric toward us. When I directed my attention toward Pearl's camp across the divide I got a sense of shielded, harnessed, focus energy, like the potential of a bomb, tightly contained. Was Pearl there? I wasn't sure she was. I wasn't sure she was *anywhere,* in a purely physical sense. Her followers, yes, but Pearl could manifest herself in ways I didn't fully understand, and that meant she couldn't be tied down to a single focus.

Not yet.

I was still searching for a sign as to what had driven Rashid on his way when Agent Sanders, looking harassed and angry, strode back into the clearing. He looked at the spot where Rashid had been sitting, glared at the agents, then at me. I shrugged.

"Djinn," I said. "He can leave when he wishes. There's really not much you—or I—can do about it."

"Your friend really doesn't value *your* life too highly, does he?" Sanders said.

"He isn't my friend," I said. "We had an agreement, not a relationship, and my life is my own to worry about."

"Yeah, you got that right. Come on. Up and at 'em."

I had been sitting cross-legged for a while, and since my hands were still cuffed behind me, it was difficult to rise. Sanders assisted me with a hand on my arm, and kept the hand there as he directed me away from the clearing, past the watching agents, and down a game trail that cut through the brush.

We emerged into an open area where tents had been erected—camouflage canvas, sturdy government issue that had probably been used for everything from disaster relief to combat. They were large structures. One held cots and a meal area; the other, where Sanders directed me, had long folding tables covered with paper, maps, computers, and equipment whose purpose I couldn't guess. Communications, perhaps. There were at least ten other people in the tent as we arrived.

Agent Turner was not among them.

There were also folding chairs, and Sanders sat me down in one for a moment to look down into my eyes. "Must be uncomfortable," he said. "Hands behind you like that. Tell you what, I'll cuff you in front, but I need your promise not to try anything stupid. I'm not your enemy. Your enemy's out there, other side of that gully."

I didn't like making any kind of deal with Sanders, but he was right; my shoulders were aching, my arms trembling from the strain of trying to relieve the constant pressure. Sitting was awkward, at best.

I nodded.

"I'm going to loosen one cuff," he said, "and you move both arms in front. No other stunts. You try anything woo-woo and my friend Agent Klein there will put a bullet right in you, are we clear?"

Agent Klein certainly was. He was a young man with curly brown hair and a semiautomatic pistol, which he held unwaveringly pointed at the center of my chest.

"I understand," I said, and looked straight at Agent Sanders. "I will cooperate." For now.

He did exactly what he said, stepping behind me to unlock one side of the manacles. I moved both hands forward, sighing a little in relief, and held them out, wrists together. Sanders reattached the cuff with a snap, and I felt a spark go through me—not enough to hurt, just enough to verify that the cuffs were still live. I lowered my hands to my lap.

"Better?" he asked. It was a rhetorical question, and that was very likely the only consideration I would get from him, so I did not respond at all. Sanders likewise didn't wait for an answer. "So here's what we know. We know that this camp over there is run by an organization of fringers. On their recruiting materials they like to call themselves the Church of the New World. They've got a Web site, bulletin boards, social networks, and a YouTube channel where they post all kinds of crazy, earnest crap about how we need to remake the world. Standard stuff, really; my team's been tracking these guys for years. But in the last twelve months, something changed with them. They were talking a good game before, but all of a sudden they've got money, they've got recruitment, they've got real physical facilities set up in at least four states that we know about. You following?"

He paused to take a drink of bottled water. When I nodded, he walked over to a laminated map of the United States, with locations circled in red marker. La Jolla, California, where we were now. An *X* mark was over a circle in Colorado, where the original version of the Ranch we'd found had been located. There were two more places circled. Both, to my eyes, looked remote, far from the nearest large city.

Sanders tapped the crossed-out circle in Colorado with the closed cap of a marker. "We were just setting up the surveillance for this place when you and your friend Luis busted the door and raised hell. Great job, by the way. Lots of dead people, missing kids, one hell of a mess left for us to try to make sense of. Thanks for that."

"I was not aware I had to clear my plans for rescuing a stolen child with you."

"Well, you do now."

"For how long?"

"How does forever work for you?"

"Better than it does for you," I assured him, and smiled, very briefly and sharply. "I don't care about your problems, Agent Sanders. I want Luis Rocha. I want to rescue the children. I leave you to deal with the rest, if you can."

Sanders dragged a chair over across the uneven ground, thumped it down in front of me, and sat with his elbows on his knees, leaning forward. He held my gaze as he said, "That's not good enough. Far as I can tell, this is a Warden mess of some kind. A Djinn mess. And we're in it now, because you people can't take care of your own shit. So read me in, Cassiel. Right now."

"*Read you in?*"

"Tell me everything I need to know."

"Simple enough. Nothing. Withdraw your people. Shut down your operation. Leave."

Sanders sighed and sat back, folding his arms across his chest. The folding metal chair creaked in complaint. He looked over at Agent Klein, who was still aiming his gun straight at me, and said, "Greg, why don't you get me and my guest a couple of cups of coffee? You drink coffee, right?" That last was directed at me. I said nothing. "Two. Thanks. This is going to take a while."

Klein looked startled, and he looked over at his boss for a moment. "Sir? You sure?"

"I'm sure. We have an understanding, right, Cassiel? You try anything with me, and I will bury you and your friend Rocha so deep that the president and the Joint Chiefs wouldn't have high enough clearance to even know you ever existed. You think Guantánamo was bad? You ain't seen nothing yet."

I blinked. "Are you trying to intimidate me?" I was honestly curious, because I had been cowed before—rarely—but it was not very likely to come from this man, with all his rules and limits. "Because for all your posturing, I don't think you are a bad man. I think you are afraid of me. You shouldn't be. As long as you don't interfere with me—"

He gave a short, hard bark of laughter. "Interfere with *you?* Lady, you've done nothing but fuck up our lives around here since you landed on Earth. Now, you tell me what I need to know about how the Wardens and the Djinn are involved in this."

"Or?"

"Or you're not going to like me very much," he said.

I didn't like him now. I didn't see how that would be much of a change.

He didn't push me. Agent Klein returned with two disposable cups filled with thick black coffee. I accepted one and held it in both hands, breathing in the fragrant steam. Agent Sanders guzzled his.

"Where is Turner?" I asked.

"Sent him out," Sanders said. "Figured that with the bad blood of him selling you out like that, you might want a piece of him. So you can consider him off the case, as far as you're concerned. All right?"

"Turner worked with you on countermeasures for Wardens," I said. "For how long?"

"How about I don't discuss classified government programs?"

"Oh, I assure you, you will discuss it. Whether you discuss it with me, with Lewis Orwell, with Joanne Baldwin, with David or Ashan or some of the others—well, that is your choice. But that will be a much more . . . energetic conversation. One Mr. Turner won't enjoy, I would think."

"Turner's our asset. We'll protect him."

I didn't like the direction this was going. Inevitably, it would end one place—with a civil war between the normal human world and the human Wardens. The Djinn would not have to take sides, but some would. Destruction and wrath would follow.

It was, as Luis would have phrased it, a cluster fuck.

Which brought my mind back to the subject I was most interested in. "I want to see Luis," I said. "Now."

Sanders and I engaged in another staring contest. He finally broke it and looked at Agent Klein, who was standing at rest, with his hand not very far at all from his gun. "Get him," he said.

"Sir—"

"Just get him."

We waited in silence while Klein was gone. I sipped my coffee. Klein had disappeared around the edge of the tent, and I'd heard a vehicle start and pull away. They weren't keeping him here, at their forward base; there was a secondary encampment, one where they would probably take me, eventually. There was no virtue in acting too soon. And the coffee wasn't bad.

Agent Sanders had sense enough to know I wouldn't speak again until my request had been fulfilled, so he stood up, drank his coffee, and conferred with other agents in the room. When he was done with that, he came and stood over me.

"You made it inside," he said. "Actually inside the compound." He sounded impressed.

"In," I said. "But just getting in is not the problem. There are safeguards. Alarms. Guards." I thought of the bear-panthers, coursing in packs in the trees, more effective than any human force that could be deployed. "If you think to raid that compound, you'll be destroyed."

"Oh, I'm not trying to raid it," he said. "Not yet. But I'm *very* interested in exactly what you saw while you were there."

"Nothing," I said. "Manicured grounds. A gravel road.

A large curved building that glowed from within. That's all I had time to see."

He tried asking me more questions, but I had already given him as much as he was going to get from me, and eventually he recognized that fact and fell silent.

Fifteen minutes later, I heard the growl of an engine, the crunch of tires, and then the silence as the driver shut down the vehicle. Slamming doors.

I stood up. That brought a change in posture from all the agents in the room—straightening, bracing, hands moving to weapons. "Sit," Sanders snapped. I ignored him, and he pulled his sidearm, although he didn't aim it. "Sit down, Cassiel. I'm not playing."

Shadows at the opening of the tent. Agent Klein . . . and Luis Rocha.

My breath went out of me, because he was being carried on a stretcher by two other men. Unconscious. The men settled the stretcher on top of one of the folding tables and, at a nod from Sanders, withdrew to wait. Klein took up his post again only a few feet away, gun drawn.

I looked from Luis's slack, blank face to Sanders. Everything seemed to have a red tinge to it, and I was having difficulty breathing.

"He's alive," Sanders said, as if that was even a question. "Whoa, Cassiel. Take it down a notch. He's going to be okay. He put up a hell of a fight. They had to go hard on him, and then they had to put him out to treat him. He'll wake up in a couple of hours."

I saw blood on Luis's shirt. I lifted the hem of it and saw a bandage as large as my hand beneath it, on his right side. Beneath it I sensed a cut, a long and deep one, that had perforated organs and nicked a bowel. The human physicians had repaired the damage with stitches, cleaned out wounds, and left him to heal.

"Take these off me," I said, and held my cuffed hands out to Sanders without looking away from Luis.

"Can't do that."

I wanted to issue the sort of threat I would have in Djinn form: *Refuse me, and I'll destroy you, your colleagues, every trace you were ever alive.* But, in human form, that would not only be extremely difficult to accomplish, it would also get me imprisoned, or shot out of hand.

"I can heal him," I said, and put a note of pleading in my voice. It was not precisely acting. "Please. Let me help him. Otherwise it will take weeks for him to get back to full strength, and he risks infection." I left unspoken the obvious: If Luis Rocha died of his wounds, or even complications of them, then he would be held responsible. Not just by me. By his superiors. By the Wardens. Possibly even by one or two Djinn with a random interest.

Sanders obviously recognized the risk.

He fixed me with a long, steady look. I tried my best to convey a lack of threat, although that was hardly my strong suit.

He sighed. "Fine. But you do *anything* I don't like, and Agent Klein here will shoot you a whole lot. Okay?"

He wasn't waiting for my agreement. He unlocked the cuffs, both wrists, and removed them. They *looked* like regular handcuffs, which was curious; I had expected some small technological addition, but I saw nothing of interest.

Sanders stepped back and nodded toward Luis, lying

silent on the table. "Clock's running," he said. "You've got five minutes."

He had no experience with Wardens, other than Turner, that much was obvious. I shook my head and put my right hand on Luis's forehead. It felt cool and slightly clammy. The left—the metal hand—I left at my side. I was no longer sure if I could control the flow of power through it at a fine enough level to perform this kind of task.

The damage within Luis had been surprisingly light, and repaired by skilled surgeons; he was, in fact, not in any danger at all, but merely needed rest and recovery. That, at least, was easy enough to fix, by simply replacing his lost energy with some of mine, although I had precious little to spare. Had he truly been badly injured, I doubted I would have had the reserves to repair him on my own . . . but this, I could do.

And did.

Luis opened his eyes. They were blank for a moment as his brain came aware and began processing information at a pace that was astonishing even to the Djinn—memory, sensory input, aetheric input. Then his eyes focused, fixed on mine, and he did nothing for a long second.

Can you hear me? I performed the Earth Warden trick, murmuring the words directly into his ear by delicate vibrations of the membrane inside. *Don't move. Don't let them see you're awake.*

He stayed perfectly still, relaxed beneath my hands.

Good to see you, he said. *You're okay?*

I was not the one who was lying on a table with stitched wounds. *Of course,* I said. *Are you strong enough to take care of half the guns?*

Lady, I can take care of all the guns, Luis responded, and blinked. *They're FBI, right? Oh man.*

Was he reconsidering? *But you will take care of the guns.*

Sure. He sounded resigned. *Might as well earn the wanted poster while I'm at it.*

I didn't waste time asking what he meant; instead, I whispered *Now* into his ear.

He sat up in one fluid movement, and as every FBI agent in the room wondered what to do next, I whirled and advanced on Agent Sanders.

Agent Klein hadn't been bluffing. He immediately pulled the trigger on his firearm, and his aim was perfectly steady. If his weapon had been working, I would have been down with a hole through my brain.

It didn't work quite that way. Instead, the gun gave a dry click. Klein blinked and immediately tried again. Another click. The sound was joined by a brittle chatter of clicks, as every FBI agent in the room attempted to fire.

I batted away Sanders's attempt to punch me and grabbed him by the throat, slamming him backward and down on one of the folding tables, which teetered dangerously and looked ready to collapse. Then it *did* collapse, in a sudden rush, metal legs splaying out unnaturally, and the table thumped down to the ground, taking Sanders with it. I followed him down, sinking into a crouch, never releasing his throat.

I let the Djinn show on my features, shine in my eyes, and I said, "I will not be controlled by the likes of you, Special Agent Adrian Sanders." I almost purred. "There is a reason the Wardens have never bent to government control. The Wardens are beyond nations, beyond administrations, beyond the rules and boundaries of your society. They must be, to accomplish their work. They police their own, and they do not need *your* particular brand of oversight." Behind me, I heard Luis take on another agent who was rushing to the rescue—possibly Agent Klein. Earth Wardens had the ability to alter gravity. This was probably news to Agent Klein, who let out a startled yelp as the area around him suddenly took on three times the normal gravity at the Earth's surface, stopping his rush in midstride and sending him crashing heavily—*very* heavily—face-first to the ground. A position from which he could not, without great and sustained effort, rise.

Luis flicked a look at the other agents, still standing near their computers, weapons in hand. They exchanged a look. "Relax," he said. "We're not going to hurt anybody. Chill out."

I was fairly certain, from the look on Sanders's face, that he didn't altogether believe that. I couldn't really blame him. The way I felt, I couldn't guarantee him anything on the not-hurting-anyone front. Especially him.

I leaned closer, pale hair drifting around my face like smoke, and whispered, "If you *ever* try to put those handcuffs on me again, Mr. Sanders, we will have this conversation again, but it won't end so nicely." Then I let go, stood up, and offered him a hand. My left. The metal one.

Sanders stared at my face, then the hand, and for a long moment I wasn't sure he'd accept the implied apology. Then he took my bronze fingers and pulled himself to his feet against my strength.

"We need to work together," I said. Behind me, Luis stepped up alongside me. "The Wardens are few right now. The Djinn are . . . largely uninvolved. But this fight is yours, too. Human children, Warden or not, are being hurt and killed. You *must* help us." I held his dark eyes, and put all my sincerity into the moment. "You must. Think of your own children, and *help us.*"

He'd been holding on to my hand, and I saw that he held concealed, on his other side, the power-disrupting handcuffs. With one move—no doubt a move he had practiced and performed many times—he could have those on me in seconds, possibly before Luis could interfere.

He didn't move. After a moment, he let go of me and took a step back. The handcuffs were slipped back into a case at his belt, under his Windbreaker.

"Don't screw me," he said. "Because I'm willing to go on a little faith, here. But not much, and not for long. You do anything that makes me doubt you're all in on this—"

"Oh, we're all in," Luis said, and winced a little as he sagged into a chair. He looked tired, and in some pain. "Jesus, how much more 'all in' could we be? I've lost my brother, my sister-in-law, my niece is somewhere out there in the hands of these assholes. We've had half a dozen serious attempts to kill us. You've hurt me, done stuff to her—and we didn't take it out of your ass, man. So shut the hell up, okay?"

Sanders didn't look particularly offended. "Okay," he said. "You want to let Klein up now?"

Luis didn't glance at the other agent, who was still straining to lift himself off of the ground against the increased pull of gravity. "Sure." Suddenly, the agent's arms powered him up from the dirt, and he scrambled to his feet, red-faced and chagrined. He retrieved his gun from the ground, checked it, and holstered it, cheeks still burning, eyes still angry. When he saw me watching him, he recovered his composure and tried to look indifferent to the whole turn of events.

Not very successfully.

Sanders took the chair across from Luis. "Let's say, for argument's sake, that I believe you. What the hell do you want out of me? I've got an FBI team, sure. I've got all the surveillance you could want. I've got eyes in the sky and boots on the ground. You think this place is going to fall to some kind of frontal assault?"

I poured Luis a cup of coffee from the pot nearby, and took it to him. He drank part of it gratefully before answering. "Show us what you know."

"You first."

"That's easy," Luis said. "Damn near nothing. Whatever Cass already told you, that's it. I wasn't even there. She's your only eyewitness. Your turn."

"Follow me," Sanders said, and led us out of the tent. I dropped back to stay next to Luis, discreetly monitoring his fitness.

He knew what I was doing, and frowned at me. "What?"

"You're in pain."

"I'm fine. It's a side effect of rapid healing for me. Nothing wrong with me." He nodded to Agent Sanders. "So you're what, alpha dog now?"

I smiled. "Humans *do* tend to run in packs. Dominate the leader, and you dominate the others."

"Cynical."

"Useful."

Sanders didn't hear, because we were both murmuring very quietly. He led us down the hillside to yet *another* tent, this one with its entrance pulled shut. He slapped it aside and entered. As we followed, I realized that it was filled with more computers, more people, and rolling bulletin boards filled with images. Some were sharply rendered satellite images, showing the area of Rose Canyon where we were; I recognized the dark slash of the chasm first, and then the manicured park of Pearl's encampment on the opposite side. The FBI tents were visible only as smudges, but they'd been marked in red to make them more visible.

The white, rounded building that I'd seen was like a moon set into the green, carefully empty expanse. Nothing around it—unlike Colorado, which had had barracks, buildings, even an elaborate playground for the children.

This was more . . . alien.

I scanned the photos one by one, looking at each in detail, surveying the entire expanse of the surface of the billboards. It took time. Luis finished before I did, but I doubt he saw as much.

He was tired.

"So?" Sanders asked. He folded his arms. "Insights from your side of the street?"

"It's not like Colorado," I said. "Not at all. That felt as if it had been built by human hands."

"That's because it was," Sanders replied. "Built by the Church of the New World. Their training-slash-inspirational camp, preaching and war games all rolled into one. Thing is, the CNW wasn't one of those apocalypse cults, originally; it was built by a bunch of hippies who wanted to do the peace and love thing. Gradually got taken over by more and more extreme elements. But even so, we never expected them to ramp up to industrial crazy. They were—" He shrugged. "Normal. As such things go."

"Until last year," I said. He nodded. "And when did this structure appear?" I touched the white bubble shown in the pictures.

"About eight months ago," he said. Same in Colorado. Same in two other places we know of. Same damn structure. This one's the largest, though. It's about the size of a football stadium, though it's not very tall. We figure all their facilities are inside, including whatever training they're doing."

"Who comes in and out?"

"In, we get individual cars and trucks. Not too many of those. Most are registered to members of the church, a few suppliers who drop off stuff and drive away."

Luis asked, "Who comes out to get it?"

"Nobody," Sanders said. "It sits there until dark. We monitor with night vision, but we never see anybody come out to get it. It just . . . disappears."

I nodded. I understood, now. "I will need a list of those . . . suppliers."

"They all check out. And yeah, we've tried putting tracking and surveillance into the shipments. No good. Everything gets blocked as soon as it's inside that dome. Some kind of interference."

"I'll need the list," I repeated. "And a weapon. Perhaps one of those large ones your agents carried in the clearing."

"Uh-huh," Sanders said, not in any way as if he was acceding to my request. "And you'd like this because . . . ?"

"Trust me," Luis said. "I don't think it's better to know the answer to that one."

"Gotta write a report," Sanders said. "Government runs on reports. So yes. I need an answer before I say yes, no, or anything."

I shrugged. "I'm going to get into the facility," I said. "Now that I know how. And I'm going to take a gun because I might need to shoot those who get in my way of retrieving Isabel and as many of the other children as possible."

Sanders blinked. "You're going to get inside. Shoot people. Rescue the kids."

"Yes."

"That's your plan."

"It is."

He looked at Luis. "Help me out."

"I think you need a little work on it," Luis told me. "Particularly in the part where you don't have any kind of backup or information about what's inside in the first place. Cass, for all you know, this is one giant fly trap, and you're the fly. You go in there, you may never make it out. And you're the one who said she's all about the Djinn. Maybe she's just waiting for a Djinn."

"I'm not a Djinn," I reminded him. "And I would happily accept backup from you. And any other Wardens you can locate and deliver quickly. But we can't wait. They know we're here. They won't be content to wait quietly much longer."

"Before they do what?" Sanders asked. His voice had gone quiet. The other agents in the tent—and they were all listening closely, although appearing not to—suddenly looked up, fixed on the answer to his question.

"Show me where the other facilities are located."

He looked nonplussed by the question, then nodded to a nearby female agent, who tapped keys on her computer and pulled up four quadrants on the glowing screen. One was labeled ROSE CANYON, LA JOLLA, CALIFORNIA—where we currently stood. One was labeled DOGTOWN COMMONS, MASSACHUSETTS, and it looked virtually identical to what was shown in La Jolla. Another said ADAMS, TENNESSEE. The last was OHIOVILLE, PENNSYLVANIA. "Show me on a map," I said. She pulled it up and illuminated the locations for me.

I called on Oversight, bringing the aetheric filter in front of my eyes, and saw the ghostly rivers of power that some humans still called ley lines.

Every one of these spots sat on a nexus, a power center. Oracles were situated on such spots; Sedona, for the Earth Oracle; Seacasket, for the Fire Oracle. Only the Weather Oracle had no fixed location that anyone could identify.

Pearl had established herself—or some aspect of herself—on the supernatural equivalent of a power grid, at the most powerful spots not being watched over by Djinn Oracles.

And all of the locations—*all* of them—now looked identical. The precisely measured open ground, freed of vegetation. The same glowing dome. Each location was bordered by geography that made it difficult to approach.

She had built herself a network, a support system, and a web of energy.

"Ley lines," I told Luis. He nodded. "You see what she's doing?"

"Building herself a power grid? Yeah, I see it. The question is, what's inside the domes? And which one is she in, physically?"

"I'm not sure she's in any of them," I said. "Or, more accurately, I'm not sure she's not in *all* of them. I think the dome *is* Pearl. But she is able to exist simultaneously, in different locations."

Luis grunted. "Wouldn't that divide her power?"

"I don't know," I said. With the ley lines, it was possible that she could draw from one location to another, move her consciousness seamlessly between the four sites without much, if any, delay. "How many other nexus points are open?"

"In this country? Probably about ten. You think she'll go after those, too?"

The FBI agent running the computer said, "The Ohioville location, there? That only came up on our radar about two months ago. Locals swear it wasn't there before. Satellite imaging confirms it."

Pearl was spreading her influence. It was an infection, a kind of disease traveling along the invisible lines of power that crisscrossed the planet's surface, and also served as conduits directly through its core. These installations could spring up like mushrooms, without warning.

"I think," I said quietly, "that if she can get enough

power, she will spread to every nexus point in the world. Think of these as blisters, holding in infection." I tapped the screen, and the white dome. "When they break . . ."

Silence. They all looked at me. Luis looked faintly sick. "How much trouble are we in, exactly?"

Enough that I was being forced, again, to consider Ashan's orders. *Destroy them all. She is powering herself through the humans. Cut out the humans, you cut her connection to the Earth, and she can be killed, once and for all.*

Her war was against the Djinn, and yes, she would destroy them and absorb their aetheric power; but her heart, her soul, her spirit was channeled through humanity, in the same way that Djinn were connected to the Oracles.

I don't want to do this, some part of me whispered. Indeed, I did not. I dreaded it with all my soul. To destroy humanity, I would have to feel their pain, their deaths, their *lives* passing through me, being removed from the world and the living memory of the Mother. I would have to unmake Luis Rocha. Isabel. Even the fragile memorials of the dead, like Manny and Angela.

I couldn't. I couldn't bring myself to take that step, not even looking at this appalling thing in front of me, and understanding how little time was left to us.

There's still time. There must be a way to stop her.

I had to try. For the sake of those I loved, for the sake of those I didn't, like Agent Sanders and his unseen family, I had to not only try, but succeed.

"We need all the Wardens you can find," I said. "All of them. We need to attack all of these at the same time, force her to fight multiple fronts. You understand?"

I turned to Agent Sanders. "There will be humans to fight, or to rescue. Can we count on you to do what is needed?"

"You want teams at each of these locations."

"Are you saying they're not already there, feeding you information?"

He was silent, watching me, and finally gave a single nod. "All right," he said. "When?"

"Let me check on Wardens," Luis said, and slapped his pockets, looking harassed. "Cell phone?"

Agent Klein stepped up and handed it over to him. Luis flipped it open and began making calls. I left him to it, staring at the shimmering, featureless domes on the screen.

Sister, I thought. *We were sisters once.* So much alike. But she had learned to love killing, and I had learned to embrace the opposite. That was a harshly learned lesson, courtesy of Ashan, probably one he had never intended. But one I valued, nevertheless.

It occurred to me that she expected me to act against her as Ashan wished, destroying humanity to cut her off from her power. Reducing me to the same state that she had once been in.

Driving me mad, because assuredly, with so much death and agony coursing through me, I *would* destroy myself. I'd become like her.

Obsessed with the end of all things.

I wondered if Ashan had thought of that, too. Of what would happen if I turned toxic, like Pearl. Two of us, rending the world apart.

I could only imagine, old and clever as Ashan was, that he'd already seen that possibility.

That meant that should I execute his orders . . . execute humanity . . . there would be someone standing in the background, waiting to destroy me, as well.

It would be the only safe thing to do.

And suddenly, Rashid's inexplicable attachment made sense. He was not Ashan's creature, but he was Ashan's hireling. Close to me not because he was interested, or concerned, but because he was waiting.

Waiting for what he, and Ashan, knew was inevitable.

My hands—flesh, and metal—clenched into fists. "No," I murmured. "Not inevitable."

The FBI agent next to me looked up, frowning. "Excuse me?"

"Nothing is inevitable," I said. "Not even death."

I left her wondering, and turned to walk outside of the tent, breathing in the fresh, crisp air. It was mostly untainted by the massive cities around us, although I could still catch the occasional stench of exhaust and oil. I leaned against the rough bark of a tree, breathing deeply, and then crouched down to place both hands flat against the ground. I could sense *something* here, something like I had felt back on the ridge where I'd buried the child. A presence, though distant and elusive. *Her* presence.

"Help me," I whispered. "Help me understand what I should do." Then I directed it upward, outward, to the greater power beyond the vast one of this world. "Help me save them."

A cool breeze drifted across my face like a caress, and I turned into it and closed my eyes. This moment felt peaceful, almost worshipful in its intensity. As if I was alone, connected once more to the life I had once led. Connected to eternity.

Then I heard a snapping of twigs, and opened my eyes to see Agent Ben Turner shove aside underbrush and step out to face me.

The Warden was not his usual, nondescript self. He'd been in a fight, a hard one; there were bruises forming on his face, and one of his hands looked swollen into use-lessness. Broken, perhaps. He was breathing hard. His FBI-issue Windbreaker was ripped—no, shredded—and I saw blood spotting his shirt. Minor wounds, it seemed, but the look in his eyes told me that he did not consider them so.

"You did that," he said. "You set that bastard on me."

Rashid. "No one commands Rashid," I said, which was quite true, albeit misleading in this case. "You drew his attention yourself, by taking the scroll. You knew he wanted it for himself." I raised my eyebrows. "Do you still have it?"

"What do *you* think?" he snapped, and held up his swollen hand. "He broke my fingers to get it!"

That did sound like Rashid. "He didn't like you turning against us. Neither did I. Neither, I suspect, will the other Wardens."

"You think I give a crap about what the Wardens think?" Turner snapped. "I did what I had to do. You people are out of control. Look at what they just did in Florida—Jesus Christ, they stole a fucking *cruise ship*. With innocent people on board. They kidnapped people, and you know some of those people are bound to get caught in the middle. That's what I'm left with—loyalty to a bunch of assholes who think nothing of collateral damage? No. No more. The Wardens need somebody telling them where their limits are, if they can't see it themselves."

It was a long speech, and he was winded by the end of it. And emotionally exhausted from the passion he'd poured into it. I wondered what collateral damage he had seen, or experienced himself. I wondered if his own hands were entirely clean of the blood.

"I have never loved the Wardens," I said, which was entirely true. As a Djinn, they'd been the enemy to me: enslavers of my own kind. Not only no better than human ... *worse* than human. When the pact had shattered between the Djinn and the Wardens, freeing the captives from their forced servitude, no one had taken more satisfaction from that than I.

But I also knew that the Wardens were what they were for a reason. They were ruthless, self-centered and ferociously competitive, yes; they were also self-sacrificing and magnificent, when necessary. These things did not make for comfortable, easily categorizable analysis. The Wardens, like nature itself, were neither good nor bad. They simply *were*. And were required to be, for the sake of the fragile lives in their trust.

"You think the government can control them?" I asked. "You think you have enough will and power of your own to force the Wardens into it?"

"I'm not alone," he said. "There are other Wardens who think things have gone too far."

"Then take it back from within. But if you think that subjugating them to the will of political appointees is a good idea, then I suggest you are allowing your hatred to blind you to reality," I said. "It doesn't matter now. We will need your help."

"My help?" He laughed, but it had a wild, dark sound. "Why the hell would I help any of you?"

"Because you're not a bad man. Because you are sworn to help, to protect, and not to run from battle, yes, but mostly because you, *Ben Turner,* the man beneath all that, wants justice. And wishes to save children. I saw that in you when we first met, Ben. You want to save them. You *need* to save them."

He blinked, but he didn't disagree with that, at least.

"There are children in that compound," I said. "Isabel Rocha is one of them. You saw Brianna. You saw Gloria. You saw the others. You *know* we can't let them be destroyed, not without losing our own honor."

He leaned against another tree across the clearing, cradling his wounded arm in his good hand. He looked tired, and achy, and a little lost. "So what are you going to do?"

"Go get them," I said. "And you will come with me."

He held up his hand. "Yeah, about that. I don't really think I'll be a whole lot of help."

Luis stepped out of the tent, looked from me to Agent Turner, and said, "Hey. Are we going to beat the crap out of this guy?"

"I think Rashid's already performed that service," I said. "What's left is healing him so that we can use him."

"Dammit. I always miss out on the beat-down and end up doing the cleanup. Sucks being an Earth Warden sometimes."

"Sometimes," I agreed, straight-faced. "Will you do it?"

"Of course I will," Luis said grumpily. "I'm not going to waste my energy on pain maintenance."

I did not blame him. Turner, for his part, looked apprehensively relieved, if such a thing were possible. Luis glared at him, then went to him and took his wounded hand. He was true to his word; I heard the tiny snaps and pops of bones straightening, being forced back into their shapes and sockets, and Turner's face went dirty-pale, and he leaned his head back against the tree, rigid and fighting to control his impulse to scream, faint, or vomit. Or some combination of those three. But I suspected Luis did, after all, put in *some* nerve blocks. He wasn't unnecessarily cruel. Merely . . . proportional.

It took a few long moments of concentration, and then Luis let go and stepped back. Turner lowered his hand and stared at it in bemused wonder. Tried to move his fingers, and winced a little.

"Yeah, the muscles will complain for a while," Luis said. "They got beaten up too. But the bones will hold, as long as you don't do something crazy with them, like hit somebody. Best I could do on short notice."

"It's better," Turner said, with a little sense of wonder to it. "I think it'll do."

"It will have to," I said. "We're going into the compound."

Turner's head came up, and his eyes widened. "What? When?"

"As soon as the other teams are in place," I said. "Luis will be able to hide our presence from any regular humans; if they have Wardens on their side, it might be a bit more difficult, but we can manage."

Fooling Pearl would be the much greater challenge. That was why I had asked for the coordinated raids on each location; if her attention was split, if she realized she was under threat on *all* fronts, she might miss me until it was too late.

Perhaps. Or perhaps she'd simply recognize my presence, withdraw from every other front, and focus on killing me.

If killing me was her intent, of course. I wasn't altogether certain of that. If she'd wanted me dead, surely she could have sent overwhelming force to manage it by now. No, I thought she wanted this. She wanted me to come here.

I didn't think it was merely for the satisfaction of watching me die, although that might easily be a consideration. No, there was something else.

Something I was missing.

Luis was watching me. "You all right?"

"Fine," I said. "And the Wardens?"

"Got them to coordinate something out of New York, but we're screwed having any Wardens on the ground for this—it'll be remote attacks at the other locations, but they'll make it as good as they can. I've got them on standby. All you have to do is give me the go."

"We go now," I said. "I will give the signal for the attack when we are in position there. Get ready."

Agent Turner raised his eyebrows, but didn't respond otherwise; he walked into the tent. A moment later, his superior burst out, looking thunderous. "Are you out of your mind?" he demanded. "I'm not letting you take people in there now. You don't even have cover of darkness!"

"It wouldn't matter if I did," I said. "Either we'll be able to hide, or we won't. Light or darkness is irrelevant to her. But if you want to be useful, make a distraction that will draw the attention of her soldiers."

"What kind of distraction?"

"Mass our people at the chasm. Make it look like you're going to come across," Turner supplied, unexpectedly. "Start using the bullhorn. Tell them you want to talk."

I nodded. I had been frankly thinking of something more violent, but that would work and expose the men and women here to less risk overall. "One hour," I said. "It will take that long for us to get across the chasm, deal with her countermeasures, and reach the dome."

"Without being detected," Sanders said. "Right. Sure."

It was not a perfect plan. And I knew, *knew* that I was missing something vital. But my conviction was that I had no time to waste, or this would be intensely worse, very soon.

Chapter 10

KITTING OUT LUIS, TURNER, and me in FBI-issue bulletproof vests—worn beneath my leather jacket, for my part, and with the FBI identification blacked out with tape for Luis—was the work of moments. Turner was freely given one of the compact assault weapons. Luis and I were flatly denied, although Sanders did, in private, slip us sidearms.

I looked at the other two Wardens in silence for a moment, standing on the edge of the chasm, as a light breeze blew across the open space and rustled the trees above us. "This will be dangerous," I said bluntly. "Very dangerous. If you wish to stop here . . ."

Luis made a rude noise. "Shut up and dance, Cass. Ibby's over there, right? I want her back. Now."

I nodded and turned my focus to Turner, who was staring into the distance as if reviewing all the choices that had led him to this somewhat distressing moment. Turner finally shrugged. "I'm in," he said. "You were right. I may hate what the Wardens stand for these days, but these are kids. Innocent kids. And they need our help."

That settled, we began to climb down.

Luis and I had agreed to preserve power whenever

possible, so the climb was managed the normal human way—hands and feet, carefully placed. Straining muscles. An ever-present, patient threat from gravity, and a fluttering fear that never quite could be brushed aside. Pebbles and dirt rattled constantly, and although I went slowly and carefully, this use of human skills was new to me. I was confident enough on trails, however steep, but this . . . this verticality was different. It looked easier, in theory. In practice, I was out of breath and trembling well before the bottom was close enough to promise a survivable fall.

A small but robust creek ran through the muck at the bottom, and we paused to wash the sweat from our faces and necks. "Don't drink that," Luis told me, and tossed me a bottle of water he'd put in a net holster on his belt. I gulped down several mouthfuls and passed it on to Turner. Luis drank last and returned the now half-empty bottle to its carrier. "She could have poisoned the creek," he told me. "I don't see any fish or insects down here."

He was right. The bottom of the chasm seemed eerily devoid of the usual creatures. Just the water, hissing on its way.

"Later," he said. He knew I was thinking of repairing the damage she'd done, if he was right about the environmental poison. "We're saving our strength, remember?" I did, but I didn't like it much. "How are we on time?"

Ben Turner checked his watch. "Twenty minutes," he said. "That gives us another twenty for the ascent, and twenty to deal with whatever's at the top and get in position. And you're sure that's reasonable, right?"

I wasn't, but there were no reasonable expectations to be had in any of this. I just faced the upthrusting wall and began to pull myself up, one painful foot at a time.

We were halfway up when I felt a surge of power coming through the aetheric. "Luis!" I called sharply, and he looked up. "Hide us!"

He took a deep breath, and lowered his head. We all froze in place on the rock face, and when I glanced down again, I saw nothing. No men below me, only vaguely man-shaped juts of rock.

Pebbles fell from above as someone leaned over the edge. There was a soft, inaudible report made in a child's high voice, and then another, adult voice clearly said, "Raise it anyway. It's good practice for you."

I rested my forehead against the stone and tried not to interfere with Luis's concentration. It was, at the moment, all that stood between us and death. We were too high to fall without serious injury, and too far from the top to launch any kind of effective attack. With one of the child-Wardens above us, we couldn't strike in any case.

Below, I heard something odd. The hissing of the water took on volume, depth, built to a roar. I felt harsh gusts of wind whip up, battering me against the rock, and the cold spray as the stream built in volume, being forced from its underground source at an ever-greater volume. In the distance I heard a sudden boom of thunder, and felt the snap of lightning. Clouds were moving overhead now, driven by the unbelievable fury of Warden magic, clumping and thickening into a storm.

Raise it anyway.

The Warden had been instructed to use wind and

water to scrub the entire chasm clean of any potential threats. I assessed our options. There weren't many.

Luis's voice suddenly whispered in my ear, in that eerie nonvocal communication. *I'm going to lock us all down,* he said. *It's the wind that's a danger. The water won't come high enough to drown us.*

Agreed, I sent back.

Beneath my hands, the rock suddenly softened, flowing around my hands, and I felt the same happening where my boots were jammed into precarious footholds. The rock solidified, trapping hands and feet into secure pockets. I couldn't fall now.

I also couldn't move on my own will, without undoing the power Luis had put in place.

The winds rose, whipping through the narrow chasm. At first it felt like shoves, then battering blows. Debris slammed through—lighter things first, then larger pieces of wood, flat rocks, discarded metal. I kept my face down, pressed to the stone, partially protected by my arms. It was all I could do.

Lightning flared in lurid, graceful fans overhead, and just when I felt that the wind would rip my arms out of my sockets with its relentless push, it began to slacken. Rain pounded down, instead, hard and silver, ice cold. I gasped and waited for it to stop.

I rose into the aetheric, anchored by Luis only a few feet away, and watched the glow of the two Wardens standing at the edge of the chasm, above. One—the child—glowed in colors that shouldn't have been possible, and the damage was awful and obvious in the persona he projected out into the world; a twisted gnome of a boy, scarred and melted. He'd been taught this. Forced into it.

The woman with him was little better, though her particular darkness glowed like poison through her veins. Her own choice, not imposed on her. She had power of her own, though not enough to have been a Warden in her own right. Possibly, once, one of the Ma'at.

The adult and the child stopped their interference with the energy of the storms, the river, the wind, and almost immediately it all slackened and fell into a confused, roiling mess. Neither of them bothered to balance the power out. That was dangerous; aetheric energy, summoned and left undirected, could trigger all manner of disasters, especially here, near the brilliant flood of energy that was the ley line, the invisible network of energy that linked together nexus points.

They're gone, I told Luis. He released his hold on the rock, and it flowed away from our hands and feet, back to its original configuration. My muscles had taken advantage of the support to rest themselves, and my pace upward increased dramatically.

Close. So close.

There.

My hands touched the grass at the top, and I pulled myself up, rolled, and immediately fell flat, facedown so that I could institute my own protective cover, which made me a slightly uneven rise and fall in the velvety green lawn. I hardly saw Luis at all, or Turner, but I knew my partner had placed the same chameleon measures over them.

Very slowly, we began to make our way, on our bellies, across the lawn. Not in the way you see in films . . . not crawling, with our bodies in the air, braced on forearms. We slid along the grass, bellies flat, pulling ourselves slowly forward with flattened hands. It was slow, tedious work, but effectively silent and almost impossible to spot, even on the open ground, with the kind of camouflage we employed.

But with the time we had lost, I was worried we wouldn't make it to the dome before Sanders triggered his distraction, drawing people directly toward us.

And then I saw one of the bear-panther chimeras emerge from the trees at the perimeter, sniff the air suspiciously, and begin to pad across the grass, nostrils flaring for scent.

Cass, Luis whispered.

I see it.

It's going to smell us.

No question of that. It already had, though it was baffled by the lack of visible evidence of our presence. It padded around us in a slow circle, orange eyes fixed on the open space where one of its senses reported we were, and the others reported we were not.

Can you put it out? I asked Luis.

Maybe, he responded. *If it gets close enough. But that leaves us with a huge unconscious problem for anybody to notice. Which is not the point of stealth.*

I closed my eyes, pushed my face into the clean, springy grass, and sent my aetheric senses out to find something, anything we could use.

I found a deer. A magnificent young buck, sharpening his antlers against a tree just beyond the tree line.

I panicked him with a pulse of Earth power and sent him bounding into the clearing, where he froze in shock at the sight of the huge, feline form of the chimera snuffling at apparently empty grass.

The chimera's head snapped up, the elusive smell of humans suddenly overridden by obvious prey.

Run, I told the deer, and released it. It turned and crashed back into the trees, bounding for its life.

The bear/panther roared after it, powering on massively muscled legs. Other howls answered it from all sides—the pack, taking up the hunt. I felt sickened, but the deer had already made the fatal error; I had only exploited it to our advantage.

We crawled as fast as such things could be accomplished.

We were not quite at the glowing curve of the dome when I heard the revving of engines on the other side of the chasm. Agent Sanders was making noise, a lot of it. Voices shouted. Metal banged. They were relocating all their tents to here, right within sight of the compound. No more hiding and playing coy.

I heard Agent Sanders's voice, magnified into a giant's deep shout, roll in a wave across the distance. "You in the dome," he said. "I want to talk to the leader of the Church of the New World in this location."

No response. I lifted my head and took reckonings. The access road was less than ten feet ahead of us, and to the left was a cleared open area, dirt only, neat as if it had been cordoned off by nature herself. The supply drop. That meant that at least one access was located right there, as close as possible to that spot; human nature and efficiency dictated that to be the case. One didn't build a road and a drop point if the access was on the other side of the building.

And Pearl, I knew, would have built access in whatever ways she liked.

Follow, I whispered to both Luis and Turner, and crawled around the edge of the supply area, almost to the dome itself.

Then we waited.

It took some time. Agent Sanders repeated his request, over and over, in a bland and annoyingly exact manner. When his voice got tired, Sanders put on blaring recorded music by a singer who offended even *my* limited sensibilities for his lack of imagination.

And after almost half an hour, an access point opened on the dome, and a single person stepped outside.

Not Pearl, of course. I didn't recognize this man. He was tall, sun-browned, lean, and with a hardened face that looked strong, but not kind. He had a bullhorn as well.

He came out of another access point, one further along the curve of the dome.

"Who are you?" he demanded, his own voice just as strong and deep as Sanders's had been. "What do you want from us?"

As if that wasn't obvious. The man couldn't be oblivious to the abduction of children going on within his own house.

See if you can open it, I whispered to Luis, and felt him crawl past me and touch his hand to the dome near the supply drop point.

While Pearl's spokesman and Sanders carried on their make-believe negotiations—and there was really no doubt how that would end—the area of the dome where Luis's hand had rested suddenly belled inward, and parted with a cool whisper of air to form a circle.

Like a mouth.

I hesitated, staring at it. The last time I had entered one of Pearl's lairs, it had almost destroyed me, and I'd been alone at the time. I hadn't had to worry about two other lives trailing along behind me.

Luis started to enter the opening. I reached out and grabbed his arm, hard.

No, I said.

What the hell? Why? We're exposed out here!

Because this was what she wanted, or she would not have driven me to this point. Picadors, and bulls. She had opened only the doors she wanted me to go through. Pearl understood me. On some level, we were the same—outcast, angry, vengeful. I had taken one road, and she another, but in parallel, not opposition.

I closed my eyes for a moment, shivering, and then whispered, *Stay here, both of you. Stay down. I will open it to bring the children out.*

Luis stared at me from shocked, wide eyes. *You can't go in alone.*

I won't be alone, I said. *You're always with me.*

He involuntarily reached out to me, cupping my cheek in his warm, dirty palm, and the look in his face was horrified, heartbroken, and angry.

Start the attack at the other domes, I told him.

You can't do this, he said. Beside him, Turner was making urgent go motions; without the Earth Warden talent for silent communication, he was left frustratingly out of the loop.

She'll have the children waiting, I told Luis. *If we go in as a group, there will be deaths. I can't let that happen.* It was what Pearl wanted. For us to be trapped in close quarters, fighting these children for our lives. The more of us there were, the worse the toll would be.

You can't do this alone, he said again. He wasn't wrong, but I also understood now that there was a price for victory here, as everywhere.

And the price was too high. She meant it to be too high.

Follow, I said. *Wait five minutes, and follow. If I'm dead, do what you can.*

I didn't bother to argue with either one of them. I just lifted my body and lunged inside, slamming the opening shut behind me and locking it with a twist of my will. He could force it, but it would take time.

I didn't think there was much left.

When I turned back, I faced an organic sweep of cool, iridescent walls—not quite stone, not quite bone, not quite nacreous. It curved as it followed the outer shape of the dome, and I ran lightly along the path, looking for what I knew I would find.

I rounded the curve and found Isabel.

"Ibby?"

I slowed my steps, my metal left hand touching the outer wall, and stared at her with the intensity I reserved for those I loved, and for enemies. I wasn't sure which she was now. Or whether she was still both.

Isabel was still, in body, a chubby little girl, but she had put aside the behavior of a child. She stood very still, very alert, watching my approach. Behind her were three other children, each older than she was. They were dressed the same, all in that durable camouflage material, which I now realized had the same properties that Luis had used in his efforts to conceal us; the material mimicked its surroundings, and now it was a shimmering ivory, like silk.

"Ibby," I said. I stopped and faced her, just as still as she was. "I've come to take you home, Ibby."

She didn't answer. None of them did. They just watched me with alert, angry eyes.

"Isabel, I don't want to fight you. I want to take you home."

Isabel slowly shook her head. "This is my home."

"No. Your home is with your uncle Luis." *And me*, I wanted to say, but didn't dare. "He's waiting for you. He's missed you so badly. You remember your uncle, don't you?"

Her dark eyes flickered for a moment, and I knew she was remembering. *What* she might remember was another question; if Pearl had succeeded in altering the girl's perceptions, her memories, she might be reliving imaginary trauma—or real ones. Pearl had manipulated these children, tried to use their familial feelings to raise barriers and drive hatreds—but she could only manipulate, not program. That left them vulnerable to the same appeals.

"Uncle Luis is dead," Ibby said. "You killed him. It was horrible."

"She's lying to you," I said. Not that I hadn't almost gotten him killed on many occasions, but it was probably not the best time to parse the dynamics of that relationship. "Ibby, the lady who tells you these things, she isn't your friend. And she lies. She wants to use you, all of you. She doesn't care what happens to you."

Isabel was no fool, and I saw her consider that. The children behind her, however, didn't have our history together. Or, perhaps, the same flexibility of mind.

"You're the liar! You're the evil one!" one of them shouted, and clapped his hands together.

A hammer of air forced itself down the narrow hallway, hit me, and slammed me backward to the floor with such violence I saw black swarms of stars, and felt myself begin to disconnect from this world. I fought back, panting, and rolled to my side to get up.

The Weather Warden child hit me again, harder, sending me face-first into the wall. I slid down it, almost senseless, and sensed Isabel stepping forward. The assault stopped, mainly because the Weather Warden—the same boy who'd almost killed us in the chasm, perhaps?—couldn't strike with Isabel in the way.

Isabel called fire into her hand. It came in a blue-white burst of energy, flickering red at the edges, and echoed eerily in her eyes as she advanced toward me.

"You wanted them dead," she said. "My parents. *All* our parents. You killed Uncle Luis. You want to kill me and my friends. You want to kill the lady."

Only one of those things was true, but it was the critical one; I *did* want to kill the lady. And however it had happened, Manny and Angela Rocha had died; Pearl could twist the facts to suit her cause, and it would be useless for me to try to deny them.

But Luis . . . I could prove she was lying about Luis.

"Stop," I said, or tried to say; there was blood in my mouth, and I wasn't sure that I had actually spoken at all. The second blow had been so hard that I couldn't get my limbs to move, other than uncoordinated scrabbles. "He's alive." That sounded almost clear. "Your uncle is alive."

"Liar," Ibby said. "I saw you kill him. The lady showed me—you hurt him, you hurt him so bad he died. And now *you're* going to burn, just like you burned him."

She pulled her hand back.

I flung out a hand in useless denial . . . and felt a surge of horror at what had been done to Ibby. To all these children. She'd watched someone—even if it had not been Luis in truth—burn. Whether that had been illusion or reality, it was traumatic enough to leave unendurable scars.

In the instant before she launched the fire at me, I shouted, "Ibby, *think*! I'm like your uncle! I can't use fire!"

Ibby blinked. She stayed there, poised on the edge of violence, fire flickering and hissing in her small, chubby hand.

"Your uncle is an Earth Warden," I panted. "I share his power. *I* am an Earth Warden. I *couldn't* burn him, even if I wanted to, do you understand? And I never would, Ibby. I love him, just as I love you."

It was much for a child her age to understand, but she'd been forced to things far beyond her normal understanding already. She understood the nature of power because of what Pearl had already taught her.

Ibby quenched the fireball with a clench of her fist, leaving behind a smear of acrid smoke on the air. She looked at me with wide, lost eyes, frowning.

"But I saw," she said. "I saw you do it. I know you did it."

Children are literal. And Pearl had counted on that. "No, my dear," I said softly, and heard the grief and tenderness in my voice. "I didn't. And I won't hurt him, or you. You have my promise."

I felt the air move behind me, a cool breeze stirring my hair, and heard running, booted feet.

And then Luis said, "Ibby?"

In the first instant there was shock, then fear. She'd seen him die. This required a wrenching adjustment of her worldview, something difficult and painful.

Then I saw delight dawn. Her eyes rounded, and so did her perfect little rosebud of a mouth, and in that single moment, she seemed the child she had been. "*Tío Luis?*" Her voice was shaking and uncertain.

He lowered himself to one knee. "I'm here, *mija*. I'm right here."

She took a step forward, then shook her head, violently, and backed away, into the safety of the other children. "No," she said. "No, it's a trick. You're playing a trick."

Luis didn't move, not even a muscle. He didn't even glance at me. "*Mija*, it's no trick. I'm here to take you home. You want to go home, don't you? I know you didn't want to leave us. I know they made you go. It's not your fault. None of this is your fault."

She pulled in a trembling breath, and I saw tears glitter in her dark eyes. So young. So fragile.

"Isabel," Luis whispered. "I love you. Please come home."

"No," said the Weather Warden boy, the one who'd slammed me into the walls. He was cold and utterly controlled, and he grabbed Ibby's shoulder as she started to move toward us. "She's not going anywhere. You're not going to hurt her anymore."

"I'm not going to hurt her." Luis kept his voice low, and as gentle as possible. "I'm not going to hurt any of you. You can all come with us."

"Why, so you can cut into our heads? Make us zombies?" The boy's grip on Ibby's shoulder must have hurt; I saw her wince. "That's what you do, we know all about it. You take us away to your hospital and you cut us up and you lock us up. We're not going to let you do that to us. Or to anyone else, ever again. We're going to stop you."

They thought they were the heroes.

Worse, there was a grain of truth in what the boy was saying, like all successful lies. The Wardens *did* operate on those whose powers were too dangerous, too uncontrollable. Some didn't survive. Some survived grievously damaged. Pearl knew that.

She had twisted it in their minds, made it their inevitable fate. Made us all evil, predatory villains.

They'd fight, all right. Fight to the death, because they were the brightest, the strongest, the most courageous.

She was turning our future heroes against us.

"Ibby," I coughed, and rolled up to my hands and knees. "Ibby, please don't. Let us help you."

"No," the boy said, when Isabel tried to pull free. He shoved her behind him, and slapped his palms together again, driving a wall of force toward us. I collapsed to the floor this time before it hit me, presenting as little target as possible; even so, the impact almost drove me into unconsciousness.

It blew Luis backwards, sliding him ten feet down the hall with a yelp of pain.

"No!" Isabel shouted, and turned on the boy, shoving him back. "No, don't hurt him!"

"That's your enemy, dummy!" he yelled back, and shoved in turn. "How weak are you? Didn't you learn *anything*? It's probably not even him!"

"It is," Isabel said, and turned toward Luis. "It is him."

As she started toward us, the boy tried to grab her, but this time, Ibby was ready, and she slipped out of his hands and ran past me, toward her uncle. Luis rose, staggering a little, and she leaped into his arms.

He was driven back a step, but held on to her; there was a flash of pain on his face, quickly buried by waves of relief. He kissed her shining dark hair, hugged her, and murmured rapid calming phrases in Spanish, only half of which I could hear. Promising he loved her. Promising he would protect her.

I hoped that was true.

"The lady lied," I managed to say to Isabel, and to the other children still facing us. "She lied to you. Do you understand? She's trying to make you hurt innocent people. I know you don't want to do that. You're better than that."

One looked horror-stricken, and backed up. He was clearly questioning everything he'd been shown, everything he'd been told; there was real doubt in his face, real pain. He was just a bit younger than the Weather Warden boy.

I saw no such doubts on that one's face. He was a fanatic. A true believer, as was the girl next to him.

"*You're* the ones who lie!" the girl shouted, and I felt a fearfully strong Earth power ripping at me, trying to clutch its fingers around my heart and crush. I batted the attack away and lurched to my feet, wiping blood from my mouth. Earth powers, I could defend against. The boy who was backing away was Fire.

The Weather Warden boy was still the real danger. He was willing to kill. Eager to. He was just trying to find the right moment, and to avoid hurting Ibby in the process—though I wasn't at all sure he would flinch from it, if he thought it necessary.

"Get her out," I said to Luis. "Go. Go now."

He hesitated. Isabel turned her luminous, too-adult eyes to me, and I saw the shadow in them, the adult understanding. The power.

Pearl had made the child old far beyond her years. Forced her to see and do things that would have damaged someone far more experienced in this world.

I wasn't sure, suddenly, that we hadn't been manipulated, once more, but really, what choice was there? Leave Ibby here, to suffer more? No. Not possible. We had to try, or there was no point to any of it.

"Take her," I said. "You have to save her or none of this will mean anything. Just go, Luis. *Go*."

He nodded and began to back away, up the tunnel.

Agent Ben Turner stepped in to fill his place, standing with feet spread wide apart, blocking any possible pursuit that might have gone after Luis and Ibby. He looked tired and bruised, but also focused and very capable. Between the two of us, we could cover two avenues of attack.

But neither of us could defend against a Weather attack.

Lightning arced from all sides of the tunnel, like a

net of energy, striking at both of us. It mostly missed me as I dove forward, but it struck Turner squarely, and he froze, galvanized by the force, but absorbing it into fire energy. Transforming it. Lightning and fire were close cousins, and although it hurt him, it didn't kill him. He staggered, fell against the curving wall of the tunnel, and stripped off his FBI Windbreaker, which had burns and melted fabric dripping in syrupy streams down the sleeves.

I hit the smooth wall of the tunnel, planted my feet, and adjusted my trajectory, adding Earth Warden speed to my movements, burning energy at a rapid rate now. Lightning continued to fill the tunnel, but I sped up my reflexes and reaction time, and although it brushed close, it never stabbed home.

The children retreated. The boy changed his attack again, pushing me back with a wave of hot wind, and the Earth child darted forward to slam a fist into my chest.

It hit with the overwhelming force of a freight train. It took *years* for an Earth Warden to build up that kind of force, yet this child pulled it in an instant, and I felt it blow through me, damaging everything in its path—ribs, lungs, barely missing my heart. I choked, gasped, and felt a burst of pain bloom like a flower made of knives in my chest.

"Cassiel!" Turner yelled, and sent a burst of fire rolling past me, forcing the Earth Warden child back just as she tried to summon up a second, killing blow. "Jesus, get back!"

I couldn't. I was already wounded, and if I didn't finish this quickly, they would.

I ignored the agony. I rolled forward over my right

shoulder, came up in a crouch, hands outstretched, slammed both palms against the foreheads of the two children, and sent a jolt of power into them that overloaded their brains, instantly sending them unconscious.

In theory.

One went down.

The one I'd held my metallic left hand to, the Weather Warden, staggered, but as I'd feared, the metal had failed to conduct aetheric power in the same way that flesh did.

It was a fatal moment to learn that for a fact.

The boy had no more hesitation or mercy than the girl at his side, who was already falling to the ground in sleep. He struck me point blank with an invisible blade of hardened air, punching it deep inside me. It was an old form of attack, one that the Wardens had long since abandoned; Weather Wardens didn't engage in close-quarters fighting, and when they did, they tried to avoid fatal wounds.

This was . . . very close to fatal. Very, very close.

I fell forward, reaching out with my right hand as I did, and slapped it against his forehead. He was a sweet-faced child, Asian in ancestry, with silky black hair cut in a careless shag around his face.

I had just enough focus left to send the pulse of power into him, and he collapsed before I fell on top of him.

I was bleeding. Unable to breathe.

"Cassiel!" A distant voice, shouting. I felt something tugging at me, but it was very remote.

It felt peaceful suddenly.

Someone rolled me over, grabbed the two unconscious children, and hustled them away. I lay there watching the red pool of my blood spread outward across the clean pale floor.

I felt the *hunger* of the place stir. It liked blood. It loved mine.

Sister. Pearl's voice, echoing in my head, unwelcome in this peaceful state I'd reached. *No, this won't do. I can't have you giving your life. That's to no purpose at all.*

Sorry to disappoint you, I replied. I felt . . . remote now. Like an Oracle myself, removed from the concerns of the world. I remembered how I'd longed for peace, for solitude, for silence.

I was finding it, breath by breath. Soon, it would surround me entirely.

You'd leave the man, Pearl said. *I find that hard to believe. You've become so human. So bound to skin. And he does so love you, already. Like the child. It was hard to turn her against you. I had to hurt her many times to do that.*

I felt a stir of hate, an echo of emotion that troubled me. It had no place here, where I was leaving things behind.

The pool of red crawled outward, spreading into a lake.

There was one more Warden child left in the hallway, the one who'd backed away from the fight once Isabel had been taken. He was an older boy, about ten years, and I saw in him the shadow of the man he might one day become, if he survived all this—if he survived all of us—to be a genuine Warden.

He would be the next Lewis Orwell. There was a light in him . . . a light . . . .

He reached out and touched me, spreading his hand over the open wet wound that the knife of air had left. "No," I whispered. "No, don't." Because as close as I had come to the edge, I might pull him with me. I *would not* pull him into the dark. "Let me go. It's all right."

Shhhh, Pearl said soothingly in my mind. *Oh my sister, he's mine to give. And I give you this gift. I'm not ready to let you go quite yet. It's not time.*

"No!" I screamed it, but it was too late.

The boy wasn't acting of his own accord. This child, this marvelous and beautiful child who would grow to be a marvelous, beautiful man, was completely under her control. Against his own will, he poured power into me, emptied every reserve. It roared into me in a fierce, white-hot cascade, burning through my nerves, spilling in a flood through the wounded tissues. Healing. Mending sliced arteries. Forcing the wound closed.

Saving me. Destroying himself.

"No!" I whispered, but I couldn't stop it. Couldn't sever the connection. I was too weak, and perhaps, at some primal level, I was too afraid. Too afraid of dying myself.

She emptied him of everything. Every tiny scrap of power, even the tiny bursts of energy that kept the cells of his body alive.

She killed him to save me.

"No!" My scream was raw, and it filled the narrow space of the hallway, raced through the space, echoed from the roots of my soul.

I caught the boy as he fell, but it was too late. He was emptied by Pearl and discarded like garbage.

I was weak, pale, and horribly damaged, but I was no

longer on the edge of death. He had gone on without me, into the dark.

Not by his choice.

I heard voices in the distance, a confusion of shouting, running feet. *You should go now, sister,* Pearl said. *I wouldn't have you waste my gift. But I won't allow you to take more of my children. I need them for our next meeting.*

"I will," I said out loud. My voice was bloody, ragged with rage. "I will stop you from doing this. *I will stop you.*"

You know how, Pearl said. *All you have to do is act. But if you do, this one child dead before you is the first of billions. Then again, if you don't act, I will do the same to the Djinn, the Oracles, to the faithless Mother who turned her back on me. Which would you prefer?*

Let the Djinn save themselves. I couldn't face another death now, much less the deaths of billions.

But there had to be another way.

"I will stop you," I repeated. "However it has to happen."

I gathered up the fallen child in my arms. My blood soaked into the boy's clothing from my own, and I staggered and fell against the wall, dizzy from the effort and a sudden, overwhelming feeling of anguish. *I am guilty of this,* I thought. *Guilty of destroying something astonishing.* I might have stopped him, if I'd been strong enough. His life, for mine. It wasn't a fair bargain.

I had to find some way to make it worthwhile. And I had to face his parents, look them in the eyes, and explain why I had failed their son.

I owed him that.

A dark shape rounded the far end of the sloping hallway, at the opposite curve from my exit—not a child, an adult. Tall and broad, and armed with a rifle, which he aimed in my direction. I had no time for subtleties; I melted the barrel of his gun just as he pulled the trigger. It exploded in his hands, sending him reeling back into the man behind him, who shoved his bleeding, screaming colleague aside to raise his own rifle and squeeze off two fast shots. His aim was poor, thanks to quick reactions and adrenaline, but the hallway was narrow, and one of the bullets caught me low in the side, in the bulletproof vest.

I turned my back as he vaulted forward, screaming his defiance, followed by a whole rank of his friends.

I ran for the exit. The weight of the dead boy was like lead in my arms, and my body felt as if it might collapse with every dull step, but I rounded the corner still ten feet ahead of the pursuers . . .

. . . and the door was closed.

I slammed my hand down on the nacreous surface, willing it to open, but it refused.

I didn't say I would make it easy, sister, Pearl laughed in my head. *I want you suffering. For a very long time, the way you made me suffer. I want to bury that tiny part of you in the ground, trapped and bleeding and aware, aware for all time. I want to feel your screams echoing in eternity. You deserve that.*

I put my back to the blank wall where the door should have been, breathing hard, and watched all the soldiers plug the hallway, blocking any possible alternate routes. Metallic clicks as they aimed their weapons, but the man in the front rank held up a clenched fist, and no one fired.

"Put him down," the man said. "And get on your knees, hands behind your head."

I couldn't disable so many weapons. Even if I could, they had other weapons, and I sensed that some of them, if not many, had other powers they could bring to bear against me.

I was trapped, completely and utterly trapped.

But I was not giving up the boy.

Or kneeling.

Not now. Not to them. Not ever.

The leader of the security force must have recognized that, because he nodded sharply and put his weapon to his shoulder, sighted, and fired. One shot.

It hit me in the leg, shattering my femur, and I screamed and almost went down.

He adjusted his aim to target the other leg. When I reached out with power to try to disable his gun, something blocked me—him, or one of his men.

The wall softened behind my back, sagged outward under my weight, and I fell as it popped and pulled aside in that eerie round mouth.

Spitting me out, this time.

"Cassiel!" Luis screamed. He grabbed my hand and dragged me around the curve of the dome, slapped a hand on its surface, and dialed the opening close in the face of the security leader. "Oh God, what the hell . . . ?"

There was chaos at the perimeter. FBI agents had driven an armored truck down the slope of the hill, and were engaged in a full firefight against a squad of Pearl's human guards, while still others were fighting off an assault by the chimera bear/panther predators. It was all lit by a hellish, fiery glow as the treetops burned around us.

Turner, panting, raced toward us, stopping along the way to trade shots with a human guard. He grabbed me by one arm, Luis took the other, and they started to drag me off.

The boy tumbled from my grip. "No!" I shrieked. "No, bring him! Bring him!" I fought them in a frenzy, grabbing at the boy's body. Luis recognized that we would all die if he didn't try to help me, and slung the boy over one shoulder as he pulled me along, limping on one bloody leg, toward the armored carrier.

He and Turner thrust me inside, along with a medic who climbed in with a pack of supplies. Also in the truck I found the two sleeping Warden children, and Isabel, who was curled up in a ball in one corner, watching the fight with bright, terrified eyes. She looked at me— bloody, pale, wild as I was—and threw herself into my arms as I collapsed on the seat beside her.

I tried to hold her as the world slipped greasily around me, but the pain came in waves, blacking out everything, and I heard the medic say, "Hold still," and then it was all dark.

Not even the rattle of gunfire followed me.

Chapter 11

I WOKE IN SILENCE, in sunlight, in my own bed in my own apartment. The covers were twisted over me. My leg was bandaged and braced, and I felt exhausted, feverish, achy.

Human, and lost because of it.

I smelled coffee brewing, and the pressure of a full bladder forced me up to the necessary task. I then seized a pair of crutches leaning against the wall and hobbled my way into the small kitchen, where I found a pot of coffee simmering on the burner. I poured a mug and drank, then refilled it, without sitting down.

From the sofa in the small living room, I heard Luis say, "You feeling better?"

"I am now," I said, and drank yet another cup to the dregs, set the mug down, and clumsily made my way to the sofa to sink down beside him. The crutches clattered down on the floor.

Luis looked . . . himself. Bruised, yes, and some the worse for wear, but I saw no serious wounds or braces. *Lucky,* I thought. Or more skilled than I at surviving it.

"Thank you for the coffee," I said.

"De nada," he replied. "I made it for myself. You got a side benefit."

He turned, arm across the back of the sofa, and studied me with concern. I didn't meet his gaze. Instead, I drew fingertips down my leg. "I don't remember," I said. "Being treated for this."

"You wouldn't. They kept you out. You were thrashing around like a caged lion. It's okay, though. The brace is on just to keep you from doing something crazy. Bones are together." He paused for a moment before saying, "Crazy being totally damn relative with you, by the way."

I sighed and let my head fall back against the sofa. "At no point did I wish myself injured," I told him. "I'm not by nature that sort of masochist. That's a human trait."

"No, you're a sadist is what you are. You know what it's like to be close to you, Cassiel? You know what it's like to feel so . . . helpless? Watch you do this to yourself?" He stopped and rubbed his hand over his face. "Shit. It's not your fault, I know that. I just hate it. I hate this. How did it get to be this way?"

"By slow steps," I said. "By nobody's will." I twisted awkwardly, and met his gaze at last. "Isabel?"

"She's all right." He didn't sound convinced of it, but more as if he was trying to make himself believe. "She'll *be* all right, anyway. They did some unholy shit to these kids, you know. They made them think—all kinds of things. Used illusion to convince them the people they ought to trust were evil. There's no pit deep enough for these bastards, I'm telling you that right now."

"And her power?" I asked.

"We're looking into it," Luis said softly. "She's got

a dual gift. Or would have had, anyway. The Wardens don't want to lose that. But they can't have her running around with those kinds of uncontrolled powers, either. Neither can I. Not if I love her. But I don't know how—I don't know how I can let them neuter her like that."

I felt that go through me like a bolt of electricity. "Neuter her?"

"You know, do the surgery. Take away her powers completely. It's dangerous, and it might be fatal if they fuck it up. Worse, it's not always effective. It could leave part of her power intact, to surface later, and she'd be even worse at dealing with it."

Not to mention what damage it would do to Isabel herself. Some Wardens could walk away from their powers safely. Others . . . others crawled away, bloody and bleeding. Others would do anything to undo the choice they made.

Isabel wasn't the sort of Warden who could walk away. I knew that already, I saw it in her. She was powerful, and she would only get more powerful.

Or more damaged.

Or both.

It was the nightmare that Pearl had promised them, and here it was, a terrible possibility. *I'd promised. I'd promised them . . .*

"What will you do?" I asked him. He looked down at his hands, flexing his fingers as if they pained him.

"Don't know," he said. "Wish to hell I did. I think—I think I have to take the chance to temporarily block her powers again. That's dangerous in itself, and it doesn't always work, but at least it's not . . . permanent. If we can delay things for another six, seven years, at least she'll have enough physical maturity to handle what happens inside her body with the Earth power. That would be the right age for that to start emerging anyway. The other kids aren't in as bad a shape."

I nodded. It sounded best to me, too.

"She wants to see you," he said. "I told her no, not right now. You need time to heal." He swallowed. "And I have to ask what happened with that boy. The one who died."

"You have to ask officially."

"Yes."

I closed my eyes. "I killed him."

Silence. Outside I heard life going on—someone mowing the grass, children laughing, radios and televisions competing for attention through open windows. The drone of an airplane overhead. Car engines on the street beyond.

Luis said, "I don't think you did, Cass. I examined the body. He was drained, just like the boy in the van. I know you wouldn't do that. I know you couldn't. It was Pearl." He fell silent for a few seconds, then said, "Tell me what happened."

I did, slowly, without any real emotion in my voice. I couldn't feel much just now. Only exhaustion. Futility. When I was finished, Luis reached out and took my hand in his, and squeezed hard.

"Oh, sweetheart," he said. "I am so sorry."

"It was my choice," I said. "To go in. I thought it was right."

"It was. We got Ibby and those other two back."

He didn't understand. Pearl had gotten exactly what she wanted.

Isabel had come back to us, and we had no idea what had really been done to her. I doubted Pearl had allowed us to take her without there being a deeper purpose in it.

And part of me had been burned black in the process— a critical part that connected me to the human race. "The boy," I said. "What happened to his body?"

"We took it with us," Luis said. "I looked into it myself. His parents are dead. He was an orphan. Disappeared from a foster family years ago. Nobody to mourn him but us."

That wasn't better.

"She's using me," I said. "Picadors and the bull. She's driving me toward something, and soon I won't have any choices left, Luis. Soon, I'll have to destroy what I love, or see everything else taken. There's no way out. She's thought of everything. I can't—"

"You can," he interrupted me. "Cassiel. Ashan didn't pick you for no damn reason. He picked you because you were the *only* Djinn who could do this. Who could face Pearl and win. Even he couldn't do it, or he would have. You're not done. We're not done."

"I'm tired of chasing her," I said. "I have to find a way to get ahead of her."

"Then we will," he said.

"Just like that."

"Yeah, pretty much. What did all those locations the FBI showed us have in common?"

I felt a stirring of something like interest. Like hope. "Ley lines," I said. "They were following ley lines."

"Then we follow them too. We start locking down places she could go. We start hemming her in, forcing her to play *our* game." Luis's hand felt warm against my face. "Look at me."

I opened my eyes and focused on him. He was close now, and the fierce light in his eyes surprised me.

"Don't let her take you down," he said. "I know you, Cass. I've seen you. You're part of me, and I'm part of you, and that's how it is, all right? You can't pull bullshit on me because I *know*. Whatever you used to be, however much of a badass Djinn, you are one of us now. Human. Fragile. Feeling. It's all right to *feel*."

I felt tears well up. Real tears, hot with anguish, with frustration, with awful fear. They burned in my eyes like Djinn fire.

His thumbs stroked them away as they fell.

"Don't let her make you the villain," he said, and kissed me. "Because I don't want to be in love with the villain, okay?"

I clung to him desperately, tasting my tears on his lips, tasting the warm, sweet light beneath of his love for me.

He meant this.

He meant it.

And for a moment—just a moment—I found that peace, that gentle whispering calm, that came from the Earth herself.

Not alone, though.

There were two of us in that place of peace.

And that was enough, for the moment.

. . . To be continued in *Outcast Season: Unseen*

TRACK LIST

As always, music is my muse—and sometimes my life-line. Here are the tracks that helped steer me through the turns on *Outcast Season: Unknown*.

"Under the Gun"	Supreme Beings of Leisure
"John Barleycorn"	Traffic
"Glory Box"	Portishead
"The Hop"	Radio Citizen featuring Bajka
"Roads"	Portishead
"My Old Self"	Wide Mouth Mason
"I Got Mine"	The Black Keys
"C'mon C'mon"	The Von Bondies
"Every Inambition"	The Trews
"Ladylike"	Big Wreck
"Six-Pack"	The Perpetrators
"Best Way to Die"	Jet Set Satellite
"Little Toy Gun"	Honeyhoney
"WannaBe in L.A."	Eagles of Death Metal
"I Don't Care (Single Version)"	Fall Out Boy
"Many Shades of Black"	The Raconteurs
"Headfirst Slide into Cooperstown on a Bad Bet"	Fall Out Boy
"U.R.A. Fever"	The Kills
"Manic Girl"	Radio Iodine
"Take Me to the Speedway"	The Dexateens

"Alsatian"	White Rose Movement
"Poison Whiskey"	Tishamingo
"Welcome Home"	Coheed & Cambria
"Tick Tick Boom"	The Hives
"Jockey Full of Bourbon"	Joe Bonamassa
"Leopard-Skin Pill-Box Hat"	Beck
"The Ballad of John Henry"	Joe Bonamassa
"Funkier Than a Mosquito's Tweeter"	Joe Bonamassa
"Happier Times"	Joe Bonamassa
"Faster"	Rachael Yamagata
"Around the Bend (Radio Edit)"	The Asteroids Galaxy Tour
"Slow Dance with a Stranger"	Danger Radio
"Ardmore"	Cardinal Trait
"Bounce"	The Cab
"Figure It Out"	Plain White T's
"I'm Not Cool"	Sohodolls
"Under the Gun"	Supreme Beings of Leisure
"All the Same to Me"	Anya Marina
"Cut Up"	Duchess Says
"Night Train (Bonus Track)"	The Kills
"The Trick Is to Keep Breathing"	Garbage
"Homecoming"	Hey Monday
"Baby, You're on Your Own"	The Steepwater Band
"I'm Not Jesus (feat. Corey Taylor)"	Apocalyptica
"Under the Gun"	Supreme Beings of Leisure
"The Little Things"	Danny Elfman
"Prayer"	Lizzie West
"Down by the Water"	P. J. Harvey
"Cruel"	Tori Amos
"Welcome to the World"	Kevin Rudolf & Rick Ross
"Lighten Up, Francis"	Puscifer
"Time Bomb"	Jessy Greene
"Ain't No Rest for the Wicked"	Cage the Elephant
"That's Not My Name"	The Ting Tings
"Goodbye"	Kristina DeBarge
"With Me Tonight"	Aynsley Lister
"As the Rush Comes (Radio Edit)"	Motorcycle

"In One Ear"	Cage the Elephant
"Top Yourself"	The Raconteurs
"Time's Up"	Aynsley Lister
"Running Out on Me"	Aynsley Lister
"Sugar Low"	Aynsley Lister
"Disorderly Me"	Aynsley Lister
"Fruit Machine"	The Ting Tings
"Take Me on the Floor"	Veronicas
"28"	Starewell
"Sugar"	Respectables
"Close Your Eyes"	Grey Eye Glances

ABOUT THE AUTHOR

Rachel Caine is the internationally bestselling author of more than thirty novels, including the Weather Warden series. She was born at White Sands Missile Range, which people who know her say explains a lot. She has been an accountant, a professional musician, and an insurance investigator, and still carries on a secret identity in the corporate world. She and her husband, fantasy artist R. Cat Conrad, live in Texas with their iguanas, Popeye and Darwin. Visit her Web site at www.rachelcaine.com, and look for her on Twitter, LiveJournal, MySpace, and Facebook.

Available wherever books are sold or at
penguin.com